Starhustler

CHRIS TURNER

CHAPTER 1

I got the transcall from Marty two days ago on Starrunner. *Meet me at Drenny's Bodega. Bring explosives.*

I was tempted to blow it off, but something in my gut told me to follow through. Business had been slow out in Veglos and the cons we had pulled up and down that wretched sector, had either blown up in our faces or been substandard. Like that smuggling op to get land mines down to the rebels on Rlenion. Three shipments, discovered at the last minute, up in flames.

Not to mention the blood-soaked debacle in the Muridon Belt before all this. Marty and I'd managed to hyper within range of Bariff's Star, escaping to some low-tech desert planet, after a series of random light hops courtesy of our wonky varwol aboard the junk freighter, *Trident.*

I'd quickly traded in that hauler for the much smaller *Starrunner*, from a rich but drunken caravan master. A deal if there ever was one. We'd hypered to Veglos, did our little thing there, now were on stopover at this slum planet, Brisis, waiting for the heat to die down on Veglos. We'd parted ways for a while, both of us needing a break from our own miserable company. Seems as if he was now longing for my companionship? Or else he had landed some deal worth chatting about. Somehow I suspected the latter.

Looking at the decadence and slummery of Hoath here on Brisis 9, capital of the supplier planet of all goods, I wasn't quite so sure now. A giant shanty town of neon and old glitter, a place I'd vowed never to return to, with its seedy dives, black markets, toothless hawkers and painted

3

brides.

What was the point of it, I asked. Without one taking a chance, opportunity always made its way to the next bidder.

Maybe that's why I was in the traders' depot. Following up on the lead just come in from Marty. That or a slump. Call it what you want, a malaise of spirit, some last desperation after the last string of bad luck.

This waiting line was taking too long. Really? That many shmucks in line for firearms? Granted, the depot was the best place to go for munitions this side of the Orbego ghetto, aside from regular black market channels. But I didn't feel like getting my legs blown off today.

The eminent sociologist, J. Markel Braeth, wrote in an informal essay, that human corruption reaches its peak during times of a dark age, after war has obliterated the countryside, after the planets, once prosperous, ache for green once again. When the worlds far and near, once so proud and with such potential, cry tears of dry sand, vomit up garbage pits and every half-baked crime lord in the galaxy.

I'm inclined to disagree with Sir Braeth's statement of tomorrow. I think it can go lower.

Rusco, you moron, who cares what you think? You're just another rambler risk-taker wanting to play it loose and fast. No different than the other hustlers in what's left of the free sectors of the galaxy, those lawless regions, the pleasure domes, the ghettos, the gang-ruled cities. The difference is you pride yourself on being one step ahead of the average con, a little quicker on your toes, a little edgier, sidestepping the dangerous beast waiting around the corner. It's a dangerous assumption, one that can get you killed.

All six-foot leathery hide of me reeked of the same starveling message. Go easy on the burnt-out con today. Here's my medallion of battle scars as proof of claim. The pale purple-tinted hair trailing to shoulder hiding the torn off ear. The wicked tear-dropped curve on the left wrist from that knife fight on Tethris. The pink scarring down the right cheek where a red hot iron had pressed the wrong way and the fleshy part of ear had kind of up and disappeared. No broken bones, no implants, no prosthetics, or anything that modern flesh-regen couldn't fix, given the right amount of funds. All it said was you were lucky.

As I scrutinized today's clientele at the depot, I felt the familiar tired sigh hiss through my teeth. What was the sod in front of me going to do with those stolen bills he clutched in his purple-veined fingers? Grab the luger off the shelf, go out and rob the local diner? Kill a couple of innocent women or some old man to feed his mescal habit?

Merc Surplus was just a hop, skip and jump down the line, stocking mint-condition gas lanterns, bowie knives, lighter fluid and rope, you name it. Great kit for arsonists or hangmen. On the other end, a pawn shop and the ubiquitous recyclo-mart distributing everything from boxsprings, old leather boots, water pumps to sex toys and tire irons. This edge of the colonized worlds had gone from seedy to seediest. Technology had all but vanished on this out-of-the-way planet. But then again, where hadn't it? The last of the space wars had gutted mother nature's belly, milked her dry. Now she sported only bands of raiders savaging the free planets. Outlaws, hoodlums, scumbags, wannabes, small men carrying big guns and wanting to be big chiefs in a messed-up world. A feudal universe of settled planets, raped of their resources; burned out cities ravaged by pulse cannons, run by organized crime thugs, crazies, religionists, every known breed of gangster the criminal world could offer.

The odd resistance fighter still roamed about, sure…freedom fighters they called them, fighting against decadence and injustice, but those were few and far between, and stupid in my opinion for risking a bullet in the head or torture by flamethrower to prove a point. For what? Wearing their crispy, blood-drenched capes to the grave. Martyrs without a cause, or hope? The slippery slope for Jet Rusco started long ago. I could have been a greater man, but instead settled on the life of a two-bit thief, trying to make ends meet, a sad vagabond, owner of a dilapidated space junker I'd won, or rather stolen from a couple of dying ruffians. Yet a part deep down in me wanted to be one of those valiant types that made a difference in this decrepit framework of humanity. I croaked out a laugh, shook my shaggy head, thinking maybe not today, Rusco, maybe not today.

The guy in front of me with the pale, haunted eyes moved off with his quivering fist clutching a handgun.

"I'll have one of those," I said across the scarred counter to the attendant poised behind the reinforced cage mesh. A lot of pulse guns and ammunition sat there, weaponry of all sorts stacked on the walls. Everything the local desperado could ever want.

The attendant flashed me a cool glance, lifted a disinterested finger to a row of black, cylindrical objects spread in a neat, tidy line.

"Yep, those ones—with the black mufflers on the ends. Mighty fine pieces," I said, trying to fake out a drawl for kicks.

"They're double-range explosives," he asserted. "Fine kick, twenty yols extra."

I flourished a hand. "Let me gauge them for weight. Two, please."

The attendant engaged the safety which ensured a ten minute lead in case of accidental detonation, passed the merchandise through the gap. Everyone knew there was no chance to steal merchandise and run. Hidden cameras worked with regular efficiency behind those reinforced panels and security gunmen posed as beggars or others traipsing about the place ready to pounce on any snatch-and-grab thieves.

I held the black cylinders in my hand, admiring the compact efficiency of their streamlined deadly potential. Juggling the canisters from hand to hand, I turned for a second, using my body to shield me from the camera, then worked my old confuse and switch gag, reaching down at an opportune time, replacing the one in my left hand with the dud concealed in my left jacket pocket. It was a ruse I'd been practicing for years. Worked every time. Oldest trick in the book.

I put on a long frown. "Actually, I'll go for the brand down, chief. These babies're a bit heavy and my pocket's a little too light."

"Told you," clucked the attendant. "Pass them back. Don't get fancy and waste my time."

I nodded and grinned and thrust them back through the hole in the cage, as if lowly equipment clerks' reprimands were the highlight of my day.

I fingered the coin-sized, scaled-down models pushed through the wire mesh, passed through twelve yols and thrust the goods in my dusty pockets as I fiddled for a home-rolled cigarette. The air was stifling and my head swam to a babel of voices. I was reaching my limit of how many shoulder jostles I could take from druggies and tough guys today. I sauntered out of the depot, whistling a tuneless jingle out of the side of my mouth. My meeting with Marty came up in the hour. A shoddy place The Bodega, but it would have to do.

As I slogged through the puddles from a recent rain toward the market, I could hear the beats of techno-music exuding from the tarped-up shanties down the way: all bass and some mid-range slurred female voice-overs in an unrecognizable mash. A glut of offworlders roamed about, a slum of small tent-like enclosures made from pieces of old rubber tires and broken vehicles. Rusty oil drums with smoking garbage burned away. Several grubby figures congregated in a huddle. An altercation broke out and knives suddenly flashed in dirty hands. Then the crash of broken glass through the grimy window of what looked a clapboard salami shop. Two ham-handed men stood arguing over who had chopped the last livers and mixed them with the pork, or some dumb thing.

As I stopped to ponder, I felt a tug at my pantleg. A mousy brown boy sat, legs splayed in the dirt and puddles, his leg missing below the knee, begging for coins. I crouched down and gave him a few of the loose yols I had, catching the dull look in the sunken, young eyes, drinking deep of the sorrow mirrored there then moving on.

My eyes wandered over him and other such sights with a familiarity that created tiny ripples in my soul. I'd had to steel myself to the suffering of others to get the jobs done that put food on the table. Only a rare glimmer of compassion did I let steal over me from time to time. The universe was what it was. Long ago I'd accepted such travesties as fate; they would continue on, regardless of what I did or didn't do.

A sickly glow permeated the sky with the sound of thunder promising more rain. I trudged through the rubble and the mud puddles, skirting wide piles of bomb debris. An air-speeder whistled past close overhead. I gave it little attention, little concerned with the comings and goings of the privileged and few. That, and the rattle of electric three-wheelers on the dingy streets whose riders wore their goggled ski-masks, racing the odd ramshackle van or lorry to the next barricaded junction.

I came to Drenny's. An eatery of fine repute, of battered brick and energetic graffiti scrawled on front, wide swoops and swirls of the lost symbols of modern vernacular. Overhead, mothers' laundry dripped and kids screamed from the balconies of squalid apartments. The city cops, aka hired mercenaries, came to this meet-place of smugglers, dope dealers and lowlifes less often than the hotter places closer to downtown. A collection of mixed sorts huddled about in drab clothing, generally trench coats and beat-up boots, sitting at tables and mumbling monosyllables or milling around at the bar. Some machines stood at the back, upright gambling units and old pinball machines, while low, distorted lounge music huffed out a muffled beat.

Marty sat over at a far table. He hunched in the dimness, bullet head and chin tipped down in the haze of blue smoke. He sat away from the hubbub and the bar. He got up and waved when he saw me. I approached with measured confidence and he took my hand with a firm grip and nodded, the faintest of grins. "Rusco, been a while. You look good."

"Could be better."

Marty patted my back with more vigor than necessary. "Attaboy! Keeping up the faith?"

I shrugged. Marty, a shock of mustard-colored hair that clung to his oiled scalp like a fish fin, was a short, heavy-boned bully with thick lips and crooked grin. But fast. Last guy who underestimated Marty lay in a shallow grave.

Marty was a good guy, well-informed but somewhat of a fanatic for odd jobs, volatile, headstrong, violent, ready to plug shells into a problem rather than think it through. Don't ever get him angry or he'd rip your head off and shove it up the next guy's ass. That's Marty. We'd put our heads together after we'd heisted that Collective ship on Nebara. We'd been drinking, shooting the shit at the local casino bar on Rega, and got to musing… 'you know, like maybe we should join forces or something and capitalize on the smuggling market, a couple of delivery wise guys like us, we could be peddling and fencing weapons and contraband versus collecting the chump change we're making now.' So we got to thinking and the old gears got whirring. Now I was a little ahead of Marty in big picture planning and could play three angles at once where he could only play one, so I humored him into thinking it was all his idea—you know, the whole let the big bad dog think he's the alpha-male, pissing on every corner, while the nice little white dog keeps his head down.

"So what's this about?" I asked.

"Got something down the line. Some easy pickings on the river way in the warehouse district."

"What, those abandoned factories and chop shops?"

"Yeah, something like that. Some small time gangsters run out of there, moving stuff new and old, you know? Big stuff."

"Yeah, like what?"

He scratched at the bridge of his nose. "I don't know, this and that."

"What? You don't even know what it is we're pulling?"

He looked away with an offended glare.

"What about transpo?" I growled. I peered over with annoyance at the two deadbeats playing old retro video games in the back shadows. The noise of buzzers and beeps and their grunts and sniggers rubbed at the edge of my concentration.

"You got your ship," said Marty, "plus we can steal some local rides if need be. They've got some air speeders I've heard."

"What, like we're just going to fly in there, gun them down, and take their goods?"

"Something like that," Marty said with a grin.

I shook my head, blinking with amazement. "You're something else, Marty, you know that? I think all that gumtox you've been chewing has gotten to your head."

"Careful there, Ruskie. The old Q himself gave me this drop. And he don't drop favors like that for nothing."

"Maybe." I grunted, licking my lips. "I just like to know what I'm getting into."

"Don't be a pussy. It's half the fun not knowing everything."

"Not really, Marty. Remember the last time we winged it, was nearly the end of us working together."

"This is your chance to make it big, Rusco. A slam dunk, instead of all those cheap little gigs out in backwaters-ville. I need ride and backup and figured you'd be good for it. I'll wait point while you nose around, scoping the place out. We'll keep in contact by bug wireless. Here—" He held up a pair of little black earpieces. "These little babies are untrackable. Shortwave or something. Tape it behind your ear."

"Shortwave," I scoffed. "Why me, stuck with the dirty work?"

Marty grinned his cat-like grin. "You're the security guard, aren't you? Didn't you tell me once you did—"

"Yeah, yeah, let's skip the little Red Riding Hood story."

"You were always good with B & E. I'm a better bullshitter and better at messing up wise guys, you know it."

I looked at him in wonder, seeing where this was going.

"Relax, this is what we're going to do, Rusco. We camo our faces, go in like cats, knock out their surveillance system. Those cams they have are ancient tech like everything on this scumbucket planet. CCTV, or something like that."

"Nighttime heists are tricky, Marty." My voice wavered between the condescending and serious.

He shook his head. "There won't be a 'nighttime'. I've been staking them out. The contra-crews and loader-boys work nights. Daytime, just a dumb fuck bunch of skeleton crew guards. Sleepy types, nothing ever happens during the day in Baer's yard. We go in in broad daylight."

"And transpo? You still haven't told me what your plan is for that. What are we going to do, fly there on our pink little wings? We're going to need a van or something to go in and truck out a load."

"You kidding me? A truck parked on the side of the road is a red flag, asking for attention, conspicious as doggy-do."

"Scooter then," I said with irritation. "We hide it somewhere in the grass and foot it the rest of the way."

"Better. From what I gather, this contraband is not needing a lot of horsepower to move it. We can always snag some wheels along the way."

"I'll think it through," I said. I bridled my doubts, clamped my jaw shut, cradling chin in my hands.

CHAPTER 2

We took an electric three-wheeler with high chopper handlebars a buddy of Marty's had stored up on the end of the old U-line in his equipment yard. I made Marty sit in the back, be the bitch for once, indicated we'd hide it in the ditch when we got closer. The wheels rolled up on the hardtop which turned to gravel as we snaked along the river. More fenced yards, larger plants, disused factories, metal-pressing mills, boatyards. Not much of anything here away from the smelly, dirty city that was Hoath. Abandoned warehouses, loading docks, crane and metal factories, food packing companies, you name it, suppliers and distributers of every manufactured product one could imagine. The river wound itself tightly alongside a service road behind those complexes, black, slimy water that back in times of older generations used to carry cargoes into town. I felt a desolate unease wash over me. The memories of old sin and dark doings lingered about these tumbledown bastions of yesteryear. Again, that nagging feeling pricked at me, of regretting I had taken on this job.

Now the river was fouled with contaminants and garbage, thick oily water that no respectable fish would be caught dead in. I looked in wonder at the sight of the makeshift shelters and wanderers dressed in tattered khaki or lumberjack shirts, with hand-made rods casting out for fish. I shuddered to think what they'd catch.

Marty tapped my shoulder and pointed at the looming warehouse. We slowed up. Beyond a fenced yard two large, gray-muzzled Behusian hounds yanked at their rusty chains by the cement block outbuilding. I didn't like the beasts' incessant yapping, so I moved away and ditched the three-wheeler, hiding it in the weeds while Marty did his best to usher me along.

We walked past that place and stared at the next yard, Baer's yard, where the docking crane lay and the chain-wired fence, and ugly looking cinder-block, prison-like warehouse with its equally rundown outbuildings.

"This is it?"

Marty opened palms in what looked like a mock apology.

"Seems kind of dumb, Baer having this kind of setup for something this big."

Marty's lips hooked in a knowing grin. "All part of the act, Rusco. Small security crew means nothing worth stealing. The bigger players don't bother. Works well, costs them less, and doesn't draw attention."

"Whatever you say, Marty." I'd only met Q once, and didn't like the man, that big shaggy mother of a criminal, with a dirty cigar hanging out of his mouth, brown teeth, b.o. and a shifty gaze.

Marty stabbed a finger over toward the far side closest to the river. "Right, we jump a ride over there."

"Okay, you can work on 'jumping a ride'. One of those air speeders?"

"I don't know, there may be something inside you can nab that's better."

I shrugged. "I'm liking this less and less, Marty. Shoddy planning, it means somebody gets killed."

"Relax, Ruskie. You always worry too much." He patted me on the back, again a little too hard. "Let's go with the flow. This is a hot lead I've privileged your ears with. We've got a few hours' lead on any other hustlers Q decides to spread the news to."

I rounded on him, my teeth bared. "So, why doesn't big Q do this thing himself, instead of pissing this lead your way?"

"Q's done with Hoathville. Too many enemies here. He'll call in his favor to me at some time. But by that time, I hope to be long gone." He gave me that moony grin I knew too well and rubbed his chin as a flicker of past dealings came and went across that swarthy face of his. "Okay, I'll let you in on a secret, Rusco. Word is 'what's going down in Baer's crib is bigger than Lwippi's spread back in '82'. Those were Q's exact words."

My eyes dulled. "Woo, think I'm going to faint with excitement."

In the end I agreed to give the scope-out a shot, though I was ready to call it quits right there. Much against my better judgment, I contemplated the wire fence, ignoring that little nagging voice in the back of my head, the one that says, you stupid horse's ass, Rusco, what are you thinking? The promise of riches to a man in a hard place though, was a hypnotic lure outweighing risk.

Baer had taken over an old welding shop. A long rectangular building—white-washed cement blocks with tall twin brick chimneys missing several pieces. Rusted metal lay ripped off the outbuildings. Some dingy cargo-holders, transports, v-gauge Cessnas with wings clipped, fly-trucks, auto-meltzers, rusty cranes, some loading docks peeked around the edges. Probably a variety of stolen goods and contraband inside, worthwhile metal parts, salvageable electronics, fuels, explosives. Baer was likely a middle man for some bigger fish up the line. Okay, I was intrigued.

One guard was way down the other end. From where we crouched by the service gate in the gravel, I could see him pacing by the wall, machine gun in hand. No dogs that I could see, fortunately. Just a single sentry.

I looked across the dark thatch of river and caught the rise and fall of heavy metal arms, moving rigs. Migrant workers toiled in the fields there, shipped in from Escaron to work those oil rigs and the strip mines. Many died there, but that was life. A source of cheap labor and cash to boot and work for them. Hard to believe, but a better place for those migrants than the war-torn planets from where they had come. Marty interrupted my reverie.

"What I figure is we take the guard down, blast the door with that dynamite I told you to bring."

"Or maybe not," I grunted. "It ain't dynamite either. Pipe down, I'm trying to think."

Marty grumbled, his fists curled.

When the guard was well down the length of the wall doing his marching soldier routine, I aimed my R4 with its muzzled silencer and took out the main camera with a single, well-aimed shot. No more sound than the buzz of an angry bee.

Marty blinked. "Why not just shoot the guard too?"

"I got something against murder."

Marty snorted. "Give me the gun."

I pulled the weapon back from him and gave him a sullen stare. "Save your groping for your boyfriend."

Marty shook his head, muttering some disparaging comment.

We checked our earpieces. We were still in good working order. Marty donned the black ski-mask; I settled for soot on my cheeks, not that either would save us if it came to a firefight.

Killing the guard early on would be bad for us. First off, Marty was all too impulsive. If he thought the guard was down, he might get some cock-eyed idea, get careless and think he could slack off and just blast his way to the spoils. I didn't feel like getting myself killed the first five minutes into our heist. Nor did I like the restless way Marty got up and started pacing from side to side. It was sloppy, and sloppiness meant disaster. More practical reasons were self-evident: cameras maybe I had missed. A dead body bleeding out on the tarmac, a conspicuous giveaway. The other thing is that sometimes these solitary guards were wired such that if their vitals failed, it sent a signal to a command post higher up that something had gone wrong.

I was banking that nobody was checking that camera very often, if Marty's information was to be believed. Our faces were covered, so nobody could ID us. I checked the kit strapped at my waist: pry tool, custom glock, penlight, blaster, explosives, medicaments, other useful knickknacks.

I hopped the steel-wire fence, taking care not to jingle it too loudly, dropped on the tarmac on the balls of my feet.

Marty followed, noisier than a dog. The sod made me wince with the racket. I cautioned him, and he nodded with a steel-eyed glare.

I threaded my way along the weed-eaten tarmac, ducking behind a generator post and an old dray-cart then lost sight of Marty as he dipped toward the back of the main complex.

Could I get at the guard from the roof? No. Too high. Drop a rock on his head? Dumbass, if you missed… come on, Rusco, you can do better than that. Blaster? Messy and bloody, undeniably noisy.

The easiest, simplest way availed itself. Always the easiest, and the best. The man yawned. Tired from a mindless day of nothing but back and forth in the sun and the drone of air speeders and bottle flies buzzing about. He was not getting paid enough to do this gig. So what if he checked out for an hour? His guard buddy down the line would pick up the slack. Just keep on nodding off, fella. I saw the double chin drop a little lower, then the hand come to clutch at the walrus-like mustache. That's it, a little lower. Probably got hammered last night and he's yawning off the hangover after his drunken lay.

I crept up behind the sap with my weapon cocked just as Poncho lifted his hand to stifle another of those cavernous yawns. One quick chop to the back of the neck along the Vagus nerve and the man fell in a soundless heap. I snatched up the fallen guard's vintage AK—it brought a nostalgic lurch to my heart—

I frisked the unconscious body, found a key ring, jammed it into the steel door, dragged him in, heels first then closed the door behind me.

The blood pounded in my temples and I forced myself to relax. I looked out upon an unmanned, dimly-lit area. A few fluorescent lights cast a dull glow on a concrete floor that stretched far back to my left, into a haze of darkness and mystery. I paused to orient myself. A loading dock spread down to my left with the usual trappings: a ramp of gridded metal, guide bars and dormant red service light above. Across the way, a gray concrete wall loomed dotted with steel doors to other rooms. I caught the vague forms of forklifts, stacked crates, machine parts and tools spread out along the peripheries. A few weigh scales stood next to a loader.

"Guard down," I hissed into the com. "Marty, anything?"

"Some rusted out three-wheelers around the back," Marty replied. "Nothing to brag about. Going to try to juice an air cart I scouted out. Slower than hell, but serviceable. Over."

"Affirmative. Over."

Marty seemed to be dicking around. I hoped he was watching for cameras.

I dragged the unconscious guard over to the far wall and tested the steel door. Unlocked. I stuffed him into the small storeroom. He'd be out for a couple of hours at least. Enough time for me to case the joint and snatch any spoils worth snatching. Hopefully a transport van of lucrative stock or contraband in some wing or bay around the sides I could drive out through the loading bay with none the wiser. Risky, and kind of a longshot, but hey, I was groping for anything at this point, and Marty assured me there was stuff here worth stealing.

No one inside; no guards to speak of. I didn't see any cameras—yet my eye was trained for them. Still, better to err on the side of caution. I thought to flush any other guards out quickly; an old trick I'd learned over the years. Basic but effective. Didn't want any nasty surprises.

Ducking in the shadows, I gripped the pebble I had snatched earlier. I tossed it lightly over my shoulder while I hid behind a wooden crate. The clinking echo rebounded throughout the loading area. I counted the heartbeats. Nothing. Only the hum of the fluorescent lights that played dim and cold over the bare concrete floor. Okay, that was a positive sign.

I crept out of my hiding place, taking noiseless steps, the guard's AK trained ahead.

The place was a little too eerie for my tastes. Kind of a grisly vibe, as if it weren't used much and had bad things happen here, like interrogation under torture. My mind replayed the dark, brown stains on the floor where I'd dumped Poncho. Sure as hell it wasn't pigs' blood. This didn't look like an abattoir or meat packing place to me.

The first creepers of disappointment tugged at my heart. I didn't see anything here worth stealing, and my doubts grew, realizing the futility of this heist. Perhaps I was expecting too much. I saw the desolate reality of this complex. A bunch of mini forklifts, empty crates on skids materializing in the gloom. The hypnotic buzz of cheap, old, electrical wiring while the stale smell lingered in my nostrils: tar, ancient dust, old engine oil.

I continued my rummaging. More crates filled with standard stuff. Boxes of grenades packed in sawdust, foot mines, circular mine sweepers, mild contraband. Military. But nothing to make any yols from this five and dime trash. The place was veritably empty.

Wtf then? That toad-licking Q give Marty false information? Maybe Marty messed up with the details? No, he was not that incompetent.

A wasted trip unless I could spring something fast. Floors bare and clean enough to eat fried eggs off.

I tapped my earpiece. "Marty, you there?"

Nothing.

"Marty, this place is looking like a dud."

Where the hell was he? I was getting more agitated by the minute. Risking my neck out in this empty coop. I whispered harshly into the com again. Nothing. I gave another colorful curse. Maybe Marty'd gotten cold feet or bailed. Was he made?

The storehouse branched out in an L-shape, and I stayed close to the rightmost wall. Across the way, I spied an electric flatbed tucked by the wall, one of the old, four-wheel lorries, riding low on its axles with covered canvas stretching over a back bed top. I slunk over. Nothing around in the back. This could come in handy if I found anything interesting, or if Marty didn't come through with a ride. The driver door was open. I poked my head in and checked the console. Nothing that wasn't easy enough to hardwire. On a whim, I tried starting it up. Ha! The engine whirred to life.

I shut it down, creeping on back to the rightmost wall like a specter.

A door loomed on my right. Blue plate steel with patches of rust caked on the edges. Grimy glass panes granted a view inside: some squarish-rectangular, cramped room. Too dim to distinguish details, but it was crowded with crates and other shadowy objects. Worth a look-see. The door looked fragile. I tried the outer U-ring. Locked. Should I blow it open? Seemed a risk, not to mention overkill. But unless I found something worthwhile here, this trip was batting a big fat zero. Maybe… I reached into my pouch. My universal pry tool gleamed in my hand, cool to the touch and very useful; I began a hack job jimmying the lock. I kept noise to a minimum, put my shoulder into it, forced it open.

A light switch on the side tempted me, but I resisted it. Others could come roaming about.

Crates and boxes of stuff lay stacked to the side. The lids of some I pried off to see weird things, looking like artifacts. Piles of them. Old technological junk, corroded batteries, wired circuits, strange bits of electrical panels, many half destroyed. But they didn't look familiar. Could as easily've been telesat equipment for all I knew. Gutted ship parts? I poked about some more, becoming more puzzled by the second. Disappointed too. Why lock up all this junk?

A set of small crates, stacked two high, aroused my attention. One was set off from the others.

I shone my penlight in the topmost box. Three small, hand-sized objects like rings with a central disc lay in the bottom of the packed cellophane. Curiosity whetted, I reached for the first. It looked like hyperized barsol, like what they made ship hulls out of. When my fingers were about to make contact, it pulsed with peculiar iridescence, like the colors of a butterfly's wings. I'm thinking it might have been something important, the way it swirled with all those alien colors, like chameleons' scales, so I wrapped the cellophane around it, tucked it into my kit, not thinking of any consequences.

Here, by the wall, stood a pair of devices, U-shaped, with waist-high parallel plates set a few feet apart. The things were balanced on black bases. I studied those plates. Circular designs like sucker marks inscribed their insides—alien tech by the look of it—with squiggles etched between its pale ribs. A chill passed over my spine.

Something warned me that this was even more important. I dragged the first parallel-plate device out back to the flatbed. Lighter than I'd thought it'd be. Gingerly, I hefted it into the back and covered it with a tarp, then crept back to the room, thinking to grab the other one, when footsteps and the light scuff of a boot alerted me. I ducked down behind the truck's rear tires.

Two guards, wearing black and white caps pushed down over their short-cut hair, came inching up to the door from the other direction. I could see they wore black chest armor and hefted AKs with murderous ease. Truncheons bobbed at their hips. Their black boots made little noise on the concrete floor. One motioned to the other and they ducked into the room, creeping forward like weasels along the walls. One stayed low to the left, the other to the opposite wall. I could see the thinner one from the angle where I crouched.

Shit, they must have been camped up in some command room watching the sensors. Could have been an infrared beam I'd triggered, which explained why the door was so lightly guarded.

Pinned like a grasshopper, I ran through my options. If I tried to start the lorry, they'd be on me. I could storm in and waste the two, but that was risky, two against one and they looked competent. Sit tight, Rusco. No need to play the hero. Slowly, I edged toward the open door, holding my weapon and breath, feeling the nakedness of my position. Only an open swath between me and death. No protection, and they'd be searching this lorry before long.

The seconds ticked by.

I heard a grunt, then an exhalation of surprise. "Mitch, there's nobody here. Maybe mice tripped the alarm."

"Right, mice just happened to jimmy the door?"

"Yeah, that is a problem; okay, scrap that." The other grumbled. "Hey, you been messing with this box? Something's tore through the wrap. I remember three of the phasos, now there's two. Maybe rats took one away."

"Yeah, rats took one and I came in like a Madonna, wearing them like bracelets behind your back, like I always do."

"Shut up, wise-ass. It's my neck on the line too. Baer hears about this and we're cooked—"

"Relax. Baer doesn't have to hear about it."

"Are you kidding me? We're fucked. Look—one of the amalgos is missing. Two of them were here propped by the wall, remember? Maybe some filchers are still prowling around?"

"Look around again," hissed the other. "Some fuck may be hiding in the shadows." I ducked lower, hearing shuffling and curses, boots laid against boxes and mutters. This was not looking good.

They came up near the door, breathing through their mouths. "Nothing. Let's check the warehouse."

"No, wait. What about the phasos?"

"Fuck the phasos, come on."

"I don't like leaving them, Mitch, if there're skulkers about." He grabbed one. "Baer said they're for Mong, the star lord—"

"I don't give a fuck if they're for Bork of Ork. Put it away, those things give me the shivers."

"I don't appreciate that kind of language, Mitch. Furthermore, I'll touch what I want, bitchface. We're living in a free world, aren't we?"

"You going to get stupid on me, Fario? I said leave it alone." And he grabbed at the other's arm, wrestled the thing out of his hand.

In a blinding flash of light, the thug disappeared. I stared with stupid, blank-faced wonder. I blinked, rubbing my eyes. No ray, no secret gun aimed from the ceiling, no Marty behind holding a blaster. The one named Mitch just disappeared. For a second, I thought someone had spiked the wine I'd swilled at The Bodega. I shook my head. The guy'd been holding the disc thing, juggling it like an ape in front of the other, whispering some wise guy stuff, then poof, was gone.

That could have been me holding that gizmo. I reached for my waist where I'd tucked the disc or phaso, then thought twice of it. Lucky I had covered it with cellophane. I swallowed hard.

So…some kind of weapon? I shifted from my hiding place, head feeling woozy. The nitwit who triggered it was vaporized and his buddy, Fario, was coming out of his stupor, eyes wide in shock, a wild quiver in his gunhand. I thought fast. A medley of plans shuttled through my head. Plan 1, get out of here asap and chuck the phaso, Plan 2, double back, get the other units and mount an escape, Plan 3, blast everybody and run.

Option# 2 had its appeal, considering the potential rewards. One of those phasos still sat in that box, so when blinky eye decided there was nothing to see and booted it, I could easily snatch the disc-ring plus the larger amalgo with parallel plates which looked like antennae, but wasn't. It didn't look homemade, more like some alien tech unless that script on it was some language I'd never seen before.

Rusco, focus.

I heard the other speak into his com, his hands shaking. "Sully, you there?"

The guard tapped his com. No answer.

"Damn you, Sully! Mitch's out. Fucker's dead. Gone. Vamoose. Where are you, you idiot? You're supposed to be watching the entrance. You let some nosepickers in."

Bloody hell. Fario was not giving me many options at this moment, scratching his head like a monkey, then loitering too close by. That box of phasos could be worth some serious dough, if I got it to the right people. Maybe Q wasn't so deadbeat after all. But where was Marty? Why hadn't he checked in? Maybe he couldn't, without being made.

A more likely scenario—Marty had fucked up and was probably dead. As I'd be soon if I didn't do something quick.

This was getting complex and ugly so I scrapped my well-intended plans. I needed to get out of here fast before my luck ran dry. These guys would kill me for whatever was in that back room. The stuff was hot, maybe too hot given my meager resources.

Fario shifted and I sighted in for the kill, trigger finger ready to deal with him. As I was rounding the vehicle door, keeping my eyes on him, a sudden waft of air tickled my skin. Boom! My left knee exploded in pain. Another guy was over me like a bad rash, kicking away my weapon. He must have been lurking there, heard my breathing or something. Or was it Mitch reappeared back like a genie? Grinning, with his AK hoisted, poised to swing it like a club to clock my other leg, I could see the gloating look in his eyes: to have scored the intruder who had nicked the contraband. Bully was written all over that miserable face, reveling in a sense of superiority over his victim, a toy he could play with.

But stupid of any bully not to take his victim out while he had a chance.

CHAPTER 3

I slid out of my painful daze as the guard's weapon came swinging down. I rolled aside. The cold metal only grazed my left ribs. I grabbed the stock and wrenched him forward, at the same time ramming my right boot as hard as I could into his groin. He sagged with a high-pitched cry. While he was gasping for breath, I reached for the syringe tucked in the kit at my belt and jammed it in my left thigh. That got me howling the banshee's yell from hell with the pain stabbing me like a longbow of agony. But above the pain I was already feeling a euphoric high. Myscol, aka Devirol, was the wonder drug of the new age and made me suddenly superman. For a moment the pain fled to a far corner of the universe, but it would come back.

I saw anger and adrenaline and invincibility wash into a blur of unreality. My attacker's face went white as he doubled over, weapon clattering to the ground. I became a fire bomb—a demon juiced up on *Devirol*, the old form of the ancient speed, or some derivative. Down he went in a tumble of tired muscle as my boot connected with his skull.

I snatched up his flesh ripper, the AK—didn't want him to use it on me, if he were to recover, unlikely as that might be.

Everything ticked in slow motion. The man's drool and broken teeth spilled out of his mouth along with a trickle of blood, his quivering cheek pushed flat to the concrete. The staticky whine of voices crackled on his com.

Fuck, there was backup coming. I shook the haze out of my head. A dark spot appeared on my leg where he'd clubbed me. I staggered to the flatbed, still clutching the man's AK, wrenched open the door and started the engine. The vehicle jolted forward, past the forklifts, down the hall, straight up the middle toward the exit. The other guard, Fario from the tickle-trunk room, came barreling after me, shooting at random. I rolled down the window, angled my weapon back at him, releasing a spray of machine fire, but I couldn't aim properly. Rotten bastard had a fast leg and caught up with me as I dodged and weaved, grasping the edge of the open window, grabbed my weapon out of my hand and wrenched it backward. Grunting, trying to jam the prick with my elbow while holding the wheel, I wrenched his arm about, snapping bone. He cursed and I kept his arm locked. The machine gun clattered to the paves. I gunned the engine straight for the sheet metal wall where I knew the loading bay to be.

A strangled scream broke from the guard's lips, as the whites of his eyes mooned in horror. The bumper sheared through the bay doors as jagged metal folded him sideways, erasing his shoulder and crushing his right limb.

The shredded gatepieces clattered behind as I crashed through the sheet metal, the wheels bucking as they took the two-foot drop without hiccup in the absence of any loading ramp. I looked back in the mirror to see his palsying form sprawled on the concrete. I burst out into the pale overcast, wondering where the hell Marty was. No one in sight. A sallow glare streamed from the sky.

Sense started to come to me. What to do with that piece of tech?

The gears in my brain worked with slow precision as I hit the gravel road and headed toward Hoath. I looked for a quick solution. Take the device to my ship at the rendezvous point, several miles out from the east end of town. A no brainer, right?

No.

An abandoned warehouse came up to my left and my heart did a little tumble.

That feeling that grips you when you're forced to make a quick decision in a time of trouble. Take Path A or Path B. The path through the woods on the tried and true trail, or that unknown animal path down by the lake you've never been to. *Step right up, folks, sign your name on the dotted line in blood.* The bad feeling that had been lurking in the pit of my stomach just suddenly jerked up a notch.

"Aw, screw me!" Acid boiling to my throat, I cranked the wheel hard, front tires spitting gravel. The flatbed broke through the rickety steel gate, and I pulled up to the loading docks.

Stumbling out of the vehicle, panting, I kicked open the rusty door of the warehouse with my good leg. Cursing, I tucked my hands in my sleeves. With hands shielded, I dragged the foreign parallel-plate gadget into the gloom, dropped it into a storeroom with only bats and mice flitting about. The place smelled of dung and mildew, but I didn't care. Hadn't been used in years. I pushed the tech deeper into the shadows and covered it with some old mildewed battered skids and tarps. One brown rat with pointed snout jumped out with a baleful stare and squeaked. Knock yourself out, rodent. Get blasted to oblivion, if you like. I limped out to the flatbed and gunned the engine, churning gravel all the way.

Forget Marty. Got to get to my ship.

I drove toward the outskirts of Hoath, following the main road. I must have driven for miles before I became aware of little oncoming traffic.

Warning bells chimed in my mind. What the hell? Minutes ago, only an odd lorry had passed, probably carrying dubious cargo. I didn't know the side roads. Might have to run some detours, which was a bad thing. My leg tingled to the barest edge of feeling as the Myscol began to wear off. To drive that piece of junk into the city—was not ideal.

The flatbed rattled over the top of a hill. Ahead and below, I saw flashing lights. A blockade of some sort: steel girders, surface cars, a few air speeders and milling figures. No way! Men in uniform, hailing down traffic, and detaining and searching vehicles. My mind raced. Baer's work? Coincidence?

Baer's boys must have called in for reinforcements—which meant I was meat if I didn't quit this scene.

I slammed on the brakes and did a full 180. An air speeder looped out after me, its airhorn piercing the stillness and scaring a flock of ducks with long spoonbill beaks. Those horseshoe-shaped air speeders looked like local law. Could Baer's reach run so deep?

I screeched down a gravelled side road. The lights flashed as an official police van lurched after me from the blockade. Now I was up shit creek. This clunker wouldn't hold up to air pursuit and souped-up cop van. In desperation, I cranked the wheel hard and ran her into the fields.

Not wise. The ground was wet and soggy with a recent rain. The engine whined at max rpm, tires spinning in the black mud. The van halted and two burly figures leaped out who looked none too pleased, grimacing through their beards. I could see their faces set and rifles in their hands. The air speeder came bearing down on me.

I bolted the doors, clutched my glock, but they smashed through the glass and hairy hands pulled me out onto the wet grass. I struggled, getting off a wild shot, but losing my grip on my gun, as it was kicked out of my grasp.

"You rotten prick," I bawled. "Pick on someone your own size."

"Funny man at two o'clock, Roy. Spike him."

I still had some juice left in me from the Myscol and I kneed the bastard in the chest just as he bent down to clobber me with his rifle. These thugs were keen on taking me alive, otherwise they would have peppered me long ago. Wrestling, I jammed his weapon in his face, breaking his nose and mashing an eye. He howled and went down in the mud, clutching at the ruin of his face. His partner reached to help him as I staggered off.

The air speeder disgorged three air guard. Husky, military boys. They looked royally pissed, a mean bunch, though nothing more than mercenaries paid to patrol and beat down whoever their employers told them to—which in this case must be Baer. I could see the blue decals with the hunting eagle on the underbelly of the craft. Not that that meant anything, the insignia of city air guards.

Rat-a-tat-tat, Three men and a rat. The rhyme worked in rhythm with the slugs that ate into the flatbed.

I wasn't going out without a fight. I pulled out a large hand-sized explosive from my waist kit. Tossed it at the air speeder. The marshals shielded themselves but I was the only one to duck in time.

Marshals and air speeder went up in a roaring flame.

I heard voices through the haze and smoke as I struggled through the wet sod.

"Nothing in the back!" cried one of the van riders. "No amalgos."

"What the fuck? Where's the amalgo? Where's that shitweasel with the bombs?"

I grinned as I hobbled away. One came loping after me through the smoke, grunting again. "Where's the bloody amalgo?"

"Up your ass, fucker. Eat shit."

A billyclub came smashing down on my head and I knew no more.

CHAPTER 4

I passed from world to world, from past to present, in a kaleidoscope of fact and fiction. My disembodied self hovered above the floor that dim day out working as a security guard over at Crystal Mindworks Ltd. Days when I entertained a notion of upholding some law-keeping role in society. Five thugs busting down the door, wearing masks.

The beat down of the guards, Frenzetti and Markus, my friends, slain in front of my eyes. Two shots clipping from my R9, one killing the first, point blank, the other sending a lowlife writhing on his back. A bullet grazing by my ear. Stumbling out the side alley, my ears ringing, blood pouring down my scalp. My one thought was to get out of here while others roved about, knowing that the bungling would be pinned on me as an accomplice. *Why were you the only one left after the robbery, Rusco?* Trying to start the air speeder to get out there, start fresh on a new world. Taking other softer jobs offworld, working star carrier baggage, playing bouncer, pawn shop security, construction crew, you name it, but it only got worse— the violence, the murder, the theft, always catching up to me, as if I were some beacon for it, with a dark cloud hovering over my soul, plunging me deeper into a nightmare of illusion. The drinking becoming more intense, the only way to drown the pain, until Mela at last left me.

Dreams have the uncanny knack of telling us hard dark truths about ourselves.

When that saw edge of reality surfaced, so began my slow descent down the road 'if you can't beat them, join them'. My looking for crime as a quick means to an end, flirting with its seductive narcotic, searching for the one big score that would never happen.

I came to, with the smell of sweat and machine oil in my nose. Some rough hands dragging me across the cement floor. In a dingy hall lit with fluorescent lights the familiar smell hit me. I groaned. Well, I'll be a monkey's fuckbuddy if I wasn't back in that shithole warehouse.

Then I discerned the sounds of a beat-down. A familiar voice. Quiet, child-like, mixed with thudding sounds like a metal pipe whacked on flesh. Only because it came through a steel door left slightly ajar did it sound surreal, like something out of a cartoon. The two goons thrust me in. I rolled on a bare concrete floor, blinking like the bedraggled wretch I was.

I took one look at Marty beside me and knew things had gone very wrong. His haggard face resembled a terrified mask. He mouthed words "had to scram or give away your position."

Marty sagged as a meaty fist clipped him in his well-purpled face. With two black eyes and lips messed up, it explained why I couldn't recognize that voice right away.

The man who'd clipped him turned his burning gaze upon me. I had seen wild animals in the zoo less feral and repulsive than that aberration who stood before me. Everything about the thug screamed bear. A shaggy ruff of black hair like the fur of a large predator coated head and arms. Wide sideburns covered his cheeks, his bared forearms exposed by rolled-up sleeves. Wide-spaced beady eyes and mallet fists. A mouthful of shark teeth. Easily could have been the most hideous creature I'd seen. Some modern-day mutant? Or one who'd experimented with, or OD'd on too many modern day transfigurative drugs and lost the fight?

"Welcome, Mr. Rusco," the man growled in his husky voice. "Glad you could make our little appointment."

"The pleasure is all mine." I spat blood, along with a tooth.

"You know who I am?"

"Mr. Magoo from the Metro Zoo. Dunno, don't care."

He flashed my long-nosed captor a meaningful look.

Long Nose grunted. "Busted up Floss and Bix real good. They won't be walking too soon. Vin's Air speeder took a hit. Some little incendiary he had up his sleeve. No amalgo."

The man sighed, a murmur of grave amusement. "Clown Hair, you've been a busy boy. Care to enlighten us on the whereabouts of my amalgo?"

"Dunno anything about any amalgo."

He paced the room, his lips getting cold and stiff, his teeth flashing as if ready to bite someone's head off. "That's funny. Fario, who lies with half his arm hanging off, claimed he saw one in the flatbed you crashed through my warehouse."

"Fario sounds like a man with an overactive imagination."

He jerked a thumb at Long Nose. "Clown Hair thinks he's gonna word-play his way out of this." He turned to me. "You know, one of the amalgos is no good without the other."

"Do I give a fuck?"

"You don't get it, do you?" he echoed in wonder.

"Sure, Baer," Marty slurred through a broken nose. "We do."

"Mr. Baer to you." He growled, turning his feral gaze on Marty. "Some clients of mine are going to be sorely pissed when they ask me where their amalgo is and I say, "beats me, Will, a couple of wise-guys broke in and stole it."

"That's a hard thing to have to say," Marty wheezed. "I can understand, Mr. Baer. Rusco's just bargaining for his life is all, aren't you, Jet?"

Baer smiled and shook his head with a sad laugh. "I'll ask you again, where's the amalgo?"

One of Marty's eyes had swollen shut. "I'm just the dog-boy here, Baer. If you want to pull somebody's legs off, you're looking at the wrong guy. *Ask, Jet.*"

"Like this sack of shit's going to tell us anything?" Baer snarled. He flashed a pistol and held it to my head. "This fuck looks as if he couldn't blow himself out of a paper bag. Last chance, Marty. You're ribbing with the wrong man, with this, 'ask Jet, shit'."

"That's rich, boss," guffawed Long Nose. He gave Marty a jab in the ribs with his truncheon that had him groaning.

"Shut up," growled Baer. "If I want you to open your mouth, I'll rattle my zipper."

I twitched, almost wanting to laugh. Marty, the faithless fucker. He was going to sell me to the dogs before long with his good-guy talk. I could see the yellow look in his eye. Fuck Marty. I'd have to rely on my own devices to live through this. The hoodlums seemed sure of themselves to have kept us unbound. They wouldn't kill me as long as I knew where their amalgo was. Torture, yes, but there was the Myscol. What was Marty's game? Was he done playing sycophant, giving up his only leverage of having something of worth they wanted? Unless, of course, Marty was being trickier still with his old good guy, bad guy routine. My mind was not thinking straight. I was in shock from the last ten hits to my skull.

Marty was stalling, always good at that, mixing fact with fiction, hopefully creating possibilities out of thin air to keep the enemy guessing and scratching his head. That it would stall Baer long enough before one of us could break out of here, was another thing. Marty wasn't looking as if he could hack too much more.

"Search him," Baer said.

"Already did. We found this little phaso on him. This big explosive too." My husky captor tossed it to Baer.

Baer nodded. "Got that. Explains the wrecked speeder. Demolitions man, are you?" he said, turning to me.

I smiled.

"Where's the amalgo? The funny little roboty-looking googad with twin parallel plates. Glows green when armed."

I tossed back my wavy dyed purple hair, trying for a gambit. Nothing to lose, right? Well, almost right. Sorry for what it cost Marty. I am sorry for that.

The Myscol, still pulsing in my veins, fueled fire to an inner strength we all have but rarely tap into. I'd taken a triple dose, something unheard of— my doctored batch, the one they had no clue I'd taken. It drew them deeper into underestimating me.

Long Nose, on a cue from his boss, stepped in to truncheon me as he had Marty. That was a mistake. My steely fist crashed into his thigh. It's as close as I could get to the brute. Left a charley horse he wouldn't forget. He buckled over with a painful rictus and my steel-toed boot caught him in the throat and that made his charley horse look like a love tap. Teeth and blood dripped on the ground with sticky white drool. Nasty scene.

Baer made his move, but I was quicker. I snatched the coin-sized explosive out of his hand, ducked in a drunken roll and tossed it right back at him, just as I armed the detonator.

The white flare caught his right side, lit him up like a candle, as he held up a hand to shield his face. Too late. The blast also caught Marty and singed half his hair and upper cheek off. Me, I was blinded for a second and my left side blood-spattered and burnt. The boss roared like a bear, clutching at his burning arm, shorn at the elbow. He'd mend it with some bio-regen, if he hurried. Doubted he had any on him at the moment.

The shaggy man staggered for the side door, coughing blood through the smoke. How he did so was beyond me; the man must not be human. I pocketed the phaso he'd dropped, grabbed Marty, and stumbled after.

I hauled Marty's sorry ass out of that burning, smoking death crib, lips curling in crazed grin at Baer's tumult. We stumbled through the gaping ruin of the loading dock. Across the tarmac we beetled like a couple of twisted scarecrows. An air speeder and two lorries stood out back of a communications tower surrounded by wire fencing. Screw the lorries. Useless against air attack. That air speeder looked like a heavenly prize, especially since it was one of Baer's.

I hopped around the other side of it with Marty all gasping and limping. The first parked vehicle shielded us from the machine gun fire that would have cut us in two. We scrambled back, ducking to the rat-a-tat-tat of stray bullets. I clawed open the speeder door, hopped in, as machine gun fire clipped the tail fins.

I pulled Marty in head down and dove behind the wheel.

Kicking the throttle full on, I veered straight up, as black smoke and pressure gauges plummeted. "Come on, baby!" I roared. "Get us out of here before old man Baer grows wings. To the air depot."

"We ain't gonna make it, Rusco," rasped Marty, caressing his soot-grimed cheek and ruined ear that oozed fluids.

I grimaced at the sight and smell of his burned flesh. "Sure we will, Marty. Shut up. Sit back and enjoy the ride. Course we'll make it."

For the first time I got a good look at Marty and shivered at what I saw. His lank mustard-colored hair was coated in slick dark fluid. His breath wheezed in and out like a terminal smoker. Coagulated blood caked the side of his head and his right arm spasmed.

"You okay?" A dumb question that I wished I hadn't asked.

He held up a quivering hand and grimaced through his pained, red-rimmed eyes. "Had better days."

"Helluva ride."

"Helluva ride. Didn't by any chance snatch up that little phaso of his before Baer was grasping for pieces of his arm?"

"Not particularly." Lies were easy to spill out of my mouth. The disc was a death curse and Marty wasn't up for what was next.

"Uh huh. Guess we could end up with nothing then after all."

"Guess so."

Marty closed his eyes and lay back his slick head against the headrest as the air speeder sputtered along, trailing a stream of ugly black smoke. The engine growled and hiccupped. It wouldn't stay airborne for long. Below us, the city came into view in all its grisly glory: broken water towers, bombed-over apartment complexes, crumbled buildings, checkerboard smokehouse slums.

"Listen, I have to set us down somewhere. We can't be caught again."

A long pause. Marty shook his head. "Ain't leaving Hoath, Rusco. You're bad luck to me. Don't want anything to do with you."

"Don't blame you, Marty. I can get you fixed up on Starrunner."

"Forget it."

"Suit yourself."

"Drop me at the nearest U-ground link," he croaked. "I'll catch a ride downtown."

"Dammit Marty, let's talk about this."

"There's nothing to say, Rusco."

I shrugged. Marty was a proud man. I couldn't blame him for despising me. The job was a cockup, we'd almost gotten killed, and in his mind, I'd screwed up and abandoned him. Perhaps that's why I had ridden solo for so long.

Marty spat out a wad of blood on the floor at his feet. I veered down over a side street on the outskirts of the Jildaree district, milling with immigrants. One of the main streets would take Marty to the old market, downtown. He could disappear in the underground like a wisp of air. Part of me hated to leave him, but it was his choice.

In his lucid moments, he'd come to see the dark cloud hovering over me, the one that had shadowed my hide for so long now. The old, painful, rat-gnawing wound in my soul that drew danger and mishap like a moth to the flame.

"So long, Jet," he muttered with a tired sigh. His crooked grin had gone cold and brittle.

As I landed in a disused equipment yard, I popped open the door and watched him ease off his seat, leaving a blood trail behind. "So long, Marty. Take care of yourself."

He limped off into the yard, catching the blinking surprise of many ragged beggars and potheads warming their hands around their fires. I opened my mouth to say something, but thought better of it. I took off into the hazy sky, doubting that despite what Marty said, the poor bastard would make it through the night.

CHAPTER 5

I glided down to the refueling-docking station where I had left Starrunner, a big sun-bleached yard with two mid-size control towers and four rusty hangars. Glad I'd paid my twenty yols to secure it—safe for a little while at least. Anything over two days wasn't guaranteed, neither here nor at any approved docks on this planet.

I set the stolen speeder down in a designated landing zone and hobbled up to the security guard at Hangar 3. I gave the gate security guard my most disarming smile. He gave me the once-over, frowning at my blackened and bruised appearance and tattered clothing, but after positive ID, he let me pass.

My ship, a sleek and gray Alpha 9 had a rough diamond shape at rear with ox horn-shaped prow at front—a balm for my soul. Many adventures we'd shared together. She'd gotten me out of jams before.

Several other ships were berthed nearby, from the dingiest rustbuckets this side of Vega, to a few Alpha retrofit models with double-flared ion thrusters, cigar fuselages and weapons defense to boot. I couldn't help but admire these vessels despite my haggard state, beauties in their own right in this day and age. One fine morning I'd graduate to a Kepler 350 or a Hexler 410 A2.

Stay focused, Jet.

The hatch peeled back after I fumbled the controls at the side. I'd rewired the thumbprint ID-pad to bypass the scan, in case my thumbs were less than thumbs.

I ducked into the hatch and stumbled to the bridge, fired up my eagle. I reached below the console and took a bottle, downed a chug of Astra whiskey to loosen me up. Then another. I needed something to take the edge off my agony when I started to really come down off the Myscol. I patted the console with all her lit-up sensors and the extra upgrades I'd installed over the years. A better version of the battle hound older models. Self-refueling, drawing the radiant energy from suns when she came close to one, replenishing the Radium-Cesium ion thrusters and wafer cells. It had less range on impulse power and less speed at sub-warp, but it saved me a lot of grief, and yols, in risking refueling at some redneck, outer-planetary dock.

As the sallow sky grew flat, stars tinkled at the edge of my vision. I heard whispering voices in my head over the hum of the engines as Starrunner passed through the clouds. Hoath became a faraway memory. A stab of bright light licked out from the sun Tiga then disappeared as I arched into planetary shadow, then the blackness of space.

At this point I'm wondering what the hell am I doing? Why pursue this gig, Rusco? Are you a masochist?

Smartest thing would be to get out of the Phaedra sector as fast as I could. To where? Beleron 6? Mixraen? Both planets were safe—relatively speaking. Mixraen, one of the less shabby worlds where I could get this knee looked after without being at risk of infection or some botch-up. The throbbing had receded to a dull ache but that likely wasn't going to go away soon.

Thing was, Starrunner wasn't protected from pot-shot hunters. Easy for Baer and his goons to do a hyperclasson trace on the heat signature, if they so desired. Triangulate from last vector before light speed. I'd have to jump worlds to give them the slip.

With such thoughts crowding my mind, I programmed the Varwol light drive for Mixraen, in the meantime coasting on steady impulse power toward Brisis's moon, knowing I'd have to clear planetary gravity before I could risk engaging the light drive.

I gazed with pride upon my rack of guns, from small pistol to semi-automatic RX series to Uzi to remodeled AK to modern high-blaster. A weapon for every day of the week. Even experimental ray guns at the end of the rack. But I tended to go for the older-generation guns. Call me a traditionalist.

My attention drifted back to the view in space. Several monstrous cylinders hovered before me. I eased past the now hulking derelict remnants of ancient planetary defense systems, orbiting Brisis. Their nuclear powerplants had winked out of existence ages ago, their pulse ray cannons, at one time able to destroy star cruisers, now iced and inert. Many half shorn barrels looked back at me. Though hollow and scavenged by junkers or freelancers for parts, they still sent shivers down my spine.

A blip appeared on my sensor readouts. I frowned. A bright object reeled in behind the nearest cylinder. At first I thought it was the actual derelict coming to life.

But no. Raiders! Clinging to the underside, piggy-backing off the defense probes like tics, eluding my sensors.

The klaxon rang from the overhead bulkhead and Molly's computerized voice began beating out an insistent monotone, *"Red alert. Enemy in pursuit. Pulser waves to hit in five seconds."*

What the bloody hell! They weren't active when I flew down to this god-forsaken planet.

I activated shields and banked Starrunner in a steep dive away from the pulse beams arching my way. It gave me a few more seconds. But the impact grazed the starboard thruster and sent me in a tailspin. Shit! The Varwol couldn't engage this close to planetary gravity, so I was scuppered.

"Great, Molly. Skurgian raiders? What this time?"

"Databanks report high probability of Skurgian origin."

Two more bogies popped up out of nowhere on my short range scanners. Three old, refitted craft with high stems, bullet noses and gray bodies. No match for Starrunner on a good day, but a risk now with her in a side slew. I maxed out the stabilizers and with help of the ship's computer, managed to pull her out of her tailspin. "Molly! Lock weapons on their engines, now!"

"Affirmative."

As the forerunner gained ground, I caught a glimpse of the raider's forecannon. Large and lethal. Nothing less than heat-seeking missiles, spiked cubes with wicked guiding systems. They'd pulse Starrunner to immobility, then blow me open like a tin can with one of their torpedoes, with the added bonus of being able to scavenge at their leisure with the crew dead.

My mind worked in furious calculation. Raiders as these went for the small fry like myself and left the big freighters alone—the big cargo transports moving world to world selling their ores, raw materials and contraband on less impoverished worlds than Hoath.

The Skurgian stalkers turned on an intercept course. I sent out a high-energy fareon beam, after Molly had done the math. The first enemy craft careened left too late as concentrated pulser made contact with metal, and a bright orange ball burst outside my starboard viewport.

I cheered. The lights dimmed and reserve power took a hit, and the shields took a beating upon the return fire. But the other two banked off.

I struggled to gain control of the fluctuating sensors. "T minus 10 to escape window," Molly droned. Like slow leaps into infinity, the seconds ticked by. Just as the next spiked missile came a ghost's breath away, the Varwol kicked in, and the universe slipped sideways. Colored lights dazzled my visual space, a million sparkles of bright light licked out at me from the void ahead. Then blackness. Starrunner had entered the no-zone of singularity. *Running again.* Rusco's signature.

Yet something was off. The last hit must have damaged the singularity stabilizers. My heart did a dive.

Odd thing about warp is that sound is often distorted. One's movements seemed blurred around the edges, as if reality is skewed, impinged by an external force. A human hand moves a little too late, or an extra finger appears on that hand but it's just a blur of five fingers moving at once. The mobilitor's tech corrected and tried to adjust for the time-dilation effect, but even that was never infallible and created little glitches of speech and movement. Exaggerated now with the mobilitors impaired.

"Molly, do something."

"Mobit tech at 82% and dropping. High impulse beam was sustained by shield at 40%. Compensating."

"Do what you can!"

A sudden dark thought edged my mind. I clawed at my pant's pocket. Still there. I grabbed a soft cloth and extracted the phaso and lay the disc on the bridge console with extreme care.

The object sat there in its weird way, shimmering with a dull iridescence. I eyed it as a tiger might eye a steel-rimmed trap. Something about the thing did not seem natural, or of any human world, with its unreadable script and its strange symbols writ along the curve's inner edge. Hieroglyphics? Numbers? Coordinates? I shook my head. Inscribed on the light hyperbarsol they reeked of heavy mystery. I daren't touch the script, for it looked as if it might be where the last schmuck had fingered it, and gone into hyperspace.

I shivered, moved the evil talisman into a metal strongbox I kept in the storage bulkhead. I closed the box with a loud clack and stuck it under the console. A spasm of pain rippled through my knee. My hand reached down, clutched at the bulged rent in my leather spaceman's garb that covered my quivering kneecap, aching and swollen.

The hydrophane from the Myscol was wearing off. Spidery pain crawled up my leg with a ripple effect, from shin to knee. I stumbled to the medicine cabinet, biting back curses, fingers arching for that place where I kept my stash of get-well drugs. My hands shook as I reached for the little pink bottle, the one I saved for special occasions. That I'd distilled from a home blend of morphine and dyzanol. I refrained from another shot of Myscol, knowing well the next jolt would send me into cardiac arrest. Muscle up, Jet boy. Stomach your pain.

Fingers beaded with sweat, I stuck a wooden rod between my teeth and champed down hard.

Eyes glued to the sensors, I watched the Varwol integrity dip down to 62%. But it held. Movement was tricky in this syrupy warp and repairs impossible. As long as it didn't get below 40% before the next planet, I was okay. If it did…ship and crew would disappear into a singularity.

I cruised for hours, maybe days, enjoying the silence of deep light travel, warring with old thoughts, aware of a nagging feeling brewing at the back of my skull. Something about this situation seemed worse than past ones—a shadow zone, as if I were staring in the black pit of the unknown. I really didn't know what my next step was, something unusual for Jet Rusco. Calm, cool, phlegmatic Rusco of the dark pool of scammers and avengers, with a million cons all ready to go. To have survived them thus far, had given me a richer confidence than I deserved. A dangerous place to be. It was a bubble waiting to be burst. That grand bungle in Hoath had been the first warning; staring down death, not once but twice. It had shaken the belief in my invulnerability, got me thinking.

Thirty-five going on eighty, melting into the wasteland of middle age. I wasn't getting any younger. The creaks in my spine were getting all too loud and more frequent. The lithe pliancy, the hard muscle that had once moved fast and rattled so many heads had toned down a peg.

The warning sensor came back and Molly's shrill voice seeped into my brain like a bullet shredding chipboard.

"Systems failure. Port wing stabilizer. Varwol disengaging. T minus 6. Impulse power at 10%."

"Molly, you doom-monger! Where the hell are we?"

"Minos sector, The Orion Zone. Coordinates T56.988234—"

"Alright, nowheresville. Target the closest habitable planet."

"Affirmative. Planetary gravity field affecting compromised Varwol." She brought up the nearest planetary datasheet on the holo display. A dusty world, of shell-shocked craters within range. Estimated indigenous population: 12,000.

"Great, okay, make for it. What is it?"

"Talyon 8A. Terraformed planet settled in the second wave of the settlers' rush, circa 2945.67.123—"

"Yeah, yeah." The fourth planet showed as a pale saffron disc in orbit around Silirus, the bright orange star dead ahead. The nearby planet's gravity was too much for the drive. The Varwol fluttered to a halt, leaving me on impulse, caught within grappling distance of Talyon's gravity. The main thrusters, already compromised, shuddered under the tidal grab, not potent enough to steer me clear.

I guided the ship as best I could down through the colorless atmosphere. Even that was rocky. Starrunner couldn't stay in the air.

I picked the straightest strip of sand I could find, between two massive mountains of what looked like monstrous garbage piles, and what looked like massive pits beyond them. I kept the nose high, tightening the straps securing me in the pilot's chair.

Starrunner's fuselage heated up to a red blur. Ship sensors warned me of further failures. I shut them off.

The ship ground its gray underbelly along the alien turf as I bashed along and watched my fragile existence flash before my eyes. No regrets, Rusco, none. Though there should have been a thousand.

The grinding of pebbles against the hull came to a screeching apex; the buffeting, rocking knocked my brain about, as I was jostled and jerked until blackness stole over my mind.

CHAPTER 6

I jerked up with a gasp, passing a hand over my brow. It came back crimson from a throbbing gash. Some loose object must have whacked me on the skull.

Blood dripped down my cheek. I blinked through the porthole at a giant mound of reddish-black crud and scummy earth glaring back at me. Whiplash, bruises and aching joints strobed in and out with red welts where the straps had held me. No broken bones. The ship's interior functions blinked in nominal condition. Better condition than what I expected. Emergency lights bathed a pale glow over the power console and sensors kept bleeping.

The pilot panel flashed like something out of a gamer's session and dust particles hung thick in the air. The ship was useless to me with the drive so impaired. Nor was I any ace mechanic. I counted the seconds as I drifted in and out of crash daze. I could sit there like a grinning statue, pretending none of this had ever happened, or I could get up and brave the elements. At some point I would have to, as my supplies were not inexhaustible. The sooner the better. My eyes traveled to the surplus space suit hanging from the wall. I visualized the sustenance I would have to gather up, stumbling about on an alien world. But who knew what horrors lurked out there? Sucking in another gasp of air, I hitched off my safety straps and collapsed to the metal-grated floor before groping to my knees and picking myself up to hobble across the bridge. The pain clutched at the heart of my nerve centers.

Readout showed a breathable atmosphere, a few decimals shy of 38 Celsius. Damn, hot out there. Terraformed likely centuries ago. But a bad feeling brewed in my gut. Shaking my head, I grabbed an R4 blaster, part Uzi, part modern tech, from the weapons rack close-by and opened the hatch. Dull sunlight struck my eyes. I staggered out, wincing, feeling the haze of disorientation.

Starrunner's fuselage smoked. I swayed on unsteady feet, struck by the heat wave. I closed the hatch, rolled up my sleeves, made the mistake of grazing the gleaming metal while keeping my balance. "Ouch, you fucking mother—" My wild curse fell on dead air. I shook out my hand.

A sandy lane disappeared around a bend between massive piles of twisted junk. Behind, a sandy streak where my smoking ship had skidded to an unceremonious halt. This looked like a vast human-made dump. Broken plastics, twisted metal, pipes, culverts, wires, charred wood, every bit of refuse I could imagine. An old dusty reek filled my nostrils, as if the cloud of slow decay had floated over here for generations. No rain had fallen here for what, decades? The dryness had ground decomposition to a halt. I reached out, touched a hank of metal, a lance-edged piece from the bumper of an old ground vehicle. The metal seemed little rusted for the time it had spent here.

The Veglos system and all the rest of the galaxy had gone to hell, but did I have to get marooned on a shit pile like this?

What were these giant mounds of garbage? Not just ass-wiping little dungcock heaps you see on the satellite, five and dime feeder worlds, but *giant* mounds. Miles of them. An ecological disaster. Not that it mattered much considering my plight on this forsaken world.

Sound to my left. A flicker of movement. I ducked behind a small heap of mangled wires and prosthetic robot parts, gripping my R4, my senses on high alert.

Two figures emerged, one tall, one short. They carried no weapons that I could see, only what looked like a Geiger counter held in the hands of the older, taller man. I blinked, shaking my head of the cobwebs.

"Billy," the older one croaked in an excited voice, "looks as if we've found our pot of gold. The sounder has found our fortune." His loose tan-brown desert rags drooped from neck to toe. "There, just like I said! A downed craft. Yahoo!" He slapped his thighs in glee, stabbed a finger of triumph at my ship, the place where she smoked and crackled.

The boy, no more than fifteen, jumped up and down like a sidekick, did a kind of jig like one of those crazy panhandlers I see back at Hoath.

"Careful, Billy," the man warned. "This thing could be booby-trapped." He pulled the teen away with a determined hand. He looked ready to cry.

I narrowed my brows. Whoever these halfwits were, I was at a low melting point with an itchy trigger. As the older fellow blinked and set down his metal detector on the hot sand, he gave my ship a careful inspection and reached within his rags, withdrew a tool of some sort to tinker with the outer hatch.

A small smile touched my lips. Good luck, pops, getting in that titanium-sealed—

My jaw dropped as the door slid open and the old man gave a victorious chuckle. The alarm sounded, a piercing intermittent klaxon whose lows and highs dripped with Molly's anticlimactic warning,

"Intruder alert, intruder alert!"

I cringed. So did my guests who stared around wild-eyed, as if monsters were ready to eat their brains. The old man's eyes kindled in desperation and he fiddled with the cowling trying to disable the alarm.

No luck. I gripped my R4, ready to blast these two desert rats. They'd invaded the one sacred place left to me in this big universe. Another voice called out a throaty drawl that made me pause.

"Back off, weasels! Mine first." The figured motioned the narrow bore of her rifle at them. Youngish to middle age, bowlegged, dressed in worn leathers, goggles strapped tight as protective eyeware against the sun, she was a sight to behold, legs set wide in an aggressive stance.

The old man turned with care and put a restraining arm around Billy's shoulder. Seemed the boy was keen on running out and getting himself shot. He snarled like a vicious animal, like some wolverine I'd seen on the nature holo-feed.

"Move," she ordered, roaring in a harsher voice, motioning to where a charred single mangle of metal hung out of the smaller mountain of debris.

Grumbling, the two hurried to stand beside a crumpled space cruiser, clinging out of the pile like some squashed insect.

She padded toward the open ship with a slow saunter, and I blinked, getting my senses together, then crept after her, my blaster raised.

"Back away," she growled. "I get first dibs on this crate, you bumpkins, then you can paw your way over it as much as you like. The grubs'll be coming out soon. Yes, the crazy boys, and you know what that means."

She leveled her sawed off black rod, a custom blaster, rigged with flamethrower and bayonet. Peeking into the entrance bay, she nodded in appreciation.

I frowned. What a filthy piece of work. Dirty as sin. Grime all over her skin and face and loose leather jacket and pants and shin-guards. Black, of all colors, in this stifling heat. Yet underneath the grime was a limber female, with lean muscles to boot.

Before she got the bright idea of staking out my ride, I stepped over and called out a pleasantry. "Okay, commander Tomboy, ease back real slow."

She whirled, lifted her weapon, but misfired a round that whistled inches from my ear. I shot off a slug that nicked the bayonet's end and made her think twice about another shot.

She held her hands up and let her weapon drop.

"That's smart. Kick it away," I said. She did, though with sullen reluctance which irked me, all that lioness pride.

I frisked her from chest to toe and she quivered in rancor. This one didn't like to be touched, I could tell. Couldn't blame her.

"You're wasting your time," she rasped. "When the crawlers get wind of this little ship, there'll be nothing left of it."

The old man clicked his tongue. "Nasty bit of luck, landing here on this planet."

"Shut up." I ducked into the hatch, entered the key code that shut Molly's remorseless voice off and whirled on the skinhead lady who seemed ready to make a move. "Who are these crazy boys you're talking about?"

She snorted. "You'll find out soon enough." I didn't like the sound of that or the lazy smirk curling across those lush lips, pretty ones in a former life.

"What's that supposed to mean?"

She licked her lips with a smirk. "Just wait, fly boy."

I gave her the once over. She gave me a once over, appraised my gleaming sinew and my doubtful looks.

Not that I was prejudiced or anything. Not my type. Too tomboyish— and dirty. The challenging stare, the tough girl stance, the stiff thrust of hip. A slight swagger that didn't quite fit her, and that mannish little brush cut— ouch, butch written all over. I wondered what this planet had done to her.

"My suggestion is, lose the butch raven cut," I grunted.

"What do you know?" she snarled, ducking in a crouch to grab for another weapon I'd missed strapped at her ankle under the dust-grimed black leather.

"Unh uh," I warned, motioning her up with my weapon, and she rose in slow motion from her cat-like crouch. I confiscated the weapon.

"Well, looks as if we got ourselves a regular standoff here," said the old man wistfully.

"The hell we do." I shook my head, flakes of soot dropping, leftovers from the explosion at Baer's crib. "From my position, you're looking down the end of a loaded barrel."

"Maybe," croaked the man, "but if you want to save your ship, you'll let Billy and me get it moving to safer ground." I saw his white mustache bristle and tassel of gray rooster hair twitch. A keen intelligence lurked behind those bushy brows. The boy had a mousy face and busy fingers, and looked as if he had as much brains as two hammers left out in the rain.

I jeered. "What you going to do, get on your hands and knees and carry it to safety?"

"Billy can run back and get a couple of anti gravs, can't you, Billy? The AGs'll lift it and we can propel it along with jet thrusters."

Snot-nose Billy gave an eager nod.

I blinked in new amazement. "Some joke, old man? Last I heard anti-gravs were quite large."

"Not mine," he called.

"How far away are these AGs?"

"About half mile back, though I think if you're thinking of following Billy, it's a bad idea."

"Why would I think of that?"

"Just thinking. Billy's a fast runner."

I exhaled a long breath, wiping the river of sweat from my forehead.

The woman grunted out a sardonic breezy sound that in no way improved my mood. "Well, now that we've got that all sorted, how be we set us up a table and napkins and have some tea and cookies before the mad boy's join us?"

"Thought they were the 'crazy boys'—suddenly now they're the 'mad boys'?"

"Happy to meet you too, space man. Name's Wren." She thrust out a hand.

"Mine's TK." The old man stepped forward.

I stared at the two of them—as if I were on a planet of crazies. The heat, the injuries were getting to me. "Rusco," I snapped with reluctance.

"Well, that's dandy," said Wren, rubbing her wrists and clapping her hands. The woman was all smiles and chuckles now.

The old man whispered some energetic words in the kid's ear who then beetled off down the sand path and disappeared around a curve in the nearest mound and was gone.

"Billy's a good boy. A little slow on the mark, but dependable."

"What's to stop your munchkin from bringing a posse down on me or some other unpleasant surprise?"

"Nothing. What other options you have? Not to worry, Billy doesn't do stuff like that anyway. Found him hiding under a mound. Burrowed himself deep like a cricket hunting for food. Shivering. His parents had been taken by the mad boys. He had the sense to hide under the refuse and I've taken him under my wing ever since."

"Very touching," I grunted.

My leg had started to quiver. The older man's eyes glowed with a trace of curiosity at my discomfort. I hunkered down to massage my burning knee. The blazing heat was making me sweat something awful, as if I had a bad fever. I must have sweat a cup of liquid in the last fifteen minutes. Tongue swelling up in my mouth, I rolled it over my parched lips.

Wren grinned. "What's the matter, space boy? Rat nip you in the knee?"

"Shut up, for crap sakes!" I lurched to my feet, rounded on her. I glared at the old man. "What if you get the ship skyworthy? I doubt if you're going to do any favors as a good samaritan?"

He lifted his chin and scratched his neck. "About time I got off this planet. How about transpo to Aldebaran?"

I shrugged. "We'll see."

"While you're at it," called Skinhead. "I could use a lift to the nearest transhub."

"Like I owe you something?" I turned and glowered at her.

The sun seemed to inch its way across the yellow sky like a big bad ball of fire kindling my insides. Sweat did wonders to help combat the pain. I pulled at my vest, snapping open the buttons, exposing my chest.

The day was long on this forgotten world—double the daylight I was used to.

My leg amped up again and throbbed. I crouched and sprawled in what was a patch of shade. Maybe I drowsed for a second then. My head lolled and I caught the woman creeping up on me with a fist clenched. "Back!" I grunted, motioning my weapon at her. Her slinking frame came to standstill, and she gave me a forced, sullen grin.

All the time I expected monsters to come jumping out of the garbage and kill us all, like those mad boys they kept yapping about. I picked up on the woman's apprehension; even the old man was edgy, making me nervous with his shifty feet and eyes darting to the surrounding dungheap. No matter, we'd all just sit tight until somebody showed.

At last, Billy came skipping out of the shimmering heat waves, eyes all a-glimmer, sporting a toothy grin like a cat that's caught a fat mouse. Three rectangular-shaped objects he clutched in his tanned-brown hands.

"That was quick, Billy," congratulated the old man. "Let me see them."

The boy returned some words I couldn't understand. Mumbles, child-like baby sounds. Was he a mute?

TK took the square blocks out of his hands, dug a small hole and fixed them up under the fuselage, one at the front, two at the back. He fired up the power on one and while I hobbled over in curiosity, he rubbed his gnarled hands. "The grav-push is heli-powered, courtesy of good old Silirus."

He went around and pressed a button on each unit and they folded in a curious way as pressure rotors kicked in and the bottom gripped the sand and the top extended and clamped to the hull. It pushed up on it, like some kind of hydraulic arm. I gaped and stood in awe as the ship levitated two feet off the ground with a blue glow shining off the flattened sand and a similar glow off the underside of the AGs. Some gravo-thrust kept the tons of metal aloft. At least some advanced technology was still alive in these days of collapse. He activated some other gizmo on the side and used the remote control he'd snatched from Billy. It spurted jets of white steam from the AG's lower flanks and pushed the Starrunner down the sandy ravine like a magno train. Wren and I loped after the old man and his prize.

"Well, I'll be a son of a bitch—"

Sand dunes curled up to the edges of the mounds on either side.

"About that ride out of here…," persisted Wren. "Shit! Incoming."

We'd barely gone fifty feet when the woman dove into the sand drift. The whine of engines roared overhead.

I swore and scrambled for the nearest mini dung pile as a flash bomb flared, nearly singeing my hide and knocking me and snot-nose and the old man off our feet. Luckily the shell had missed Starrunner by a sliver and her reinforced battle plates took the shrapnel.

Two ships came angling out of the sky: lean, grey with cannons locked. I opened my mouth in a startled cry but Wren was already moving. She was skipping under my line of fire before I could do anything and jumping into the hatch. The first ship dropped down in the space between us and the mountain of crud.

I fucking knew it. Baer!

I got to my feet, dazed from the blast. I gimped along, somehow twisting my already savaged leg in the fall. My eyes stung, blinded by the bomb's flare. The second ship waited in the sky, weapons trained.

"For fuck's sake!" I was shaking my head, aiming too late before a blaster beam clipped the barrel, and I dropped it as it became sizzling hot.

The man, Baer's man, wearing helmet and blue body armor, jumped out of the hatch, pointing his blaster at me. "Easy, chief. No stupid moves. Drop the other weapon. Edge back away from the ship."

"Relax, no need to get excited." I let the mini-glock that I'd tried to snatch from my belt fall at my toes.

"Move away," he snarled. Two more emerged from the hatch to stand at either side.

While TK and Billy scuttled sideways like crabs, my mind worked to come up with a plan.

I caught a movement out of the corner of my eye—some slinking, mummy-wrapped shape. "Dung mite!" I cried, motioning to the pile to the man's left.

He whirled and with a snarl, shot the head off some grotesque figure dressed in rags in a spray of blood and brains.

I licked my lips. "Good play, chief. Aim for the head, always the best percentage shot. Good thing I'm watching your back."

"Cut the cute talk, smart man."

"Let's cut a deal here," I wheedled. "You can see I've nothing. If I did, think I'd be hanging around with these grubbers?" I made a sweep of hand toward TK and the boy huddled in the refuse. "You go your way, I go mine. Maybe we can come to a solution."

"You're a dead man, Rusco. Baer wants you dead, and I do too for wasting Kriegs, plus a cut of the reward money on your head. Rub is, we have to bring you in alive."

"Isn't that interesting? I'm suddenly a celebrity. Worth more than Marvin K. Dicks."

"Shut up. You're a dead mother fuck—" The right front cannon of Starrunner lifted and a hell of a blast came spitting out from her barrel to fry the man on the spot.

Hot damn, that crafty skinhead knew how to shoot! I rolled as blaster fire came a hair's breadth from my throat. The two other thugs crouching by the ship, rained fire at anything that moved. Hunched like a beetle, I ran up to the pile, grabbed my weapon, emptied it on the closest merc. He crumpled with a shot-out leg just as the damned mummy people, who I guessed might be the mad boys, crawled over them like ants and the downed ship. Must have poured out from some lizard hole behind the ship. There were thuds of metal on metal, broken glass and screams as mummy flesh met thug flesh. Then followed only the harsh breathing and hillbilly grunts like some redneck rape scene out of a bad horror movie.

Misshapen men, women, or neither, it was hard to tell, came streaming from out of the garbage pits and stinking heaps from all directions, clutching black batons like truncheons, hunks of metal, any weapon they could forage out of those refuse piles. All wrapped in rags, bandaged like lepers, only their fingertips showed, clawed nails glinting through the dirty brown wraps of cloth. Snorkel masks frogged their mouths, black-rimmed goggles on the eyes. Metal caps on the skulls.

The mummy people were coming for us next, but the second ship banked in and sprayed pulse beams at them. They took care not to wipe our ship out. Red fire exploded into the mass of moving figures. Limbs and heads separated from bodies. Starrunner's rear cannon swiveled, aimed and shot the ship out of the sky.

"Yeehow!" I yelled at TK to get Starrunner moving. I could detect faint motion, for activity still stirred amongst that rubble. The sad, stark reality was if they got the ship, we were sunk.

The old man came huffing and puffing around the side of the smoking metal, hauling Billy by the arm. "Get a move on! More ships can drop on us any second."

Wren jumped out of the hatch, a fresh AK in her hand, breathless, flushed at her kills. I was warming to this lady.

"Let them come. We'll let them blow the crap out of these dunghill rats." She kicked at one of the mummy-wrapped things lying in a smouldering heap after I'd blasted it, their albino heads gleaming ghoulishly in the sun.

I winced.

"The sun eated them up," crooned the kid, all smiles, the only thing he'd said so far.

"That's right, Billy. You know it, don't you?" TK said with a sad laugh.

The mad boys seemed occupied with their spoils, rustling like rats. Two smoking ships and a trio or more of fresh corpses. Needless to say, I kept an eye out for more unexpected crazies as we jogged along Starrunner's moving flank, putting the hustle on to get the ship away from here.

We left the smoking rubble and the dead vestiges of humanity behind. Despite my gratitude for the quick bloodshed, I almost wished Wren hadn't blasted both Baer's ships out of commission. At least then there'd have been an alternative means of escape off this planet, if the old man couldn't get Starrunner operational.

Rounding a bend out of sight down another sandy corridor, TK aimed the AG jet spurts to guide us between great mounds of crud and garbage.

"How long before they catch up with us?" I asked.

"Half hour, maybe less."

I pawed at my grimy grimace.

"Don't worry, I have protection," TK said.

"It better be good."

I looked at the old man's billyclub, the firepipe he clutched in his hand that he'd pulled out from his desert cloak. "That's all you got? You're going to get killed with primitive junk like that. Stop the rig."

He did. I jumped into the hatch, motioning him to stay put. "There're weapons in the hall aft. Wait here."

A few limping strides and I was rummaging around through the spare armory rack. Old man didn't listen and came stumbling down the main aisle with wide eyes, blinking in the semi-dark of emergency light. "Wow, this ship's something else."

"I told you to stay out," I rasped, pushing him back down the hall, leveling my weapon at him.

"Sorry." He gaped. "Been a long time since I've seen an Alpha Explorer, anything remotely like the interior of a working ship."

Something about the comment made me feel compassion for the man and his plight, marooned here on this trash planet.

"She's a vintage model," I said grudgingly. "Couple of gangsters heisted it. They're no longer with us, so I took the liberty of being its ward. Renamed it Starrunner."

"A fine name."

"I thought so." I tossed him an R3A, a short-range blaster that would kill anything within a twenty yard range.

The kid came in, pointing and gibbering. I backed the two out into the hall by the hatch and gave Wren a helping hand up into the ship. I urged TK and his boy with strong words to get Starrunner moving along with full speed. I didn't need to repeat myself. This way there'd be no tracks. As long as we gave the mummy boys the slip, the scavengers couldn't follow us.

CHAPTER 7

We wound through sandy paths with TK and Billy guiding Starrunner. TK sat legs dangling out the hatch, looking up along the line of the hull. Wren crouched, flashing me weird, curious looks, until the mounds to either side became less massive and we arched up over a wide, well-trodden path along a ridge. The distant teeth of broken buildings spread below us down a long valley, the settlers' city: toppled towers, blasted squares, a sight all too familiar for me—some war-torn urban wasteland abandoned for generations.

We came abreast a large mound and TK halted the convoy. We climbed out while the ship hovered two feet above the baking sand. A ruined building hulked to the side, only the corner posts and a few girders showing like the ribs of a desiccated whale.

"Why're we stopping?" I asked as TK flicked off the jets, leaving a heavy silence over the desert.

"You want to circumambulate the entire planet?"

"Why here? Where's this safety you promised?"

"You're looking at it."

"This broken pile of cement blocks and pillars?" I reached for my gun, temper short, guessing that the old man was pulling a fast one on me. Wren was looking straight at me with her raven-pearl eyes glinting with something of mirth, watching what I'd do next.

"Relax." TK held up his hand. He herded me over to the ruin and got me to take a closer look at the pit yawning below. The floor had collapsed long ago, but I saw in the depression below a basement or somesuch, a section of one side which had crumbled. I stared at it for a long time. What my eyes didn't first register was that it had been tarped up with clever handiwork to blend into the sand and conceal a large space behind.

I looked up at the four stone pillars and a spider-web roof framework. This place could have been a cathedral as easily as a warehouse, or some eccentric's mansion.

Scratching my head, I watched as TK worked the remote control with a wink at Billy. The propellant steamed and the antigravs guided Starrunner down into the pit.

TK clambered down a steep, crumbling staircase and I followed, gripping my gun with a ready hand. He moved over to the tarp, cranked the handle of a hidden wheel cached in the earth and up ratcheted the tarp. A huge work area burrowed within that far side of the pit.

I gave a low whistle. "Well, I'll be a damned monkey."

TK did a little bow. "You can congratulate me later, Rusco. Here, Billy, help me guide this thing in."

I stepped inside the darkened quarters, suppressing a grunt. The place projected deeply into the back of the pit. Old engines, machine parts and housing lay strewn on the sand, rotors and gears and panels, whatnots, some on workbenches and tables. The old man lit a pair of battery-powered lights near the door while Billy guided my ship over the sprawl of engine parts then let her rest by the wall. Wren scooted in before TK closed the flap. "Never can be too careful," he said with a worried grin.

I could see the desert man had built something of a garage for himself. Tables with hammers, drills, electrical gauges, hoses, cables, all salvaged from the rubbish heaps outside. Old vehicle batteries were linked together to give him the power to do his tinkering. "I charge them from solar panels rigged out back where no one can see them. From time to time I need to change them."

He motioned to a series of jigsaw cutters, pry bars and twisted pieces of metal. "I salvage whatever's useful from the dump, always more to find even as the years roll on."

"So I see. Very clever."

"Never gave up trying to get off this heap," he said wistfully.

"Some grand little shop you have here, old man."

He nodded, beaming with pride. "Never had enough of a working engine to get off this rock though. Believe me, friend, I tried." He picked up a mini pneumatic drill and smacked it on the table. "Been scavenging parts from these dumps since as long as I can remember. Still haven't given up on the mother lode. You can appreciate my excitement when I saw your Alpha coming down out of the sky."

"I bet."

He laughed at the memory. "I once got an old Rixen Eagle space probe up a hundred yards into the air before she crashed past the washboard wastes other side of these mounds. She still sits there collecting dust. Nearly killed me and Billy."

"How long to fix this thing?"

"Depends on what's broke."

"Well, I can tell you the mobilitors are in bad shape, probably dead. Less than 60% before she went down." I eyed him, checking to see if the term meant anything to him.

"Mobilitors, eh? They can be tricky."

"What isn't?"

"Let's have a look-see then." He crouched beneath the underpanel while the AGs kept Starrunner aloft. He unscrewed a panel, crawled up the conduit a ways, gave it a shifty glance. "What have we here?"

He knuckled a fist at the twin Barenium cylinders. I poked my head in and blinked. Barenium cylinders…That much I knew. About waist high. Green in a liquid medium, with a golden glow around the edges. Some unstable isotope discovered way back, the liquid masking the radiation somehow, from what I gathered.

"All gunkum to me," growled Wren, crowding over my shoulder.

"That green liquid there," he said. "Think of it as a compact potent pressure pump. When excited with photons from that light gun at the end, you've got yourself warp power to go." He waved a casual hand like a professor explaining something to a young child.

"Left one's shot. Explains why you were down to 60% integrity."

I sighed. "So, what's the damage?"

"Won't know until I look inside."

"Okay. Let's check it out."

While Wren poked around the cowling, I watched over the man's shoulder like a hawk as he hiked her up higher on the AGs and got Billy to monitor the power.

He stood back, poking an elbow in my ribs. "Oi!" give me some breathing space, will you?" I stepped back with a reluctant grunt. I didn't like anybody prodding around my ship. Especially the engines. Not to mention, I wanted to learn something in case I needed to tinker with Starrunner myself some day.

"What gets me is we're light years from Brisis. How the hell they tracked me so quickly—"

"No mystery there," interrupted TK. "Your enemies traced the residual Barenium from those leaky seals—Couldn't have had a clearer signal, active dust on the outer cowling from the burn warp, a clear heat signature. The failed mobilitors would have made even more of a dust trail. You're lucky to have gone any distance at all."

I gave my head a sober shake. "Just my luck."

"In my opinion, Rusco, you've had plenty of luck. Nine lives of it." He squinted hard at the canisters. "I can fix it at 50%. Enough to get you to a proper station."

"Better than sitting around here waiting for Baer and his bounty hunters to nab us."

TK grunted. "Let's get to it then. Show me to the bridge. I'll check the warp engine controls."

We went on board, down the main service hall lit in dim crimson by the emergency lights, past the cabins and the head into the bridge, with Billy and Wren trailing like kites in the wind.

I shuttled TK over to the pilot's chair where the console still blinked and lay bathed in the eerie glow of the emergency lights.

TK sighed. "Bring up the warp panel. These modern interfaces are a little more new-fangled than I care for."

"As you like." I hit some side bars on the keypad, showed him the utility menus and he played long fingers along the touchscreen, bringing up a menu. "*Varwol 6.0. Mezanine 3.4 kbs. Waxrin thrust gain, nominal.* There, Barenium seal. See, you're too low."

He played with the sensors and he couldn't help but notice the iridescent disc that lay three feet away below the auxiliary console. It must have flown free from the strongbox during impact. Could have been it or the box itself that hit me on the head. "What's this shimmering disc you have here on the floor?" He reached for it.

I snatched it out of the old man's hand before I remembered how dangerous the thing was, and dropped it like a red hot coal. "Nothing. Just some artifact." I lanced the old man a wary look.

He did a double take and jerked back his head. "Artifact, my eye." His eyes narrowed. "That's why those men were chasing you, right?"

"Forgot to tuck it away in the back. Kinda hard when you're crashlanding in a garbage pit." I grabbed it up with my sleeve, laid it out on the control board with care. Something told me to trust the old man, as he'd figured most of it out anyway.

"It's a small version of something else I saw back on Brisis. Some sort of weapon, I figure. Careful, it's dangerous."

He flipped it over in his gloved hands, while Wren came to stare over his shoulder, peering at it with doubt.

"Any more of these things?" he asked.

"None aboard. A larger version of something that looks quite different is locked in a safe place," I said cryptically.

"What you've got here is a phase shifter. Moves atoms around from one time or place to another. How it does it, the physics is beyond me, but I've read about them."

"Even you?" I guffawed. "Thought you were Mr. Fix-it-up and Encyclopedia man."

"Not me," he barked, "still a long ways to go. This here's a remnant of another newfangled tech before the galaxy went to shit."

I grunted, a thoughtful murmur on my tongue. "Explains how one yobo dematerialized to nowhere-land in front of my eyes." I wondered how Baer and his idiot hirelings got it. They must have stumbled on it somewhere digging through the many crates of contraband going through their warehouse. Holding out for the highest bidder, like the vultures they were.

TK mused, "In the hands of ruthless people, this device could mean trouble."

Wren blew air out of her nose. "Don't you think we're already on the road to hell, old man? As a species we should have been stamped out long ago."

"No argument there," he laughed.

"I think that sinking ship has already sunk," I said.

"See those key codes or glyphs, bug script?" TK said. "Somehow they set a location. But they're scrambled or encoded in some cryptic language. Nothing like I've ever seen before."

"Bug, what do you mean, bug?" I croaked.

"Mentera tech, lost long ago—an old alien insect race. Rulers of the galaxy. Good luck finding a translator key."

"So it's useless?"

"I wouldn't say that. The technobrains could probably back-engineer it. Someone with the yols and the clout to organize a think tank."

"Hence your friend Baer, trying to fence it to someone," muttered Wren.

Some star lord, if I recall.

"See, I think—" I reached for the thing without thinking, and wished I hadn't, because TK had somehow armed it with his handling. As soon as I made contact—Zap. I came out in some other place, clutching that thing, blinking like an owl.

A sallow dawn greeted me, a snaky loop of smoke misting on the horizon. Cold dry air entered my lungs, very hard to breath. I clutched at my throat, gasping. Aphid-like shapes moved with slow synchrony across a steely grey sky. I saw more there than ever I cared to see in any lifetime.

The eye can only process so many things at once. I dropped to my knees, fiddling with the device, trying to get it to push me back to the world where I had come from. But nothing seemed to work and it just pulsed that eerie, iridescent glow all the stronger, like an evil eye while my lungs croaked for air. Clouds, strange life forms flitted over the horizon. Birds, aliens, far-off alien craft? I didn't know, nor cared to guess. Maybe I was hallucinating. The future, past, present? Could have been all or none. From the corner of my eye, I caught glimpses of desiccated human bodies lying about. Whatever I did next, fiddling with the script, something jarred the thing back to life.

Zap. I was back in Starrunner, peering up at the hazy forms of figures prodding me. "You okay?" Wren snapped. "You just blinked out there for a second."

"Holy crap!" I gasped. I sank lower on my knees, chucking the thing aside, as if it were radioactive. "I was out there—somewhere. Some putrid, rotten world. A ruined city. War was in the air, out there, somewhere in time. Alien wars. Strange things roved on the horizon. Decayed bodies all around, leathery skin and old bones." My voice quavered. "Maybe it was all a dream of the past."

"Easy, Rusco," said TK.

"That's nutso," scoffed Wren, shaking her head. "Either one or all of us is on some kind of drugs."

"No trip," I growled. "It was real, right down to my bursting lungs."

"Your eyes went wide and staring, as if you were a ghost, fading fast. My hand passed right through you," she said.

TK muttered, "Phase shift, to some far world. Could have been any one of the desolate planets out there."

The old man placed a hand on my arm. "Can't let this get into devils' paws like those after you."

"Like who?" sputtered Wren. "Some rich, wicked little buyer trips out to his favorite planetary resort for holidays? I'm shaking in my boots, TK."

"No, you fool! I mean, by installing one of these devices on a drone or a mechnobot, they can blast any city or space station to smithereens and come back out of it without a scratch. An army of these could—well, make ruin of what's left of the populated worlds."

Wren scoffed. "Yeah, just like these bug-like things you talk about that are now extinct. Fat lot of good this tech did them in taking over the galaxy."

"The details of the Mentera's demise are lost in time."

My trembling reverie came to an end. "Let's just keep it out of anybody's hands for now." I shuddered to think what a brute like Baer would do with it, or who he might sell it to. He'd talked about some star lord wanting to buy it. It now dawned on me what had happened to Mitch, the guard back there. The phaso seemed to work its mischief when some combination of the alien script and its surface was touched. He'd gone to one of those worlds, but without the device, he couldn't get back. I only managed to get back because I had a firm grip on it. Mitch didn't.

I couldn't help notice the hungry look in TK's eye as he studied the disc, despite his gallant words. I quickly gathered the strongbox up from under the conference table and locked up that evil, little treasure. I kept it clasped in my arms, thinking to hide it away somewhere on the ship.

Mumbling, rubbing hand on chin, I stepped back a few paces, while he rubbed his brow with a dirty cloth. "I'd better start fixing that drive. All of you, leave me alone. Sit on your thumbs, swap tales, play tiddlywinks, I don't care, just don't distract me. I need space and quiet to concentrate."

"Sure thing, pops," I said.

"Billy! Change up the batteries. Load the spares that I charged yesterday. We're going to need more juice to incite the Barenium."

I granted the old man his space. Leaving him to his tasks, I wandered through his workshop, staring in a daze at the maze of machinery. Wren was at my heels.

"So what's it like out there?" she asked. "Always dreamed about going to the planets."

"Lot of poverty and corruption. Believe me, you haven't missed much." She was all for asking a bunch of questions, but I waved her off. My mind was preoccupied with Baer's bounty hunters and if more would be on their way.

Some time later TK came to us, rubbing his oily hands with a soiled rag.

"So, I did a full scan and mustered what I could. The Barenium'll take time to settle in those canisters. I'm guessing about eight hours. We give it a try after. If it starts up first shot, we're lucky, if not, we've got ourselves a problem."

"Let's hope it starts up then." I wished it was sooner, but realized the settling was out of my hands.

We edged back out of the workshop, the bright light stinging our eyes. "So what now, professor?" I asked him, squinting under the glare. The sun looked as if it had not dipped a degree in the sky.

"Time to eat," he said. He and Billy ratcheted up the tarp. "This way." He pointed a forked hand to another place, far away from the workshop. "It's a forty hour day on this world, so it's easy to get hungry."

I could see the method in TK's madness, keeping his residence far from work, in case one of the 'mad boys' happened to stumble on his crib. He'd have a temporary place to lie low in, if that wasn't compromised too.

CHAPTER 8

TK had made his residence in the side of one of the dung piles, like an igloo of crud, indistinguishable from the rest of the other compost.

I stepped closer to the fifty-foot-high gummed mass, recoiling at the sudden cloying stench that hit me, but a skittering sound had me turning around wild-eyed. Aiming my blaster at two mean-looking scorpion-like knee-high crab things scuttling across the sand straight at us.

"Fuck! What are these things?" I got off a shot, but didn't do any significant damage.

TK let out a shrill whistle, his finger to lips. He slapped down my weapon before I could get the next shot off and waste it too. The creatures bobbed back, springing on their spindly, segmented legs a foot away. They hissed and clicked, barbed stingers coiling over their scaled backs. The pincers out in front looked like capable clipping machines.

"Protection," TK explained. "Come on, inside."

I realized the scorpion dung at the side of the mound was the source of the smell. Gingerly I stepped around it, eyeing the six-legged crustaceans with a wary eye. Clear translucent exoskeleton, eyes perched on stalks, armored carapace, one could see right through to the lungs pumping, heart beating, and some black red, kidney-shaped organs.

I shivered and Wren ducked in a defensive crouch, muttering some foul words under her breath.

I whirled to another sound, my blaster lifting. A mummy-like shape hobbled out of the shimmering heat waves, a walking stick in hand. Brown-wrapped rags hugged the sleek body, up to the high hood; white albino eyes shone through the black oval of a cowled face. The scorpions didn't budge.

"Relax." TK pulled down my weapon. "I know him." He lifted a hand in greeting. "Oi, Toog. Some new friends I'd like you to meet."

He introduced the wary figure to us. The newcomer was about five seven, thin, wiry like others of his kind. Only his eyes showed, white pools into nowhere. Even his hands were mitted as if he had scabies. Those eyes, as white as an egg, mesmerized me.

"Toog's been a friend for a long time. Ever since Billy caught desert fever and almost died two seasons back." My foggy, tired brain pondered on how long a Talyon year was.

"You're welcome to join us, Toog," he said. "We're just sitting down to a meal. This here's Wren and that there's Rusco."

Toog dipped his head in thanks, accepted Wren and I as equals, seeing as we were friends of TK's.

A trap door led inside the igloo of sanctuary, camouflaged to look like the other junk metal and plastics in the pile. Inside it was dark and surprisingly cool, protection at least from the mad boys.

"Toog's one of the few who fled from the crawlers, searching other ways. He's one of the good ones, Rusco. You've nothing to fear." He glanced at my clenched fists on my assault rifle.

To my relief the house pets stayed outside.

"Raised those dervishes from babies. I fed them, tamed them and watered their backs. Now they're loyal to me, as long as I keep feeding them."

"What do you feed them?" asked Wren.

"Dead meat. Anything I can catch. I look for the condors or buzzards circling overhead. Anywhere they're circling means fresh meat is about. Sometimes they sight a sick crawler wandered off to die or some fresh carrion. Rest of the time I hunt whatever I can for food with my bow."

I nodded as if nothing could be more natural.

The floor was fine white sand, the ceiling beamed with girders; the walls, dried mud, making it cool and dry inside, and a relief to my pounding head. Billy went running over to a shelf of pots to gulp water from a beat-up bucket. I saw the old man kept a crude, fire-stoked stove complete with chimney. Buckets of water ranged around, dozens of them; a chest of junk for fuel, elsewhere a few potted cacti, some low cots. Spartan but serviceable. A mystery where TK got water.

He motioned us to a low steel table with woven place mats in the middle of the room. While we sat around it, the old man fired up the pot-iron stove, rustled up some food, banging various pots and before long he served us a piping-hot soup of green vegetables and some crunchy brown sticks.

I dove in, famished. Munching away, I lifted my spoon to him. "This is not half bad, TK. What is it?"

"The green stuff's cactus, high in trace minerals and nutrients. The desert insects, those brown sticks you're shoveling in by the forkful, are common to this region, easy to catch and super high in protein."

I dropped my utensil on the plate, coughed, and my mouth hung open.

Wren smirked. "What's the matter, Rusco? There're more in the pot where that came from. Grasshopper is a novelty on Talyon."

Loosing a sigh, I studied my company. Toog with his quiet, diminutive movements, never taking a mouthful too swiftly, Wren, her challenging stare, as if everything was wrong in the world, and TK, a glint of amusement in his gray eyes, watching us as if we were all a study in social experiment.

TK read my mind about the next question about the water. "Don't worry. I have to manufacture my own liquids. I have a rig further down. I call it the hydrophon." He grinned. "My back's not what it used to be in the old days so I rig up the AGs and get Billy to help me haul a barrow of filled buckets to this place."

I nodded. "Seems as if you have everything worked out. Except maybe the bloodthirsty scorps and the zombie mummies lurking about your doorstep."

"Them…well, I have my ways of keeping them at bay. Xig and Xag, those two brutes outside, help me with that. They've killed many wandering crawly boys who've come nosing around. If word got out me and Billy were holed up here…" He let the idea hang in dead air.

"So you've survived," I said. "I'd count that as impressive. Was there ever a better yesterday?"

"Dezran City used to be a self-supporting community. A bunch of us used to live in scattered settlements. Along the foot of the desert ridge, not like the big metropolises you see on the settled planets. Talyon was different, had a fresh start, even though it served as the recycling center of the solar system. Then they came and burned up the town."

"Who's 'they'?"

"Some glory-seeking warlords out to make a name for themselves. Heard this place was fair game, rich in mining, beryllium and other elements, and laid waste to the city."

"Sounds like any of a dozen lowlifes I know."

TK shrugged. "The strongest of us banded together and we became fighters. In the end, ultimately refugees, living hand to mouth. Many of us drank poison water, I don't know what else: some became the mutants you saw out there. Messed up their heads, burned their skin, deformed their bodies. That's why they're all wrapped up in rags. Used to be human, but they went—feral, let's say. If you saw them—" he shuddered and cast a sharp look at Toog.

Toog stirred and spoke in a lisp. I caught a flash of harelip beneath the cowl as if his teeth were set the wrong way. "Some genetics company had been brewing toxic bio-mixtures. They got mixed up in the water supply when the outlaws were blasting the place all up."

TK loosed a choked growl. "That and the toxic waste dump burning and smoldering and seeping scum into the water table. Don't forget that, Toog. A toxic jury-rigged slurry, a disaster waiting to happen, courtesy of the growing recycle piles!"

"Where did all this junk come from?" I asked.

"Shipped in from innumerable planets. All the worlds far and near used Talyon as their dumping grounds. For generations and generations. That all ended when the wars started."

I drummed my knuckles on the table. "So how come you guys aren't all twisted up like our mummy friends out there—no offense to our friend Toog here?"

TK held up a glass bottle of pills, liquid capsules on the table. "Quizanine. Methyl basene—plus a smidge of isopropyl alcohol."

"Well, aren't you the clever one," I marveled.

"I pride myself in knowing things."

"I can see that." I frowned and turned to Wren. "What about you?"

"What would you like to know?"

"Why didn't you turn into one of our mummy friends?"

"Lucky, I guess. Always added a bit of vinegar from fermented cactus to my water."

TK laughed at the notion. "Some of us are just resistant to the effects."

Wren shrugged, apparently not in the mood for arguing with the old man.

"Family?" I turned to her. "How have you been surviving?"

"Dodge and blast, nothing else. My crib's hidden far away. On the other side of the pits. I saw your ship come down. Then I came to look. My rod's been keeping me alive, no thanks to you, losing it out there somewhere in the sand. Built it myself."

"Treat that new piece at your waist as your new improved 'rod'. You still haven't explained how—"

"Nothing much different from TK's story," she said in a harsh voice. "My family was killed, my daughter too."

"Sorry to hear that."

"Don't be. You didn't know her from Eve. Bad shit happens to good people. Happens all the time. I got over it."

I could see that Wren hadn't and probably never would. But I was no grief therapist and so I moved on. "If we get my ship running again, I'm inviting you all out for a ride—you too, skinhead." I shadow-boxed her playfully on the shoulder. Her body remained rigid. My sudden act of charity was not just in good nature. A little bit of self-preservation was mixed in with a whole lot of scheming. "I could use a resourceful bunch of entrepreneurs like you."

TK swigged down a gulp of water.

"So, you've never made it off this rock?"

"Nope." He shrugged. "I've been off and traveled at lot in my younger days before the space docks and starships were wiped out and communication towers destroyed. A few rogue ships have dropped out of the sky over the years, but on seeing nothing here but desert ruin and mummy freaks they speed off in a hell of a hurry."

"Nobody's come to this planet since I've been a girl," croaked Wren in a faraway voice. "Even then the memory is dim. I remember a silver, cigar-shaped craft angling down in the plain once, before it became another toxic waste dump. I watched from one of the recycle hills." Her eyes clouded over. "They landed, let out a bunch of people—prisoners, I reckoned, with their arms bound behind their backs. Three tried to make a run for it, and the captors blasted them in cold blood." She shivered. "The rest they let live. Then they flew off."

"What happened to the survivors?" I asked.

"Dunno, I scrambled away, fast as I could, being just a little kid. When

I came back, they were gone. Sand dervishes must have got them."

I stared in grim silence. "And you, Toog?"

"I kill mad boys as easily as TK here. Sometimes they hunt me, but I lure them to my special place—where an army of dervishes nest. They feed nicely that day." He gave a snorting exclamation. "Was just checking on TK here, seeing that he's feeding his pets properly."

"And was I?" TK asked with a crooked grin.

"Seemed so."

"A good trick," I said. "Letting the dervishes control your mad boys. Surprises me you'd kill your own kind though."

Toog grunted, the first real emotion I'd heard from him. "I owe them nothing. They killed my family, ground them up, ate them for stew. Made me one of them. But I escaped. Now I kill them on sight."

"You're one against an army," I pointed out.

"Doesn't matter."

"I admire your spirit, Toog. All of you. Just think you're on the wrong world."

"What world isn't 'wrong'?" grunted TK.

"I invite you to come with us, Toog."

He stared at me a long time. "No, this is the only home I've known. Call it sentimental, but I've a kinship here. There are others like me, like TK and Billy."

"Knock yourself out." I shrugged. But in those eyes I saw the sadness of generations, as I had seen so many times on many worlds. Worlds ripped apart by senseless violence, and privation, sunk in the deepest mire of decadence.

While TK and Wren went off with Billy and Toog to fetch water and look out for more mad boys crawling about, I drifted off in the opposite direction to the repair shop, my Uzi slung over a shoulder, thinking it better to be closer to my ship. I followed what I remembered of the route we took, wiping my brow in the baking sun. No number of nervous glances over my shoulder allayed my suspicion that those damn sand crabs weren't following me.

The ruins came in sight and I heaved myself down on a sand drift at the edge of the pit. The merciless sun beat down on my head and my mind wandered on how I'd always wanted a tan.

I lay the Uzi on my lap in case a mad boy decided to make a move. It was a good compact submachine gun, modified to fire a heat-swath plus bullets, frying anything within a twenty yard range. Lumo, infrared scope for night fight and laser lock, cool smooth barrel, compact hand stock—I liked the lighter feel, its quickness to slide off the shoulder and into the hands.

The throb in my knee had receded to a dull ache, that or I'd gotten used to it. Nevertheless, I up-ended the last of the pain pill-bottle I'd pulled from Starrunner into my gullet. Seemed I was about due for another dose. I glanced down at the pit: a stark, baking hole with crumbling earth on all sides. No soul would ever guess a hidden workshop lurked down in that abyss holding a Class A starship and stocked with tools.

I shook my head with an amazed grin, hardly aware that I was starting to doze off.

I awoke to the drop of something in my lap, a black-leathered figure crouching before me with a wry smile.

"Must have drifted off."

"Dangerous place to do that," Wren admonished, dropping the handful of pebbles she'd been tossing.

I gave a careless grunt, rose to my undignified half crouch, squinting in the obnoxious glare.

"Boring over there hauling water," she bantered. "Thought I'd bug you instead." She squinted down at me. "You serious about taking me with you, if the old man fixes the ship?"

"Why not? I'm generally not a liar. There're things to discuss first. Like business. Not just a free ride here; work to be done."

"Like what?"

"Let's cross that bridge when the time comes."

A stiff silence came over us and I could see her pouty frown moving across her fine lips, so it prompted me to mellow somewhat.

"Listen, I'm sorry for what I said back there."

"About what?"

"About saying you had a butch cut."

She laughed. "Well, it's kinda true, isn't it? Though I'm no butch."

"Think you'd look a lot prettier with a whole head of hair though, instead of a few bristles like a porcupine. Not that you aren't pretty. Just saying."

"Opinion noted," she said dryly. "This brush cut is more for practical reasons than anything. It's cooler on the skull."

"Those leathers sure aren't."

"They're for protection, Rusco. In case I run into some dervishes. Their pincers are deadly."

Voices drifted from down the path and a scuffling of moving figures.

TK, Billy, and the mummy-ish Toog came trundling up the hot sand, with the old man wearing a worried frown. His two scorpion friends scuttled at his heels.

"Bad news," he said. "Mad boys are on the prowl. Saw 'em skulking up the ridge farther on. This is the closest they've come to this area." He gave a brusque flourish. "Let's get into the workshop."

"Don't need to convince me."

We were hardly down the crude stair and moving across the pit when a ghost of motion caught my eye.

I gave a choked cry, shielded my eyes from the sun's glare up top the pit.

TK lifted his head, swearing a wicked curse. "Into the workshop!"

Shapes came prowling around the edge and began to drop at our feet. Crapola! Our tracks must have led them right here.

"Get down!" I hissed.

Too late. I blasted one as they threw metal spikes at us and I lunged in the same motion. Another tried to gut stab me with a chunk of metal. I whirled, grabbed my knife from my belt, and slashed it soundly across the chest. Steel ripped up to its chin.

Dark blood sprayed over my open shirt and a white pulpy face fell flat at my feet. I kicked away the grotesque corpse.

More malformed shapes gathered in numbers. Wren crouched in attack, fired a spray of bullets into the faces of swaying, reaching mad boys. "Die, you bitches!" she cried. Billy uttered some Neanderthal sound and scrambled back behind the old man.

I tossed Toog the extra weapon in my belt. He opened fire with a bloodthirstiness that seemed uncharacteristic of his mild manner.

Limbs parted and mummy shapes rolled in the sand with mewling sobs. Fresh blood dripped on the sand.

Silence. Heat. The shimmer of an unnatural stillness. The cry of a carrion bird echoed overhead.

Swarms of crazies crawled everywhere, peeking over the rim like feral spectators. I lifted my weapon and opened fire, peppering any I saw. Somehow the presence of Starrunner had lured these ghouls here. And somehow the old man had known they would come.

Hordes of them dropped down on us like monkeys, only the whites of their eyes showing in ghostly, blotched faces partially hidden under brown, cowled hoods.

TK's two sand dervishes scuttled down the path after the cloth-wrapped zombies, their stingers raised. A pincer clipped out to clamp on a brown-garbed leg, then a stinger fell and arched into a rag-garbed neck.

I blasted two between the eyes but a slinking shape crawling at my legs got hold of my weapon and yanked it out of my grasp. "Motherfucker." I pulled my knife out, only to reel as a chunk of pipe came angling for my skull. I dodged back, but the thing ended up thunking on my shoulder. I cried out in pain. Wren was yelling at the top of her lungs. She blasted mummy flesh left, right and center.

Shoots of agony rippled up my arm, but I recovered, grabbed my spare glock, slashed out with its butt end and kicked the gnashing scavenger away in the fleshy part of the gut, before blasting open its skull.

"Get to the ship," I cried.

TK and Billy fought in a wild muddle of bodies. Wise thing that I had given the old man that R3A, else he and his world would have come to an abrupt end.

I slashed a hole in the tarp, pulled aside the burlap and raced through the maze of machine parts with Wren, TK and Billy staggering at my heels.

Toog was too far away. The man was doomed unless he cleared a path. I saw the head of one of the dervishes squashed by a giant rock. Brown shapes pounced on it like bobcats and pulled off its legs and ripped it apart with their bare hands, metal weapons in their clawed fingers. Like the ghouls they were, they stuck the fleshy pieces in burlap sacks and carried them away.

I reached Starrunner and thrust open the port hatch. Pushing Wren through, I yanked TK in last who had shoved Billy in before him and jammed the door shut just as a mass of flesh thudded against the plated metal. One of the scumbitches rolled in with us and Wren stomped its neck and face. I shook the blood out of my hair, scrambled to the bridge. I got the thrusters warmed up, praying to god that those deep space engines would fire—at least, the impulse drive.

Wren raced to the weapons console and aimed the starboard cannon still operating under auxiliary power.

The clunks of weapons into the metal hull and thuds against the port glass caused me to wince.

"Bloody hell! They're going to break the glass!"

I reached for the thruster impulse to give it max juice, but TK reached to pull my hand away. "It's too early to task the ship. The Barenium hasn't settled yet. Sudden acceleration will—"

"Fuck it! We either get out of here, or those mummy fiends of yours bust through the glass and we're dead." I forced the lever up.

Wren cried, "He's right! Hundreds of them out there. They won't stop at a few blaster shots."

Billy stared wild-eyed, holding his head, whimpering like a child. Menacing shapes clustered at the windows.

TK ground his teeth with a fatalistic groan.

I gunned the engines. The impulse drive made an unwholesome growl, but fired up. Starrunner's curved prow broke through the top of the low ceiling, raining crumbling earth down and scattering tools and benches while hordes of mad boys clung to the fuselage like bloodsuckers.

"Woohee! That's what I want to hear, baby." I cranked the thrusters.

I wasn't worried about finesse now. Those leachy-ghouls wouldn't last long once Starrunner got going. *If she got going.*

I cleared the pit and circled back, watching the crawlers fall to their doom. I reamed a generous spray of pulse blasts on those stinking vermin, grinding my teeth in vindication, hoping to give Toog a fighting chance, if he were still alive. Saw no sign of him. Only those hooded creepos parceling up their own dead for the evening stew. I lifted off into the bright sky, a grumble of exultation in my throat. I was glad to see the end of Talyon...or at least I hoped it was the end.

CHAPTER 9

The Barenium held. After clearing Talyon's gravity we jumped to warp. The nearest shelter was the outpost at Skeller's Run, a massive space station in the Wizrin sector on the far edge of Orion. Not a first pick for me, the space station, but it would do for now. We needed supplies, particularly water.

TK paced back and forth on the bridge in a huff, face contorted at the risk of the compromised Barenium. "The liquid's not settled. Besides, they're still going to trace you."

"Right. Have to get that fixed."

He shook his head and threw his hands in the air.

"Okay, Beleron then," I said, "but first things first. We make it to the outpost. Go and play cribbage with Billy or something. You're making me nervous with all your pacing. We've got time to burn aboard this ship."

TK didn't budge. Wren occasioned to bump her hip against me as I was swiveling to check the log coordinates on the nav. I turned to cast her an inquiring glance. Her cheeky smile culminated in a lush rise of black brows. It intrigued but also irked me at the same time. I ordered her to scrub down in the shower. On the next stop, our second priority would be to get her some proper clothes. She didn't seem to appreciate the hint, and stormed off.

"Molly, get us info on the next destination."

"Orbital station, class D. Captive of gas giant Orves. Inception 2362. Fueling and supply center for inner, terraformed worlds Megal and Vylnos."

TK's mouth dropped. "Molly?"

"It's as good a name as any," I growled. "My first girl if you want to know. You've got a problem with that?"

"No, but—"

"Good, then check out the landing protocol on the station, if you want to make yourself useful. See who's on duty, what they're looking for, and on guard against. Sometimes these stations can be funny about deep space cruisers coming in out of nowhere, with skeleton crews and ones without papers."

TK grumbled and tapped some holo keys on the data console. It was something Molly could have told me in an instant, but I needed to keep TK busy. At the moment the man was a nuisance. Judging from his hobbies down on his home world, his mind was too fertile to be idle for any length of time.

"A certain Roga Flann is the designated contraband checker," TK muttered.

"And?"

"They seem to be particularly intolerant of bombs and peddlers hassling clientele in transit."

"Good. Keep digging, TK. What's Flann's official's game? Credentials, past history. There's more info lurking about on what they're looking for. Not that we're carrying anything illicit, but sometimes these officials try to pull a scam where they plant stuff on an incoming ship like ours then shake the captain down for yols, a bribe not to report us."

"How's me digging for stuff going to help if—"

"Just do it," I grunted.

He clamped his mouth shut and set to work. Billy was moving at his side like a spider. Damn, that munchkin, shadowing the old man like a leech. The kid couldn't sit still. Another source of frustration for me.

Seemed we'd been flying forever. The Varwol disengaged and the course coordinates finally became a reality. The ship lurched, bucked like a crotchety old mule. The slow corkscrew out of warp had minimal hiccups, I suppose.

In the viewport, the station loomed—a gigantic figure-eight with hundreds of birthing docks, bays and pods, with untold shield meshes, solar panels, tracking stations. My jaw dropped. Hundreds of ships passed in and out of the ring. So many? Another unexpected sight, these masses of ships converging on the space station. "What in—?" I wheezed.

TK grumbled, "Looks like a mass run on the station."

"Something must have gone wrong on one of the nearby worlds. Look at those space junkers and tramp freighters. I sense desperation here. They're ready to fall apart."

"Should we try somewhere else?" Wren asked.

"No, we need supplies. Some news wouldn't hurt at this point."

I eased Starrunner through the bee-like swarm of traffic. We approached the far side of the station. From what I could see it was going to be slim pickings for berthing docks. Lucky to see two free stalls. I made contact with the ground personnel.

An officious voice resonated over the com. "Alpha Explorer XU6, proceed to reserve dock A2. Berthing will be restricted to two hours."

"Two hours?" I croaked. "That's not nearly enough time to either piss or shit—"

"Sir, we do not appreciate vulgarities. The station is under high volume. Do you wish to cancel your reservation?"

"No," I growled. "But—okay, book it." I cut the connection.

"Like a mass exodus," said Wren, her eyes glowing in wonder.

"Never seen so many ships in my life," mused TK.

True, every space vessel in the vicinity seemed to be seeking refuge.

"Seems we picked a bad time to dock. Okay, we'll touch down, get our supplies and move on."

Light seeped through the cracks as the circular gate opened and I docked Starrunner in berth A2-983. A snug fit but workable. Deep in the mooring bay, robot arms secured the prow. The hatch closed behind us and the chamber pressurized. I took my small hand weapon disguised as a small pen, and tossed a like model to Wren.

"Machine guns aren't allowed, for obvious reasons."

We de-boarded and I attached the water cable from the utility wall to Starrunner's underbelly. After I'd inserted ten yols in the dispenser, the green light came on and with a grunt of satisfaction, I could hear water flowing into Starrunner's bare tanks.

"Let's hit the observation decks, since we have such a brief time. The water'll shut off on its own."

TK nodded and herded Billy down the wide hall. Wren looked about with wonder, smelling much better after her shower. Her eyes flashed on the polished chrome railings, imitation marble floors, small potted trees and dust-free cleanliness. "This is a snazzy station." Seemed all these sights were new to her.

"Not really. Skeller Station's been around for centuries. But it's improved over the years. Megal's a rich world; they can afford to pay for some luxury."

"Why so far out from Megal though?" TK asked, as if to no one in particular. His eyes wandered past the glass over Orves, the gas giant, looming below. Our orbit was hundreds of thousands of miles out, yet still the giant planet arched below us like a monstrous white and red banded egg.

I shrugged. "Tradition? Who knows? Probably its ore-rich moons were the first mining interest before the inner planets were settled. I think they were more interested in mining rights than terraforming the inner worlds. Over time the place became a resort stop. You'd have to ask the builders, but they're four hundred years in the grave."

"I'll pass, thanks," said TK.

We passed the first checkpoints, me sliding through with my breezy confidence. *No, sirs, we came directly from Wiesen in Cassiopeia. No sirs, no illicit drugs or firearms. These are a couple of travelers I picked up on the ride roster en route to Alphanor. We're more interested in getting repairs than any layovers. Thank you, sirs.'*

All kinds of outworlders milled about, from those with hair piled up on their heads like donuts, to those in trim, tight space jumpers: pilots, shuttle monkeys, cargo couriers. Some were in worse shape than others. A babel of sound hummed in the background, making conversation difficult.

From the port window, a security docker ship, squat and unsightly like a gray bloated toad, floated with ominous import. Such a ship would be looking to maintain law and order—shakedown any runners peddling contraband or out to leverage any of the station's business. Skeller's Run would not be an easy place to work scams.

I tapped a tall outworlder on the shoulder, carrying a parcel in one hand and a paneled, cameo briefcase. He looked like an Arkadian on official business caught in an inordinately busy rush. At any rate, someone who knew what was going on. "What's up, chief?" I asked. "Why the hubbub?"

He turned a high forehead to me crowned with a sculpted drift of tan-colored hair. "Haven't you heard? Ah, you just came in, didn't you? Megal's been attacked. Some rogue bandit just declared war and flew in with his stealth craft and took over the planet."

I blinked. "Planetary defenses?"

"Minimal and antiquated. This Mong's got state-of-the-art equipment, and know-how."

"Who?" I croaked.

"Mong."

I frowned, recalling that name. "Why attack the space station? Didn't they just nab a world?"

"Out of the way. Easy spoils." The man's eyes darted to the destination boards, as if distracted. "He's taking ships and men, everything. Laying waste, crippling any offenses, moving on."

TK mused, "That sounds like a tried and true formula, repeated throughout history, like the Vandal hordes and Blitzkrieg of Earth's early history."

"Another petty warlord come to make life miserable for everyone," the man spat. "Just another power-monger rising from the ashes of doom."

"Mong," I grunted. "So, that bastard changed his name, did he?"

"What do you mean?" the outworlder demanded.

"I knew a Ging or a Gong on Hazzerot planet—the scum planet of the universe. Raged bloody murder and mayhem there, tore it to pieces. Drank human blood from the victims' skulls."

"That sounds like a bit of hokum to me," said the outworlder.

"You mean old wives' tales?" hissed Wren. "Try visiting Talyon some time."

"Yeah, tell that to the victims' families," I said.

TK pulled at his whiskers. "I seem to recall a legend of a degenerate warlord out of old Earth history savaging the lands, a Googis Khem. Took over half the ancient world before he was killed."

"That's Genghis Khan," I corrected him.

"So maybe this Mong guy takes after him?" asked Wren.

The outworlder shrugged. "No doubt he's a role model."

"Haven't had the grace to meet the man," I said with a low mutter. "Hope I never do."

"Let's just get our stuff and go," Wren asserted. She wrung her hands, clutched her sides and flashed impatient looks.

"What else do we need here?" asked TK.

"Just packaged goods. Dry packs, meals of any sort, add water and you have instant nutrients. Here." I tossed over some thirty yols and motioned him to the confectionary section to get the supplies. Billy hopped after him, his ferret-dark eyes blinking in adoration. I shook my head. It's as if I'd given his mentor a 'prize of the year'.

I directed Wren to the clothing shop, passed her a handful of credits. I further noted it would be taken out of her share when work was divvied up and the spoils came in. She trotted off with a haughty air and came back from the change rooms a new woman. Leathers hugged her slim hide like a sleek leopard with a fit pleasing to any eye. I wished I could get a real wig for her or something to cover up that blasted bald crown...

In fact... I shuttled her to the hair salon down the way and tossed a thick black wig into the basket at the sales counter.

"That'll be three yols," the attendant said.

"What's that for?" Wren demanded suspiciously.

I smirked. "Nothing, really, just part of my plan. Relax, all good."

Moving onward deeper within the terminus, we came to a giant rotating rotunda milling with people. A high dome spread overhead with reinforced glass that overlooked a lovely view to the stars. Service shops, eateries, hair stylists, outerwear, everything the casual, weary traveler could want, young or old, rich or poor. Step right up, folks. There was even an executive pad on the upper level like a casino royale, stocked with fancy restaurants, shave and a haircut, shoe-shining parlors, rent a courtesan by the minute. My mind reeled with the cons I could pull up there. But I reined myself in. Not the time or place. Keep your imaginative skull on hold, Rusco.

This was like something out of time, from an older generation before the slums and ghettos had edged over the bloodied city ruins.

Meanwhile Wren and I hustled over to the general section for a last minute stop, some Devirol to make more of my homebrew. TK pulled Billy along and scoped out the dry goods. This section of the Run, a giant circular revolving wheel with port windows every fifty feet, was unusually busy with traffic. All kinds from the surrounding sectors.

I bumped shoulders with a lot of impatient folk from duty officers to transients, all milling about and talking a lot of hokum in loud voices. I caught snippets of conversation that were not entirely of reassuring nature. Drought on this world, killings on that world, planetary genocide. Gang takeover. Refugees from Megal, merchants from Vylnos, down and out speculators from any of the mining worlds and prospectors scoping out asteroids, uncharted moons, any chunk of rock that could churn out a dime. Any number of garden-variety drifters and hopefuls looking for a new life on a new world. I heard them all, like the buzz of angry bees, haggling over prices of basic commodities like soup, drypak, underwear, which seemed to have escalated in the sudden demand created by the exodus. A tense expectancy hung in the air; a flurry of desperation that made everyone edgy, like a massive feedback loop, the threat of scarcity and the fragile security of their lives.

"Let's get out of here," Wren muttered, after I'd paid for the two bottles I needed. "The vibes are getting a little out of hand."

"Agreed."

"What's that glass bottle? Little bit of a garden cocktail?"

"Something like that." I cast her my chilliest grin before I surged ahead.

Suddenly there came a low drone, pulsing through the air like an air siren out from an audio-net nightmare. The station alarm. Eyes darted up, dull whispers broke from dry lips.

A security monitor next to me spoke in a clipped whisper. "Advance armada—Early distant warning. They'll be coming out of warp in two minutes."

The monitor's partner spat out a curse. "Shit, they're already here. Why?"

TK mumbled, grabbing my shoulder. "Bad idea to berth here, Rusco, bad idea." He shook his gray head.

I snatched at Wren's arm. "Let's get back to the ship."

Out the porthole I saw the docking security ship take a turn and bank away, her weapons lights streaming on her foredeck.

That was not good.

Orange lights winked over the shops and service counters. A robot voice pealed over the loudspeaker: *"Amber alert. All dockers aboard Skeller's Run report to emergency bay. Lockdown in process. All docking bays from A1-T3 will be closed in T minus 2 minutes. All boarders proceed to emergency support bay. Repeat, report to emergency bay."*

"Jesus, can you believe it?" I bawled.

The attack came in less than two minutes.

Several stealth raiders came out of warp like banshees and flanked the station. Long beetle-like prows with glass eyes surveyed the station with predatory menace. Their tapered purple-grey hulls pulsed with malignant energy.

The emergency alert was as useless as tits on a bull.

A group of frightened souls snarled curses at the vanguard. White fingers gripped wrists; pale-faces goggled at what faced them.

The battle cruisers came arching into view. The lead craft glowed an ominous grey with triangular nose and bulkheads racked on an octagonal rear body like a souped up war freighter. The *Galaga*.

"Holy mother of god—" a bystander cried. "That's Mong's devil ship. Enough firepower there to wipe out half of Veglos."

More and more of that name 'Mong'. It tinkled in the back of my mind like a shaman's death rattle. *Hoath*. That two-bit guard. He'd dropped the name. Some star lord or mega star-mogul.

A black-bearded man, clutching a bag of drypak meals, crowded close to the glass. The man looked like a pilot, judging from the eagle logo on his blue spacer uniform. "He's an ugly brute. Some kind of cult leader. Whatever the case, you don't want to mess with him."

"Founded the Temple of Tirith on *Ciros*, I heard," croaked another. "Priest, nomad, witch-hunter, warlord, jack of every trade. With some weird kind of powers to boot."

"Like what?" I snarled, whirling on him.

"Don't know, like moving stuff with his mind. Weird shit like that."

"That's all crap," I scoffed. "He's just a flesh-eating shitter like the rest of us." But somehow I knew not, and my greatest fears were realized, remembering the tales of blood and rapine that Ging fellow on Hazzerot had committed. But it had been so long ago.

"Maybe, but that's what I've heard," said the outworlder. "Whatever, you don't want to mess with him."

Seems as if I already had, if Baer was mixed up with him—and I had provoked him by rifling his secret stash and blowing off his arm.

I moved off with a grunt, feeling a tremor of sick unease crawling up my gut.

"Rusco, we should—"

I waved TK off.

Without warning all hell broke loose. It seemed any communications' parley had failed. The wasps surged in with amazing dexterity, making retaliation impossible.

The security docker opened fire but stood no chance against so many enemies. The attackers pounded it to chipboard, its shields blinking red before dying.

The security vessel and companion ships rocked under the firepower. The enemy looped around them like blackflies circling a wounded deer, peppering them with rays, penetrating shields and shearing cannons.

The flagship blew the main security docker ship to dust. That gray-bloated pig with antennae, towers and cannons was no more.

TK paled. "They just nuked the main security vessel."

"No kidding," I growled. "The thing's really just show and glitter. A sitting duck for those smaller spitfires. See?"

The wasps roared over the last of the defenders, taking out crafts, military and civilian.

"Why? What's their purpose?" cried Wren. "Why take a station when they can have a planet?"

I shifted uncomfortably. "For show, kicks, greed? Teach the refugees there's no safe place to hide?"

I stood in helpless awe as the invaders employed that blitzkrieg technique TK'd mentioned. It was devastatingly effective.

"Get to Starrunner, before it's too late," I mumbled.

The first smart bombs struck the upper decks of the Run, rocking the floor under our boots and knocking us off our feet.

Screams rose from all quarters. Metal crumpled around us, glass shattered, and smoke rose in a shower of sparks, spraying me with debris.

I picked myself up and ran with Wren down the littered terminus, picking my way through the stampede, against the flow.

Pandemonium hit the rotunda. Most tried to scramble for the main avenue to the emergency bay—a mistake, and soon it was a clot of writhing, fighting hordes, crammed against themselves like lemmings.

I grabbed Wren and pushed TK forward. "Back to the ship—"

"But they said—"

I waved him off. "Forget it. Follow my lead if you want to live."

I ran right into a checkpoint station guard crouching, holding an R2 at my chest. "Get back. You can't go in there!" he bawled. "Lock down."

One thing I hated was protocol during life and death situations. I pretended to bow my head in submission, then upended him in the chops with an elbow, knocking him flat on his ass. I kicked the weapon out of his reach and lifted my pen blaster.

His buddy crouched and aimed for my head.

Wren lifted her pen and blew the man's head off without a second's hesitation.

I blinked. "Let's go."

We raced past the checkpoint for the A2 dock where Starrunner berthed; fortunately she hadn't been destroyed, only trembling to explosive rumbles and flecked with silver metal plates fallen from the ceiling. Smoke curled from down the hall and cries of the dying reverberated with sparks raging and metal beams crashing down.

The docking arm still hung clamped to our bow. I swore and jerked open the hatch, raced for the bridge, got the engine running. The others were not far behind me. I pulled Starrunner out, breaking off the docking struts and the arm. The water connection severed, sending pipe and water spewing like a fire hose. Sparks flew where pieces were still attached. I turned the cannon and blasted a hole in the stubborn berth gate. I gunned the engines and she ripped through the jagged opening and under impulse power shot up on a ninety degree angle straight out of there. Pulse rays tore across our beam and flared around us like firecrackers with enemy ships on our tail. Bug-shaped marauders with two wings fore and aft, like two ice picks end to end.

Odd sounds streamed from Billy's mouth in a disturbing manner. Wren, flush-faced and grimacing, manned the starboard guns.

"The hostiles are coming too close for comfort," yelled TK.

"Quit blabbing and start shooting! Do I need to coach you? Is there no compliance in this universe?"

"You been praying to the wrong gods, Rusco," gibed Wren. "Maybe you should quit squawking."

I whirled on the old man whose arms were trembling. "TK, man the auxiliary starboard guns. Wren, you take the port. We're going to have ourselves a dogfight before this is all over."

"We've got multiple bogies on our tail," she called.

"The manuals are in the console, if you need them," I said.

"Warp out of here," she cried.

"Can't. That's a gas giant down there in case you didn't notice. Gravity galore. I have to clear another 100k miles away before I can even think about Varwol."

"He's right," TK groaned.

Wren stared in disbelief. "Why is this happening? How could we have warped in within orbital distance—"

"Shut up. Fire!"

Other ships burst from their stalls, some of them hopelessly damaged and catching fire in the process. I winced as they became incendiaries, ripe prey for the enemy stealth ships bearing down on them. Some tried to jump to warp too soon and became stretched discs miles long before they shimmered blue and winked out of existence forever. I saw a Vega 6 ultra light cruiser go up in flames, drowned in pulse fire. Others followed suit. Fat pulse beams whipped so close to Starrunner they almost tagged her flanks as the black and grey starfleas bombarded us with every weapon they had. All I could do was urge every ounce of speed out of Starrunner before I could trigger the Varwol.

I pondered the motive of any man to unleash such wholesale slaughter. Target: all the refugees from that doomed planet. Truly a vengeful bastard in the extreme, this Mong character. On the chance it was the same Mong I'd heard dropped on Hoath, we'd better be wary. My thoughts were interrupted as a larger, blue wasp-enemy came vaulting out of the ether with fareons locked. What were the chances it was the same Mong?

"Molly, give me live feed and max juice."

"Affirmative."

The holo display came up. A target zoomed in and possible missile trajectories for intercept. I targeted it and smashed it broadside on the rear thrusters, near the heat-sink. "Die, fucker." But my mouth sagged. The wasp-like fuselage flared in a red aureole then faded down to standard gray. I whacked my fist on the weapons console. "Why don't you die, fucker?" I launched another fareon. Now those stealthguard cannons were aiming straight at us. No wonder those bee-stinging, bitch-faced flydirts had defeated an entire planet. "Molly, we'd better be getting out of here pretty damn fast!"

"Affirmative. ETA T-1:36 before Varwol can engage."

"That's an awfully long road to hell. Molly. Snap it up!"

I whirled on Wren. "Give that bitch your best shot. If we combine blasts, maybe our attacks can penetrate those crypto-shields."

"10-4! On the count of three. Three—two—one. Now!"

Our blasts coordinated at the same point, a four-foot square on the underbelly of the approaching, offensive craft. The thing glowed for several seconds, one baleful crimson, then began to flame around the edges. My mouth quivered for a second, then curled in triumph. "Hot damn! Wallow in oblivion, you bandit shitweasel—"

Fareon beams came arching from the two attacking ships at the flaming ship's heel which I dodged as other escaping craft died in our rear sights. Shields held but upper panels began to smoke and the Varwol was beginning to shiver and kick in.

Maybe, just maybe. Multiple beams arced out across the gulfs, but Starrunner blinked out in a haze of nothingness as the Varwol, miracle of science, kicked in.

CHAPTER 10

We all took a time out, and celebrated over a bottle of gin I had tucked in the forward bulkhead I called the 'back hamper'. Starrunner was off to the Norios belt or some never-never land, and I hoped to hell the Barenium would hold. After the backslapping and congratulations were over and Billy had finished his powdered milk and munched his synthetic cookies, we sat down for a fireside chat at the circular conference table on the bridge. "I see the Varwol's already degraded 2.5%."

"Sad thing that," muttered TK.

"We survived this round, but next time might not be so pretty. I'm not saying that was a typical day in the life of an honest crook, but if you're running with me, it's not going to be easy."

Wren shrugged her sinewy shoulders. "All the same to me, dads. I've been dodging mad boys and dervishes most of my life, so this just felt like home." She adjusted her Uzi on her shoulder at a better angle.

"First of all, I'm not dads, and it's not grey hair, it's purple, in case you didn't notice."

She reached across the tinted tabletop and patted my hand, as if to console my feelings. "There, there, Rusco, just horsing around. Don't take it the wrong way."

It was a nice addition, even if it was a touch condescending. "Forget it, Wren. None taken. Now, way I see it, we can run scams and cons up and down the populated worlds, starting with the most prosperous planets. I got one in mind now, where we play tag team at the rich dives and the casinos, looking for manageable marks. We showboat them around, give them a good time, make ourselves out as easy marks, then take them for all they're worth."

Wren shrugged. "It sounds easy, but I got a better idea. Why not fake a shipwreck, set up a distress signal, and let them come to us, then we nab their ship and goods."

TK muttered, rubbing his chin, "It has potential, but too many variables and violent possibilities. I don't have that many years left in my old bones and don't feel like cutting them short, lying in a pool of blood."

"Good luck with that, old man." I chuckled. "If you're running with bad boys, blood there'll be. Tell you what, we can always let you off at Beta Aquilae or the nearest hub."

The old man gave a withering grimace. "Billy and I'll stay on here, I think."

"Good choice. But I tend to agree with your rejection of the shipwreck plan. Wren, as much as I like your idea, I'll have to downvote it. Let's stick to plan A."

She shrugged, gave a surly scowl. "All the same to me, Rusco. Go for it."

"On another note, Starrunner's due for an overhaul. New stabilizers, Barenium seals, whatever. You contribute your share and we're all fine. I've facilitated your escape and'll put in for the bulk of repairs. After that we share in the spoils."

TK blinked and growled, "I can live with that, Rusco, but I'd rather you pay me hard yols for the repairs I do, and give me a garage, diagnostic equipment and tools."

I smiled. "See, there's the rub, TK." I put my arm around his shoulders. "Things like hangar space and tools, cost money."

"Why not dump this silly crate and buy a whole new kit?" grunted Wren.

I stared at her for a moment. "How do you figure that? You think quality spacecraft are just lying about, waiting to be plucked from trees?"

"Steal one."

"Something unethical about that," I said, in my most deadpan voice.

TK snorted.

These rubes didn't appreciate a good joke. "I need to take a nap, sleep off these wounds. Knock yourself out, the bridge is yours.

"Wait!" cried TK. "Let's talk more about these heists. If you're serious, why not start on Vasel or Perseus? Lot of trade up there, or at least was, when I was touring."

"Perseus is a high draw," I admitted. "I've heard ripe business goes on up there. Some money to milk at least."

"Another place comes to mind is Skguron."

"With Skurgian raiders coming up your ass out of every nook and cranny in hyperspace. I think not."

"Scrap it then. Perseus, it is."

"We'll talk about it more later." I yawned. "Plenty of water in the dispenser and dry food in the paks, and some more cheap gin under the bulkhead, if you need a kick."

"Thanks, dads," said Wren with unveiled sarcasm. "That's a great package, the dry meal included."

"Don't mention it," I said, tipping my head in salute.

Exhaustion had more than taken its toll. After showing Wren and TK to their quarters in the spare cabins, I thought to hit my bunk. But first I locked the controls on autopilot for Beleron, with only a key code that I knew. Didn't trust them farther than I could spit. Yet.

I flopped down on my hard foam, locking the door tightly by remote. I caught some restless sleep, but awoke in a cold sweat some hours later, feeling the gnarling pain in my knee, a gnawing ache which was like a saw penetrating to the bone.

I descended to the hold, checking things over, sauntered back up the service hall where I saw the bridge lights on. Wren had already retired, but as I approached, I caught TK snooping by the controls, rummaging for something. He seemed to be fiddling with the auxiliary panel. It looked as if he were searching for booze, but on second glance, he pretended to tie his boot lace. Then I got suspicious with his head snapping up like that with a stupid grin, fingers tapping some keystrokes into the data console.

"Says here packed Barenium will hold up 50% longer, Jet, if it's nazolene-pressed vs raw-treated. You know what era your Barenium's from?"

"Not rightly, TK. Wasn't given the proper maintenance papers by the lowlifes I snatched the ship from."

"I can imagine that. Well, seems as if we should make some effort to track those papers down, shouldn't we? I was searching for them in the utility cabinets below when you startled me—"

"They aren't there." I curled up my lip. It might have been a legitimate story but I thought not. TK was slier than he looked. Seemed he had pulled up some info on the free data stream via holo net. Kits which included diagrams, well-marked-up color-coded map, step-by-step instructions with two young, vivacious birdies giving a servicing tutorial on the finer points of Barenium and handling fresh product in vacuum sealed canisters. Nice girls. Pretty looking, but it looked much like a cute trick to sidestep me, and a feint to cover his real intentions.

"Bridge is off limits while I'm not here," I muttered in a cold voice.

"I thought you said to make ourselves—"

"I said no bridge access. New rules." I'd have to make a point of moving that strongbox with the phaso to a more secure location. The last hungry look I saw on the old man's face had that wild, eager edge that stuck in my mind. The phaso was already hidden well in the forward bulkhead, but one could never be too sure.

* * *

We skipped Beleron and docked at Zanzadeer, known for its mech shops and abundant ship parts. Also gambling houses, party houseboats, rave depots, plenty to placate the varied vices of humankind: sex sports, needle games, you name it, they had it. I opted to kill two birds with one stone, repairs and profit. Not the best place to dock for a leisurely layover. Lots of mishaps reported on Zanzadeer: missing bodies, child abductions, random blast attacks, but we couldn't be choosy with Starrunner acting up as she was.

The repairs were complex, items that even TK couldn't fix, despite his protestations to the contrary. Without a proper garage, his skills were limited. But he said he'd look over the mechanics' work after they were done to check for shoddy service. I nodded, muting my skepticism of honest-dealers. Meanwhile, we needed funds. I was sadly lacking, after shelling out for the supplies, and it was not as if any of the hangers-on aboard, my new crew, had a yol to share between them.

"We need to go out on the town and rustle up some coin."

"Anything in mind?" asked Wren.

I nodded, worried my lip. "We work the gaming boats on Lake Yoe first. Follow my lead, stay low and alert, and you two may learn something."

"Yes, Captain Ruskie," said Wren with a cynical salute.

No mention of the phase-distorter from TK, though I knew it was on his mind. Billy was useless to us so he stayed back on the ship. I just hoped the halfwit wouldn't trash the place. I'd disabled all the controls, and left him with some crude magazines to pore over, unbeknownst to TK, but one couldn't be too sure.

After scanning the ship's database for loopholes in the Zanzadeer gambling systems, I discovered we needed some updated props; new games were in play on the boats. I went to work on some loaded die and some fancy cards. Been a while since I'd been to this planet so I had to refresh my memory. My mind worked over the endless scams I could pitch: the spinners, the loopers, the big sting. In that way my brain was like a computer. I could soak up cons like sponges water: spin a mark's mind up so tight, he's wanting to get scammed. Or, the big lie, the loopers, the ones almost impossible to believe, but the reward so high that the mark can't resist.

A simple con came to mind: Me and Wren'd work the game houses along the wharf, a husband-wife team, 'Emmie and Hamber', newly-weds, playing the amorous duffers.

Wren, determined and proficient, played the part a little closer to the mark than I expected, but if it earned us credence among the big players, I was game. All the flighty little moves she contrived, the touches, the pets and kisses, pecks on the cheek at the right moment, seemed credible enough. Been five years since I'd worked that scam. Did it with my ex-girl, Katie, back on Kalsinar, but that had ended on a bad note when she got roughed up; it'd soured any attempt on my part to revive it. I was superstitious that way—no raising of old ghosts. But now was not the time for superstition, or to sabotage this venture, seeing as we needed funds so I could get Starrunner back in space.

I was surprised to see Wren wearing a black skirt, tight-pressed that showed her upper curves well, all dolled up, very sexy; she cleaned up well, in my opinion. She must have bought that garment back at the station. The butchy, skinhead look would never fly, so I pulled out the wig and plopped it on her head. "There, black, just as you like." I patted it down roughly. "Matches everything else on your hide."

She groused about it, but only a little. I turned her to the mirror and told her she looked beautiful. With a reluctant grunt, she accepted the wig.

With my last instructions to the mechanics, telling them we'd pay them later, we took a tram from the service garage into the glitter and glitz of centertown. The place made Hoath look like a complete scumhole. But the crumbled buildings, gang-graffiti and blackened, shell-torn smokestacks rising beyond the old quarters demonstrated otherwise and still lurked around the edges as we got closer. Much was hidden in Zanzadeer city.

We scouted out several joints, me and TK in disguise, and separately, so as not to attract any outriders by association. We came up with a system, different than others, for the games had changed as I had remembered them, and so had the management. One thing about the con business, never make any assumptions. Do your research, check your facts, figures, plans, and recheck them at least three times before committing. Something I'd failed badly at back in Hoath, trusting Marty with the particulars, and almost getting the two of us killed.

Yoe was a shallow lake and a bunch of entrepreneurs had got together and formed the novel idea of setting their gambling houses up on the water. A flotilla of fun. Dancing, music, the works, house games like Monster, Juju, Bluewrack, and names like Barney J's Lil' Ole Boathouse and Iggy's Pop, and my favorite—Popcorn. Goofy names, but Zanzadeer was a goofy place. Disarm the sheep, separate them of their money. Only moneyed folk could afford these floating mini-palaces, but they were here in this town, as I had discovered early on in my prior visits. The organized crime leaders, the ones with the private guards and the refitted space yachts all dressed in mahogany and marble complete with private bars and waitresses, made it a dangerous arena, but a lucrative one for the clever artist. I'd overcome my fears of fencing with the big boys long ago. All a matter of confidence, a mind over matter thing. If I stripped every vibe of doubt and radiated confidence, there was nothing I couldn't do. Such a mindset overrode fear mechanisms which got even the best cons killed. Even in the toughest situations I could worm my way out. I used to get juiced up on Myscol before a swindle in my younger years, to build up enough nerve, but I got over that kid's ploy when I realized it was a losing battle, a battle of addiction that I'd never win. So, I sucked it up, took a deep breath, visualized how it was all going to go down and practiced my affirmation, and my mantras. Most importantly, tried to work with competent players in the game. Now TK and Wren were untested, and I assumed had no experience with real scams, though that Wren was a mean one on her feet, but so far they had shown promise. Let's hope my instincts were correct about them.

After scrutinizing several games on various boats, TK the

mathematician, ran the numbers and figured out a workable system. We put our heads together to select the best possible outcomes.

The house had rigged Juju, so that was out of the question. But Bluewrack and Monster had potential. They were group, not house games and promise for some tidy profit. Of course, we'd need a point-scout. That's where TK came in who'd agreed to devise hand signals.

The ten-sided dice were new to me, geared to throw off sharks who had already polished their scams.

"Seed the aces," TK said. "Half the die are loaded. We insert our own in play. At drop fifteen we play full out and win, then drop back, lose a little so they don't get suspicious."

"Okay, old man, we play one against the other. I'll engineer a way to signal so nobody figures it out and pulls the alarm on us. As I see it, the house will always win in the long run, but short term gains are possible. The more players, the more likelihood of a gain. It's a matter of getting out at the right time."

"We're on board then. Let's establish a coordinated plan of exit."

"Right."

"How's your Bluewrack?" I grinned at Wren.

She shrugged. "Never played it, but I became proficient at something like it back when I used to trounce my brothers."

"Oh, yeah? It'll have to do. I needn't remind you that the stakes are high here—broken legs and fingers are not uncommon. Fates get worse than that for cheaters."

"Don't sweat it, I've got it under control."

I didn't like the nonchalance in her voice, considering the stakes of the enterprise; it could get ugly very quickly.

We practiced several rounds on the bridge with my own weighted die and marked cards. I coached Wren on the finer points of the game, when to toss and when to roll a losing hand and when to go for the jugular. She learned fast. Like she said, she seemed to have experience with the game before.

"Throw them without getting intimidated. Get them to land a certain way. You dig your nail in the three-spot on the heavy side and the magnets kick in and the dice'll fall the other way."

"Not bad, Rusco. Some clever rigging here."

I shrugged. "I've used these scams before, engineered a way to peer in on other's hands, putting a reflective strip of polyeselon, a reflective bit of glass, on the opposite wall where I sat and kept chatting to divert my opponents."

TK shook his head. "Risky. If they caught you—"

"They're not looking for it, don't you see?" I said. "Without a point man or some nondescript posing as an innocent spectator, they're looking for other things."

"I don't know," said TK. "The strip sounds easy for a roving eye to pick up."

"What I did was photograph the wall pattern prior to playing and mock up some reflecto-pad to follow its blend. I'd brush against the wall, elbow the pad sticky side out when no one was looking. Voila. Stuck there like an invisible stamp. The thing's thin, so there's no visible evidence, and it's slightly convex to show a wide view."

"Don't see how that would show you anything."

"I wore a kind of contact lens to pick up the faint reflection."

TK shook his head. "I'm just glad we're not using a scam like that. I can blend in easy enough, a sad alcoholic wanting a piece of the action but no yols to play."

"Good, simpler's better. BJ's is busy, lots of players there. Small timers too, so it won't be as hot."

"Any idea of how long we'll be out on the floor?"

"As long as the tables are dealing, we work up some stash, then we skip to the next boat. Or I give you the signal to cut for the night."

I saw TK's hesitation. "Any hint of anything going sour, we bail, agreed?"

Grumbles. Shrugs. Looked as if we were on track.

CHAPTER 11

We were finally ready to deal and I picked BJ's to start. The place was popular, busy, a buzz of pleasant excitement in the air. Bright lights lit up the back that hurt the eyes, made you feel tired and radiated a lot of heat, leaving a lot of hot sweaty residue on the skin. Geared to get you to make impulsive moves to release that excess discomfort, blow your money while munching complimentary nuts and salted tidbits at the tables so you'd feel thirstier and drink more of the local brew. Slot machines jingled to the side; group games progressed toward the front. Live band at the back, playing an upbeat techno-jazz with juicy electro frills unfamiliar to my ear. The clink of glasses caught my attention, the titter of women's voices as they watched the big players toss glittering die or spread fan-colored cards in front of their faces, hoping for the big win. The hustlers latched on to the winners, blinked in derision at the losers.

Wren and I wended our way to the happening section while TK stayed back. The alpha dog at the head table of four had at least two guys working for him, or watching out for him. I could tell by the subtle eye movements and stiffening of shoulders. I earmarked that information.

We sat down at the Bluewrack table, in between two of the foremost gamblers, Wren as Emmie, all smiles and giggles, looking a little tipsy, but as sober as a shark, me on her other side. I was a different story, not so easily able to fake drunkenness, despite the local juice giving me a flushed face and a fuzzy skull. I had an uncanny knack of keeping my thoughts coherent, even though my body language might show the influence of drink.

Sitting aside Wren, I gave the players my most disarming smile and nod. I'd slicked back my long hair like an old hipster and had it knotted in a ponytail so it didn't look so beatnik. That look wasn't going to fly at these highbrow tables. I'd lost most of the purple tint but let a few of the violet traces show through, figured it might make me look more like a groovy, middle-aged trendster, momma's rich boy, making his second attempt at life with a new bride swinging on his arm.

The game was a combo of dice and cards, iridescent pieces which showed up like magic tricks, and danger to boot, dazzling the eyes.

We'd rehearsed our signals. Blink twice for a move to up the ante. Once, plus a pause to fold. We'd switch it up to a parting of lips and scratch of jowl, then back to the double-blink when TK'd take a swig of his local liquor and lick his chops.

The boats or overhauled barges were packed really close together along the shore and lit up with bright neon. Red, yellow and white light streamed across the dark waters. Fireworks arched across the lake—faraway festivities were in the works.

Other pleasure boats plied the water like gaudy floating birthday cakes. The waters were dense with salts and minerals and gave greater buoyancy to the gambling houses. The draw on these flat-bottomed boats was a whopping twenty-six inches. Not much speed. They could pull in at three knots, slow as turtles, but why go fast when you're making yols by the minute? Better to keep the fat fish aboard slapping their chips onto the tables.

All the while I kept a wary eye out for trouble. Those hard faces around us, laughing and wisecracking, were the faces of killers. Violent repercussions could be the result of one failed gambit, should one be caught. We'd be thrown to the monster moonrays, feral eels that haunted the salty waters. Heard horror stories of cons weighted at the ankles and thrust into the deeper water, while the gangsters watched the disappearing act from the comfort of their yachts, eating surf and turf and sipping martinis.

Wren, who looked less suspicious, would clock up most of the wins, while I'd sit back on my thumbs and tank hands and blame it on wifey. Wife and Hubby team. Rich and spoiled from moneyed families who had struck out on the ill-fated expedition of marriage, then made the naïve mistake of wasting their yols on these nice gentlemen.

It was important to give the right cues, not to set anyone's suspicions off. I was reading these guys as best I could while Emmie chattered on about nothing. She was doing well; one would never know the woman was a cold-blooded killer. Fatty, directly opposite me, with the dimpled cheeks and airbrushed hair, was all smiles amid peanut eating and shell cracking. Munching away with his quail-ass grin while he won hand after hand. Pissed me off. But it was part of the act.

Patience, Rusco. Keep losing.

The skinny one with the black suit and dour looks paid me no heed but managed a nod and grunt from time to time to his crony. No less crafty, I could tell. The older one was harder to read. Salt and pepper hair, serious type but not so serious. A blank, bulldog face with strong lines on the upper cheeks, sometimes crinkling in a smug grimace; other times he'd drop a line of philosophic rhetoric straight from Goethe. Because he was the boss, he was the most dangerous of the lot. They called him Elmer. What kind of jackleg name was that? Either it was a gag, or I was missing something. Still, I gave Elmer his due respect and played the happy hubby, drinking more than my share, wincing with every gasp of the local swamp water laced with distilled spirits, twice as potent as normal alcohol. I let the flush rise to my cheeks, a healthy pink—the gambler's flush they called it—pulled at the sweaty fabric on my collar, made a half-hearted smile and little coo at my beloved wife—who the others seemed to dig, despite the horrid wig job. Amused me, while my brain worked overtime trying to figure out how to stall the game and lose some more.

TK was doing his part, wandering about to different tables, chatting, letting us play out our tricks and hands, so it didn't look as if he was feeding us any information. Also letting us lose a lot while he was there, to create a negative association with his presence. A clever diversion.

That tingling feeling between my shoulder blades told me that our window of opportunity was closing fast. Time to cash out. Emmie had accumulated a good stash on the last hand. I'd lost the next round deliberately, and badly, though I had put in small bids.

"I told you not to lead with that flush!" I yelled at her.

"Sorry," she giggled. "I'm not thinking straight, dearie. Must be these highballs. They're stronger than what I'm used to."

Layering it on a little thick perhaps, but it got some chuckles from our card crew. Husband and wife team, wife stricken with a case of the tipsy giggles and an excess of yols.

I threw down the dice in a huff of disgust. "Emmie, I'm out, need a break. You'd better come too. You've won quite a bit."

"Nothing doing, Hamber, I'm just warming up."

"Beginner's luck," I grumbled at her with unfeigned jealousy. "We're not inexhaustible, you know."

"Hush, dear," she cooed, "I'm just getting into the game! Don't be a prig. I'm sure these nice gentlemen'll go easy on me—if I start to lose."

One of the shark eyes leaned in with an oily, but genial tip of the head. "To keep your charm in the game, madam, is our modest pleasure. It's Lemmy here you have to worry about." He nudged the man next to him in the ribs and gave a harsh guffaw. "We still have to earn back some of the yols you've taken from us."

Real rib ticklers, these sharks.

The faint, seaweedy smell continued to ooze off the dark water, drifting in the window, making me feel slightly ill.

When Wren played coy at leaving the game, I made a scene, pretending to get in a drunken huff and stalked off to the bar.

Weaving a little as I walked, for effect, I could hear Wren murmur some gracious, bubble-headed words, giving a whole spiel of effusive apologies for her disgruntled husband whom she felt *compelled* to nursemaid from his griefs—the big sullen, drunken baby—while promising to return to the game asap. TK edged slowly toward the other games in progress closer to the exit.

Good girl, cash out your chips, hit the ladies' room, then make a beeline to the back door while those sods await your return.

Drink in hand, I pushed through the double doors and hit the deck, glad of the fresh air. The sky was dark, starless; the air cool and musky. The shots of the local spirits, clouds of nicotine and the bebop beat had started to eat away at my skull.

I counted the moments, listening to the laughter and the revelry and disco beats carry on across the water from the other boats. Wren came out, her cheeks flushed.

"You got the yols?" I grunted.

"Nice job, Rusco. Seems your scheme worked."

"Where?"

"Right here." She tapped the inside of her thigh where she had taped it. "Peachy."

A good act, but maybe not good enough. The door flapped opened.

Elmer tripped over with a grim smile. "Hey, girlie, game's still rolling. Well, what's this? Hubby and dollface taking a little timeout by the water? Charming." Elmer, with a smile that'd kill a grouper, slapped an arm around my shoulder.

"Just came out for some fresh air, Elmer. Be back in in a sec when I get my second wind."

"Don't rush. You don't look so good, Hamber."

"Think I ate some bad fish."

His head bobbed as he smiled. "You know what, I think you guys are a bunch of shamsters. Funny how I take a dislike to scammers, on account that I live here. Own a legitimate business, have some genuine friends. Makes me and my chums look bad. All the stories you jokers'd tell of how you conned a couple of the local fish." He laughed and TK took the unfortunate moment to breeze out of the swinging doors and give a gasping breath. Catching wind of the little gathering, he turned to hustle back in.

"Wait up, gramps." Elmer snapped his fingers. A couple of his thugs, all murder and glares, intercepted and pushed TK back to the rail in our direction. Elmer moved over to TK and threw an arm over his shoulder, as he had done to me. "I like you, gramps. Very slick of you in there, giving signals like that as if you were swatting away flies. Nice gig. These two I don't like, especially Hammy here with all his glib talk." His boot shot out and kicked me in the bad knee, as if he'd known it was my weak spot. I went down, crouching in agony. "Smarts, doesn't it, Hammy?" He laughed. "Suck it up, you pussy. Doesn't look good in front of the missus." He grabbed Wren by the hair and pulled her down to his crotch with his other hand rubbing his knuckles hard across her wig. The piece dropped off to show her skin head.

"My, my, surprises by the minute. Didn't know you went in for baldies, Hammy."

I was groaning, cursing myself for my stupidity. Fucker'd taken me by surprise. Innocent old uncle Elmer, a thug who'd whack you with a tire iron before you could blink and you'd still be wondering what hit you.

"Don't want no trouble here," TK stammered, looking as if he'd seen a ghost and was going to piss his pants.

"Oh, no trouble, gramps, just a small misunderstanding. See, we're going to go back into the gambling house and continue our game. We'll let you join for free."

I got to my feet, swaying, pretending a show of drunken bravado, as Wren struggled in Elmer's grip and I took a half-assed swing at Grease Hair to his side, making it easy for him to block. He gave a clown's laugh and pushed me into his henchmen while I flailed away like a jackass. He thought I was an easy takedown and grabbed the cuff of my sportman's jacket. Mistake #1. Never leave yourself open to attack, against even the dorkiest, most ham-handed drunk. One small tap on the throat or other sensitive area and the stars are spinning in your head. Then up comes the knee into the nose, pushing back the bone and cartilage into the brain. Then it's lights out…which is exactly what happened. One step inside the left leg and I was all over Lemmy with a chop to the neck for added measure.

I heaved the limp body over the rail, wincing at the splashing and flapping going on as something large and gurgling did their work. Elmer grimaced and licked his chops. Luckily the music was loud, or there'd be more fuss. But scattered couples were coming out to catch the next houseboat and watch the free show. I like putting on a show as much as the next wiseass, but all facts considered, things were not looking too good for us. We were in poor disguise and on a foreign world. Anything could escalate into bloodshed.

Wren gurgled out a throaty cry and kicked Elmer in the groin while I sprang to toe-tangle with the other fellow. She dropped to grab her concealed gun taped on the inside of her black-skirted thigh as TK pushed through the gathering crowd to get to the boarding dock. Wise and heroic move, TK. Leave your team behind while you make your escape.

I stumbled after the old coward, cursing and grumbling and hopped the rail as he did, making a flying leap over to the next boat, but my midriff struck hard against the hull, knocking the wind out of me. Meanwhile feral critters thrashed below. The alcohol gurgled up in my throat. TK was spryer than I imagined, the wispy-haired codger, fingers clutching the varnished wood just as Wren vaulted over and grasped at a higher point along the rail.

Quick, neat, but we weren't out the frying pan yet. We had to skip this houseboat in case more of Elmer's goons noticed the boss's absence. That second boat was angling to shore.

As soon as it bumped against the pier, we were off, tramping our way through the red light district and the back alleys, avoiding the downtown tram stops, in case Elmer's thugs had eyes on them. I had to fry some enterprising vagrants who jumped out at us, looking for spare coins. Hell would freeze over before I'd let all that work go to waste while almost getting killed, only to get sacked by some backalley punks.

We doubled back toward the lake on a zigzagging course and caught an air taxi farther up the line back to the repair shop. As we flew away from the boats, I let out a sigh of relief, knowing we had escaped a deadly scenario relatively unharmed.

Billy, turns out, had gotten himself in a bit of trouble, locking himself out of the loo, running back and forth not knowing what to do until he had finally wet himself. Was a while before one of the mechanics heard him banging on the hatch and had let him out. A sorry sight.

We got Billy cleaned up and squared up with the repairmen. Back on Starrunner, I took a bit of Myscol to help with my reinjured knee. The familiar tingly warm feeling overshadowed the throbbing agony as my eyes glazed over. Okay for now, but that leg was taking a beating. I'd have to see some doctor. Wren, who had been eyeing me with more than appraisal as the night wore on, took advantage of the success of our little venture to attempt some familiarity of flesh. She leaned in, brushing against me to snake her arm about my waist, a gesture so intimate as to feel almost passion-driven. Her voice dropped in a husky murmur, "Well, hubby, a good night's work, let's do it again real soon."

I leaned in on my good leg with only slightly less languid intent. "Tigress, you're being a naughty puss. Let the law of thuggery prevail. While the heat's on, lie low."

TK chose to blunder in on us like an ox at that moment. "I don't like this town, or their greasy games."

I blurted out an oath. "You and me both."

She slumped, turning away in frustration that the moment had been spoiled. "You know, you two are real wussies."

I shrugged. I could see that Wren was hedging for Miss Prickly of the Year award. TK and I moved off to the bridge.

We'd just about broken even after dispensing the funds for repairs, coming out a few hundred yols ahead. Not bad, but not good either. Split three ways, that wasn't much. Well, strictly speaking, I took 60%, considering it was my ship and I was doing them a favor, saving all our asses by getting out of dodge twice now.

The rear fin stabilizer was working so we couldn't burn up or wobble ourselves to death upon reentry. The warp drive was still an issue, the Barenium canister still with a hairpin leak, but it was an old part that couldn't be replaced too easily, the lead mechanic had told us. "We can put it on order, but a used part like that would be only 85% operational."

I slapped my fist down on the nav console at the memory as we warped out to Baile's planet, somewhere far away in Yanadar.

TK growled, "I know I should have monitored those greased monkeys better. I don't believe the drive was 'irreparable'."

"Good luck hanging around Zanzadeer while Uncle Elmer is on the rampage," Wren groused. "We should've killed him and all his thugs while we had the chance."

I waved a hand. "Don't get too trigger happy. Do no good anyway. His business associate rats'd still come out of the culverts and get us. This is the problem with being a traveling huckster, Wren. No time to do fix-it-up jobs. One chance, and it's vamoose. We'd better suck up our losses and move on. Bigger fish await in the pond across the way."

I felt glad to be away from Zanzadeer and the boats.

Wren caught up with me in the hall as I was stumbling my way to my cabin. She pressed her mouth hard against mine. I was surprised, for she was up front to a fault, but she was a tomboy after all. Pretty no-nonsense and a convincing one at that, despite my initial non-interest in her. It didn't feel proper to resist.

Back in her cabin, our clothes quickly became unpeeled and after the inevitable, 'Ew, what happened to your ear?' we were right down to business.

The woman had a luxuriant figure when stripped of her hunter's-gauge black leathers. I suppose our first joining was fated. The cabin vibrated to the sounds of our lovemaking. A long sweaty dance of push and pull that had both of us gasping and sucking in the same lungfuls of air. It seemed Wren had always wanted to get it on with me. Okay, I'd bite. I couldn't admit to the same, but I humored her all the same. It took the edge off the loneliness of a con-artist's existence, with no hope for tomorrow.

I awoke some hours later to a tangle of limbs. Her soft breathing on my left shoulder, a warm breast pressed to my chest. I rolled over and my lightly purple-tinted hair brushed her neck like a horsehair fan. Her long legs twitched, a moan pattered in her throat. The memory of some horror of the past? I rumbled out a lion's roar and squeezed her tightly and ran my tongue along her neck which prompted a murmur of escalated breath.

She seemed amused by the animal roar and gave me a playful slap. "Enough, tiger. Let's sleep it off. Plenty more time to play bride and groom in the days ahead."

CHAPTER 12

We'd been scamming up and down the Zaion worlds for a few weeks now and after several false starts, began to turn a profit. We'd finally repaired the Barenium leak and equipped the landing shuttle on Starrunner with extra space suits. I'd got my knee looked after at the local regen clinic on Gainor, one of the six habitable, terraformed worlds. Some regen—not cheap, and a loving pat on the leg by the stony-eyed medic. After scouting down a new-old Barenium cylinder on Gainor, I gave a praise to the good Kazoo that I no longer had to worry about Baer tracking us. As for the blood-hungry pirate Mong, we'd keep an eye out for him. The man had discovered a superior form of armor or shield technology that had given him a significant edge over his enemies.

I walked onto the bridge to catch TK and Wren glued to the holo screen. The free store planetary press was having a field day with the latest sensation—always a new goldmine of cheery information. The face that stared back at me with those eyes black as charred coal had me cringing.

The broadcast came over the public channel—Mong, in all his glory and ceremonial garb, black-braided ponytails and leather shoulderpiece. His cheeks flushed a ruddy bronze, but that face was set as serene as an avatar.

"Citizens and people of Questra! Surrender your government, your ships and your wealth, or I will unleash a rain of fire that will send you to hell!"

The image cut out and the screen panned back to the announcer. "And that is the latest ultimatum from warmonger, Kaibus Mong, known as the 'star lord' or the 'dark lord of death'. His latest conquest on Megal orbiting Tiran's star turned the landscape into a fiery, feudal wasteland. Will

'Questra', another of the inner planets, suffer the same fate? No one has come to offer aid to either Megal or Questra. Experts say that nearby governments and planetary United Nations are reluctant to defy Mong, fearing retaliation with his blitzkrieg tactics."

"Turn that fucker off, please," I ordered.

TK hit the switch. "See, this renegade Mong is bad news, Rusco. Doesn't look as if he's going to let a few petty worlds satisfy his greed."

"No kidding." The transmission had cast a shadow over my mood. "No different than Genghis Khan, from what I gathered from history. Snatching up territories as if they were candy for the taking." I shook my head. "No matter. Nothing we can do except keep a wide berth."

I finally decided to quit Gainor and scout out crime leads in my old haunts on Tarsus, the second innermost planet. The gigs we were pulling out in the hinterlands were but two-bit shams, raking in a few yols, mere milk money, in retrospect. But they were stepping stones to test out my team, iron out the wrinkles, so to speak, see where TK and Wren's weaknesses lay and how we could improve upon them. Wren was always too impulsive, a natural hothead, but brave and for the most part, unquestioning. TK, on the other hand, was a cautious worrier and a slightly lazy sort. But smart, and his input on cons, particularly timing and logistics, had given me an edge. Even that caper down on Zanzadeer had been a cockup, truthfully, a little bit too convoluted for my ragamuffin recruits. Had almost blown up in our faces. Not that I was Captain Gohimbo or anything. TK and Wren were rising in my estimation and I felt I could trust them with some bigger fish to fry. After purchasing some explosives down on Gainor with the gambling money from Zanzadeer, I decided to reach a little higher.

An old acquaintance of mine in Haifor City gave us our first genuine break. A Gigor Knox aka 'Blinky', who worked as the concierge at the Big Apple Hotel was my lead. He was a middle man up to his ears in larceny and schemes, from black market to sex trade. A contract job had come up through the grapevine, orchestrated by a certain gangster, the Dancing Slugger, Pazarol.

At the hotel and after a few words of catch up, Blinky took me aside. "I can hook you up for a meet down with Pazzy, kind of an open house." He spread his arms wide, and I saw brown rotten teeth rooted there in his grin.

"Sure," I said. "Whatever you say, Blinky. Just looking for a few opportunities here."

"That's the spirit, JR. That's why I like you." He patted my back with his ham-like hand.

Risky, making the contact with Pazarol, knowing the man was on a par with Baer from what I'd heard. A faint watery voice, a very distant one, told me to back off. But not a loud enough voice for me to take heed.

I did my research and checked out his modus operandi. A jack-of-all trades: arms, clothing, slaves, mercenaries for hire, anything that he could use to turn a profit, which in these days of gang-run, war-torn cities, was mostly contraband.

The gas cloud in the holo view coalesced and morphed into whatever 3D stimulus the ship's computer willed of it. The holo image, drawn from the public free-store, showed a series of dingy warehouses in a seedy industrial neighborhood with broken antennae prickling its rusty roof and decaying load lifters scattered in the yard with flat balloon tires. Inside, the secret cam, highlighting bootlegged clips from the free-store darknet, revealed some old sewing equipment. Outside, a wider pan revealed a few aging dumpsters and cargo ships. Junkers. Didn't think they would fly. A good front.

"You coming with me?" I muttered at Wren.

She shrugged. "Why not? We can go down together, but no wig this time."

I smiled. "Suit yourself."

TK grunted, "I'll stay put with Billy."

"As you wish. Keep an eye on our progress. We'll be wired for sound and video. If things go sour, that little red button'll glow. Hit the override sequence, fire up Starrunner and blast that piece of shit warehouse to shreds. Then I'll know my death was avenged. I'm not planning on Pazarol being that much of a shyster—but one can never be too sure... In the meantime, put that big brain of yours to work devising new and wonderful scams."

"I'll do that," he agreed with a laugh.

Keep old TK busy, out of mischief.

Those holo data dumps, part of the free store, came in handy. Someone had told me that far world data was updated by a simple file-sharing algorithm, courtesy of the ships' computers that came into proximity of a star system. Every time a ship made the Varwol leap, the local network of a new world would collect any updated info and merge it with its own local database while uploading new data to the ship's computer. Hence the system stayed current. Ingenious, but not 100% real time. Of course, worlds like Wren's on Talyon would get nothing of this, having no traffic to speak of nor any network infrastructure.

I met Pazarol and his gang down in his crib out in Tarsus in the decrepit town of Belgen, liking none of it from the get-go. I hoped to hell TK and Billy came through if there was trouble. Wren seemed indifferent to the meet, as if she were immune to danger. I think the days of violent terror she'd lived through in early years, with sand dervishes and mad boys had made her immune to fear.

I landed neatly in the service yard and debarked. As the engines wound down, the wide gated shutter of tin fluttered up and eight men of a standard merc detail jumped out and escorted Wren and me inside. A large echoey warehouse was busy with motion, tall upright machines and long low vats, looking like stitching and dyeing equipment to me, and some robot assembly machinery stamping out circuits. Pazarol met me with a meaty hand, a big rubicund man with a gleaming pate and a fuzz of blond hair at the back. He wore a starchly-ironed blue plaid suit, polished black shoes, gaudy necktie, all smelling of cigar smoke. Protruding buck teeth dominated his face, goatee hanging from a snub chin. I had no reason to dislike the man on first meeting, but nonetheless I did.

He motioned to his assembly plant with what could have been a gesture of pride. "This is my side business," he said, spreading a sweaty palm at the production line of boys and young women working fingers to bone to manufacture heavy clothing and boots, others fastening bolts and small latches to what looked like equipment scanners of some sort.

"You mean, 'front'?"

"Sure, whatever you want to call it, Rusco. Why argue over details?"

"No reason." A half dozen gunmen idled by, toying with their remodeled Uzis, lazy yawns on their thick lips, evincing casual interest, sleeping lions, but I knew better. I could sense they were wire alert, their lazy, easy steps too light, their sleek bodies too toned, their quick fingers too close to the triggers. To Pazarol's side, two of his men seemed to be paying more attention to the banter, one tall, swarthy, and sleazy looking with short greased hair; the other shorter, stockier, with down-turned brows and slicked back grey mullet and wearing small round glasses.

"A man needs a legitimate business in this world," asserted Pazarol, "otherwise he's got nothing, right? A few scams giving him a bit of bread now and then. His heist money always running low; no investments, nothing to fall back on, and the wolves, the opportunists, the terrorists, the hired government guard, whatever's left of them, coming out of the woodwork like termites, asking awkward questions."

I just smiled.

"Something tells me you never really got a business going yourself, did you, Rusco?...you should try it."

"On the to-do list, Mr. Pazarol, earmarked for a rainy day."

"That's good!" He wheezed, slapped me on the back. A bad smoker's cough. I'd give him five years, no more.

I wondered when he'd broach particulars about the job. This was his game, feeling out his new personnel, gauging the reactions, sparring with bullshit, testing reflexes, even though he was doing all the talking.

"Hire 'em cheap, work 'em hard," he went on. "Rusco, that's my credo. Watch and learn. No labor costs here. Look at these patsies. They're a bunch of dumb, happy freaks. I give 'em room and board—for the price of protection."

It was a sweatshop in the worst of ways. I saw frightened eyes, young boys, battered women with bruised cheeks or a blackened eye, the cocky guards walking about with Uzis, cracking jokes, ogling the prettier women.

"Get out your lumo pen, Rusco!" Pazarol laughed. "I'll let you take notes for a limited time, no extra charge."

I clenched my teeth, a part of me vowing to come back to this dumphole and free every one of those slave laborers. Blow Pazarol's enterprise to kingdom come. "What's this they're making? Looks like army clothes."

"Boots and combat fatigues. Guerilla outerwear for all sorts. High demand for merchandise like this in these times. A lot of traditional guerrillas, aka war thugs, are doing assaults on land."

"No doubt." I moved over and hefted a boot on a rack. Brown leather, durable, super light. Fast for runners in the bush, swamps or other onerous terrain.

"There's an extra kick in those babies, for sure." Pazarol shook out his fingers, bragging. "A barb with nerve toxin stub on the toe. One kick to exposed flesh and the victim is paralyzed, dies in twenty seconds."

"Nice." I set the boot down, wincing. He picked up a pair of fresh fatigues a nervous woman had sewn a battery pack to and motioned to the hand-sized circuit box wired to the back collar.

"This khaki blends into whatever environment a combat soldier is in. Brown bush, grey concrete, red sunset, don't matter. A phosphoro-gluten plant-based resin coats the inside surface. This doohickey on the back, a black box, sends the signal down to the plant membranes or whatever, telling it what form to take. Right down to the color, texture. Big seller. The rage these days. Touch it. It's realistic."

"I'll pass. Seems impressive though."

"Ah, a cautious man."

I offered no comment.

"I'll throw in a pair for you as a freebie, my token of appreciation and good faith. What size? Oh, you look about a ten." He grabbed a new suit off the storage rack and plunged it too into my hands." He eyed me, seeing how I'd react.

"Who's this lovely young lad you got here? Hiding behind your skirts like a bashful choir boy."

"This here's Wren—as in the bird."

"A mighty fine bird, that. Got her all dressed up like an army brat and what, with a fuck-boy cut? Surprises me, Rusco. Didn't peg you going for that. I'm liking what I see. Got to get me a fuck-boy."

"Very funny," I said and Wren growled her contempt. In spite of the rudeness of the remark, I let a dog snicker of grin brush my face. *Get on Paz's good side. It'll give you an edge in this fencing. Let Wren get a little sore, no harm.* Dressed in khakis and looking as unlady-like as possible, Wren was well, Wren.

"How 'bout it, sister?" He motioned to the fatigues. "You want a pair?"

"No, thanks," she said. "Might make me too sexy in front of your boys and give them some unwelcome ideas."

He snuffled out a laugh. "A good wit on her, Rusco. I like her. Better hang on to her. She's a good one."

"That she is."

His expression turned serious in a second.

"They're a trigger happy bunch of bitches down in the desert where you'll be going—desert mongrels, primitives holed up on a hot planet too long. So don't go getting any ideas to wise-guy them or do a double-cross.

You'll guard the shipment, make sure things go smooth as olive oil. They'll string your nuts up on their voodoo-crossed banyans faster than you can spit prune pits out your ass, if you get on their bad side."

"I'll keep that in mind."

"Take Raez here with you. I want him and Gris to report all operations direct."

I looked over at the shifty man with the cold grin on his face. "No deal. Don't know him from Adam."

"Tough titty. Either Raez goes with you or no deal and you can walk and we'll never cross paths again. A one time offer."

I chewed my lip, pretending to hem and haw over it. I studied Raez, with the slicked-back hair, thin nose and beefy cheeks, wondering how I could dislike the man even more than Pazarol, without him having opened his mouth. The wide stance, the 'I don't-give-a-fuck' attitude conveyed through the animal eyes, the challenging, bad-boy posture, it was a subliminal code of 'screw with me and you die' I'd picked up from experience. I ought to discuss it with TK and Wren, my partners, but there was no time. If I waffled here, Pazarol would look elsewhere and the deal would disintegrate, and a part of me vied to play longer. I gave a slow nod.

"Wise choice, Rusco. Now, more facts of life: Grisheimer, aka Gris, will be called in to run the main freighter and oversee a team of my own boys—hand picked." He motioned to the older shiftless fellow with penetrating owl-like eyes, the slack jowl, gangly limbs, but no less violent a man than Raez—the kind that would slit your throat and ask questions later for less reason than a dirty look. "He'll act as navigator on the Urgon, the freighter out back, and backup for the handling, pick up and drop of the cargo. In case things go ape and you fuck up, Rusco, Gris will carry out the rest of the plan."

I could see Pazarol was a prudent man, an arranger, despite his fat, friendly airs. He liked to cover his bases, though with an arrogance and pride that stank up the air from here to Perseus. Nor did I like the idea of 'brother' Raez hobgobbling about my ship with his foul breath polluting the air. Something odd about the man, and something odd about this job in general; it seemed off from the start. Raez's greasy look, Paz's all too easy gestures and his quick impulse to fast-track this job and dish out roles without any discussion at all. A wiser man would listen to advice and input from the players, and never take on a fresh hireling so readily, at least without a test. Perhaps that was in the works. I got the crazy idea Paz'd gotten wind of something I wasn't aware of. So my first warning was triggered. "You still haven't told me what it is we're carrying or where it is to be transported."

"We fly Urgon from Besi 6 to Jasmel, plus your ship to guard. It's enough to transfer the product. Fareon beam replacements, extended range, kills starfleas dead. That and raw Beryllium crystal needed to manufacture the beams. Need you to pick up raw product in Gizren on Besi then deliver that plus a full load of the replacement parts to Jasmel. I got me some full fareon beams in the back for shipment to the same source. But that's another story."

I stifled a grimace. *How's it feel, Rusco, to be giving your friendly neighborhood warlord like Mong a helping hand in the arm's race? Maybe it could have been you down on Megal when the bombs dropped?* The automatic voice rattled in my head: *Well, if it isn't you, it's some other slimeball playing delivery boy.*

Yet somehow these circular kind of reasonings didn't soothe me. More than ever I wished I'd never walked into Pazarol's warehouse.

"Sounds pretty heavy. What's in it for me?"

"You'd be looking at 10 Gs if everything works out. As for risk, plenty of raiders out there. Those are lawless territories. We'll need firepower to keep our investment protected. The ore freighter can move at impulse power only, sub warp, no more. It's more than she was made for, but will move her from Besi 6 to Jasmel space in a week or more."

"Skurgian raiders always find a hole."

He chuckled. "As for the split, it's a three-way deal. The Tanza boys at Gizren'll take their cut plus a few bribes along the way. I take mine, and you get yours."

"So, why don't you do this yourself?" I asked. "You seem to have capable men. What do you need me for?"

"That's the complex part, Rusco, nothing's ever straightforward. I got other business commitments going on. My team's maybe not so savvy in foreign affairs. Blinky says you're competent. You wouldn't be here if I didn't trust him and his good word."

"Sure, and what's the real reason?"

He looked at me for a second, wearing a feral scowl, gripping his goatee. "I need a shamster down there to grease the wheels and make this work. Dammit! I don't trust those Tanza boys—always fighting and scrapping amongst each other like a pack of wild dogs. Stringing each other up in banyans and letting the buzzards gnaw at them. This's a rush job here. We need the crystals right now to make fareon boosters. Or this buyer, a certain 'Dark Angel', will go elsewhere. I don't want to lose this deal. As I've said, you've got a reputation. So I took Blinky's recommendation to heart."

"I'm flattered."

"Don't be. Just get the job done and everybody's good, and maybe there's more where that came from."

"Let's cross that bridge when the time comes."

"Don't get cocky, Rusco. You're wanted by a dozen agencies and cartels around the galaxy. Men who'll have you snuffed out for a yol if they catch up with you. On lists galore." He snuffled a laugh. "A bounty hunter's dream. Your reputation precedes you—grand larceny, willful destruction of property, first degree murder, assault, border jumping, explosives, on and on." His face took on a brighter cast. "What I'm saying, Rusco, you're my kind of shyster. Welcome to the club." He patted my arm.

Somehow I was not liking being on Pazarol's 'good' side. The man was a slimy *douchebag*, even slimier than the lower echelon of thugs I sometimes did business with.

"The Tanza boys won't just take a simple cash deal. They'll want to escort the load too, or some fool thing like that. I want you to thwart them, if possible. It just muddies the pie. Convince them otherwise. I don't care just as long as the shipment makes it on time and in one piece."

"I'm mulling it over, Pazarol."

He gave me a cold inspection. I'd seen less predatory looks on steel-fanged viper fish.

"Tell me more about the product," I asked.

"Fresh tech, a quarter price. Fresh off the black market. Double the range, fareon state-of-the-art. Got a bunch of the devices here."

"Do I get one?"

"If you say pretty please and suck my dick." He looked around, enjoying the snickers of his henchmen. "For you I might swing a deal, with that lady friend thrown in on the side. One of the boys at the other end might equip you with a choicer one, once you've got the job done."

I shafted him a glare much like a wolf before it leaps in to rend the rabbit.

"Just kidding, Rusco. Wipe that murderous grimace off your face. Geez, you're a humorless man. This client I've got a deal with'll take the crystals and enhanced beams without fuss. An up and coming space bully. Thinks he's Captain Jojo, going to take over the universe."

"One of those at every transhub."

"You betcha. Keeps us in business." He laughed it off, a sour, hacking cough. "Wants raw crystal as well to manufacture his own weaponry. I shake my head, say, 'I can do it for you cheaper' and he says, 'no, I want to manage the trade myself'. I say, 'Okay, I can deal, half in advance', he says, 'Fine'. First rule of business, Rusco, is please the customer. Clichéd, but true. A sale is a sale." He looked at me with a cock-eyed grin.

I didn't know why he was telling me all this. I think it's one of those good guy ploys: let the new guy in town think he's more important than he is, some bigger part of the overall picture, then he'll work harder for you, stay loyal.

Pazarol's harsh voice tipped me out of my musing. "Okay, that's out of the way. What's your plan of operation?"

It was too late to back out. That time'd passed an hour ago. Suddenly I didn't want to deal any more.

"We'll go in as negotiators, me, Wren, Raez, pack weapons and explosives, in case things get ugly. We don't want things going haywire."

"Whatever, just as long as you don't damage my product."

"What do you think I am, an amateur?"

"Just so we're on the same page," he grumbled. He patted my arm a second time. He put his mouth close to my ear, spoke in a confiding whisper. "Take care, Ruski. On the off chance you sidewind me, I might become one of those mean-ass bounty hunters after your hide."

"We wouldn't want that, would we?"

CHAPTER 13

Back on the bridge, things were escalating. Wren was all over me about what went down in pig Pazarol's crib, even though I assured her it was all just show. We'd suffered another close scrape under impulse power by what I guessed were Baer's bounty hunters: two ships we'd barely evaded before a jump to hyperspace'd saved our hides. Why was Baer riding our asses so closely? Then again, I had blown off the guy's arm.

"Those bastards are everywhere at once," I muttered under my breath.

"And why shouldn't they be?" Wren growled. "Either they must have tracked us prior to the last repairs, or the Barenium's still leaking."

"Maybe somebody tipped them off," suggested TK.

Wren waved a hand. "If you hadn't brought that piece of shit microchip bad luck aboard, we'd be in none of this mess."

"That again?" I groaned. Shaking my head, I wished I'd never let them in on that tech. What one didn't know, couldn't hurt him, right? A shuffle of boot sounded behind me. I turned, scowling to see Raez hovering there like a ghoul. "What do you want?"

"I just wanted to check if we were good with the transshipment. We're going in tandem, right—or you going solo? Think you should put me on lead. Wren as backup, you to man the ship. What do you think, Rusco?" He gave her a lascivious look.

My fists clenched in an involuntary ball. "We already discussed that, *Raez*. I go in with Wren, you're backup. You keep your mouth shut. Remember, you're only here as a courtesy."

"Just wanted to double check."

Yeah, double check my ass. Any bit of eavesdropping you can do, you'll do, you piece of shit. I flashed Wren a warning glance, but she didn't seem to pick up on it.

Raez was one of those weasely types, slicked-back hair, thin jaw, who hangs out as a lurker, the smiling, grinning predator who looks for any trusting person or piece of interesting dirt that he can dig up, one that can be useful. I feared his sleazy habit would spill over into his work.

I had to put this apprehension aside. This was business and once the deal was over, I'd set the bastard down on the nearest transhub and be done with it. "Okay, let's go through the motions again. I don't want any margin of error."

Within moments, Raez sighed and threw down the map I'd drawn out painstakingly by hand. "Listen, we pick up the merchandise from this Gizren place on Besi, at what, 08:00? Why's it so hard? Dolgra or Dogface, and his Tanza boys'll be there with heavy guns, wanting insurance and money up front. We move in, take it aboard, guide the freighter, do whatever the hell those monkeys want done. If we get our jobs done, nobody gets hurt and everything rolls like a greased wheel."

"Yeah, exactly, if everyone gets their jobs done." I leveled him a stare.

"And what're you insinuating?"

"Exactly what it sounds like. It means let's study the map another time, and a hundredth time if we have to. I don't want any screw ups on this."

"Alright already. Don't get your tubes in a knot."

"Up yours, Raez. I'm sick of your wise-assing about. Either you up your game, or I ship you back to daddy Paz. Let him cater to your moods."

The others tensed.

Raez glared at me for a time, his mouth working in a mincy little line. He did his huffy routine, shifting from foot to foot, quivering and looking all mean, as if he were some big shot mobster. Then as I stared him down, daring him to go further, he backed down like a coward. It wasn't a subtle thing, just a change of psycho-physical energy in the air palpable to all. One I knew well. One of which I seemed to be in more command. He settled down in a snit, shook out his grease-slicked hair. But I could tell his nose was out of joint on this one and he'd be looking for some way to gain face. Let the man sulk, for fuck's sake. What did I care?

* * *

Besi 6 was a sparsely-populated, impoverished world closest to the sun Jesra. The biggest city, Tyaan, had more outdoor markets than any in the solar system, the bazaar capital of the solar system, but the rest of the planet was just scattered villages in a dry, windswept sandbath.

Because of its poverty, Besi had been spared the scars and gutting of war like the multi-citied worlds. But there were some heavy players with goods to sell and hustles to go. We were going straight into the heart of the wild, trigger-happy western tribes that spanned the arid gulches, the parched, baking wasteland.

Pazarol had mentioned the dominant tribe, the Gedra, known to extort the smaller clans of their exports, which they called 'protection fees' or some kind of fool tax for being in their territory. The Tanza of Gizren, of course, refused to pay, so I hoped we didn't have trouble with any of them this day.

Starrunner and Urgon rode low over the dust-cloaked valley. It was wide and swept with low dunes of fine, white sand. To the side snaked a ridge of pale red outcrops and black-flecked rock. On the other side, a long, thin lake, or what looked like a body of dark, greasy water, lurked. Probably caked with alien salt and poisons of high concentration.

Urgon landed at the base of the ridge where a group of rusted tin outbuildings clustered and what seemed an abandoned oil rig. But I kept Starrunner back, closer to the oily water for reasons I attributed to pure instinct. Two ships parked off to the other side of the rig: a sleek silver Sphinx, and a grey Markest, both looking in good working order.

The engines wound down and Wren and I jumped down in the stifling heat to meet the sellers, with Raez trotting at our heels. Wren carried the funds Pazarol had given us in a black bag. Raez seemed quick to make a show of the armed bulge at his hip, the R4, as if he were a real cowboy. I forbore comment on that.

The Urgon's loading hatch dropped and Grisheimer, efficient as a bulldog, clumped out with two of his heavily-armed men to stand at either side. Their AKs gleamed in the sun while the pilot stayed on the bridge, keeping the ship online in case a quick getaway was necessary.

Eight Tanza guards stood loitering about the rig, carrying a mix of submachine guns and semi-automatics; a few might have been women among that motley lot. Hard to tell from this distance. Their hair was tied up in flat brown fur caps, and no help either the baggy clothes that hid a lot of telltales. Rake-thin desert types, bronzed skin, yellow-bleached hair from decades of sun.

The steel-mill trestle-thing poked up from a low mound in the sand, like some twisted grasshopper of an earlier age. The gears worked, and a grinding, back-grating whir of an engine at high rpms brought a giant, metal, pear-shaped gourd up on heavy chains. An operator worked a side lever; chains and clamps tipped the thing lengthwise into a massive lode cart, dumping the raw, small blue crystals in without ceremony.

Some of the miners did not look good—pale, haggard and hacking with dry, rasping coughs. I only guessed the beryllium or whatever derivative of it they mined, was not the healthiest of substances. They started up the six-wheeled tractor that hauled the massive lode cart.

I caught a fleeting glimpse of the dark stuff as it tumbled into the loader, sending shrill echoes up the rugged ridge. A rare mineral combo of emerald, beryllium, quartz, and something else. Whatever the case, it didn't look too stable. I was glad the smugglers' freighter would be carrying it, and not my ship. Maybe I'd take a rain check on the 'enhanced' fareon beam for now.

The Tanza crew met Wren, me, and Raez at the foot of the loader, as the freighter's engine, noisy in age and construction, ramped down and its four landing struts sank deeper into the sand. Grisheimer signaled for the man inside to shorten the ramp to facilitate the cargo transfer.

Hardened, blunt-nosed men worked the ore cart's hatch to get the stuff dropped inside.

"These thugs look like regular guerillas." I whispered, indicating the foremost gunmen, wrapped in their tan, camel hides, roped at the waist, each with an Uzi slung over a shoulder, another gripped in hand.

Wren snorted. "More like the local terror guard hired to keep the crystal from getting snatched."

"And? You got a problem with that?" snarled Raez. "What universe do you subscribe to, woman?"

"Shut up, both of you," I hissed. "They're coming closer."

The young chief, met us, waving in gruff, blunt manner. "Welcome. I didn't expect you on time. I'm Dolgra. On Besi, nobody is on time."

"Well, we are," I grunted. "My name's Rusco."

I couldn't help but notice the patch of trees, three stubby ones, on which hung grungy patches of blackened flesh of what had once been human.

The chief peered to where I was looking. "Those are ones who thought to betray our interests. Reminders of doom, a powerful incentive for obedience on Besi."

"No doubt."

Dolgra seemed smaller than the other tribesmen, lighter boned and with a face that at first glance seemed feminine: the fine nose, the soft eyes, the delicate lashes, all were testament to a misconceived gender. But on deeper inspection the layers of sinew on his oiled biceps and forearms showed muscle that'd been amassed after years of hard discipline. One of his dog-faced men pulled off his cap to wipe his sweaty brow and I saw darker hair underneath. So, they were not all fair. Many were lank-limbed with shaved chins, and there was a curious slant to their eyes, wide-spaced like oxen, but their skin and bodies were as lean as greyhounds and toughened from generations of stinking hot sun.

"You have all the Beryllium crystal?"

The chief held up a hand. "Here... Wait, you fools!" he yelled up at his loading men, then faced us. "You have the money?"

Smoke from a nearby village curled farther down the valley. I guessed they lived up in the rugged hills. The 80k yols they were due, and the 120k later when the buyer paid out, would be nothing less than a small fortune. I jerked my head to the bag Wren clutched. "In there. All 80k yols."

"Good. Let me see."

"I unzipped the leather bag and held it up for the chief's inspection.

His emerald eyes twinkled with greed. He curled a finger in beckoning. "Pass it over."

"First load up the merchandise," I insisted.

The chief shrugged. He gave a brief signal to his men. The loader jerked forward.

I frowned. There were only five hulking bins sitting tucked away to the side that looked anything like a stash of valuable ore. "Is this all of it?" I demanded. I'd expected more.

The chief scowled and fluttered his fingers. "There were complications. My workers are this minute digging out the last of the beryllium crystal." He motioned to his other loader and his men began tractoring the five heaping carts into Urgon's hold.

Raez's mouth quivered in slack-jawed anger. "Is this a joke, Dolgra? We had an agreement."

Dolgra showed a line of brown teeth. "Couldn't be helped. You're getting the goods at a fair price, so consider yourself lucky. Be patient."

"Patient?" Raez cried, flinging a hand down at his bulging hip. "We're running on a tight deadline here. If this deal goes south because of your incompetence—"

"Relax," I growled at Raez, grabbing his arm while lancing him a warning glare.

Raez grunted and wrenched his arm free. "Don't patronize me, asshole. Lay hands on me again, Rusco, and you'll regret it. These fucking grease balls are trying to dick us around, don't you see it? Pazarol is going to be eating monkey nuts for breakfast when—"

"Shut the hell up," I hissed. I turned to Dolgra, showing my most amiable face. "How long for the rest of the shipment? Two hours, maybe four?"

He shrugged. "Probably longer."

I wagged my head. "Well, nothing we can do about it. We kick back and relax."

"What do you mean, 'kick back and relax'?" uttered Raez. "No we can't just 'kick back and relax', you lamebrain. Paz said—"

"I don't give a flying fuck what 'Paz' said," I rasped. "Things are never optimal, Raez. Paz should have allowed for some contingencies."

"And he didn't." The thug's hand went for his R4. The clink of metal sounded all around as Dolgra's men trained barrels on us.

I held up my hands, smiling like a cornered cat. "Okay…let's all calm down. No need for violence." *Shit, this is going badly. That pissbrain, Raez. No wonder Paz-ass couldn't trust his own men to handle this.*

"Control your dog, Mr. Rusco," said Dolgra, "otherwise, there'll be blood on the sand today."

I glared at Raez. "You heard the man."

A whine of engines came screeching out of the sky. Two V-Zon cruisers arched down armed to the teeth with glinting armor. I shook my head in dismay. *What else could go wrong?*

"Who are they?" Wren croaked.

"Gedra." Dolgra swore. "They'll want a cut." He whirled on his aide beside him. "Vespie, I thought you said we were clean? Didn't you scout out the area?"

"They must have slipped underneath our radar, chief. Cloakers."

"That's unacceptable!"

"How much do they want?" I asked.

"Probably 30% which is the usual Gedra tax."

"No fucking way, Dole-face," Raez snorted. "Stall them, or kill them. It's up to you, or this deal's off."

Weapons came up, half on the approaching ships, the others cocked on Raez and me. Dolgra scowled, face curling in an indecisive snarl. "The deal stands, or you'll be strung in those trees minus two arms."

"See, I told you so," whined Raez. "While these morons were out sunbathing by the lake, we could've loaded up and been out of here. Now what's your plan, Rusco? You going to leap around, do a rain dance or something?"

"Shut up, I'm thinking."

"Think fast, because—"

The first Gedra ship landed nearby kicking up dust; four armored men stormed out, clutching rifles and home-grown grenades in fists that were big, ugly, olive-colored weapons, the size of melons.

The first man spoke in a guttural accent, "This is most irregular, Dolgra. You know Chief Jzrend's policy. Report all goods to the central authority—or…."

"I can pay next time, Avloz. Not this time."

"Famous excuses." The Gedra smiled and gave his head a sad shake. "No deal. Make that 40% cut this time, for insolence and wasting our time."

I approached with a breezy confidence. "No need to bat heads, gentlemen." I hefted the bag of yols. Putting on my most disarming smile, I let my words spew out in typical Rusco fashion. "I bet you boys are getting what, a tenth of a percent of your shakedown? if that, even if you are on salary? Let's sweeten the pot." Let a competitor think he's getting a better deal, he'll be all for it, and think you're on his side.

But there was no chance to explore that angle.

Raez whipped out his R4 and sprayed bullets into the midst, taking off the head of the first Gedra. The others in his troupe fired, dropping two of Dolgra's guards.

Weapons exploded from all sides. Grenades launched in the air. I ducked. Reached out to pull Wren back. Shrapnel tore at the closest Gedra and skimmed off Starrunner's back plates. Lucky that I'd set her down farther away.

Another grenade landed closer to our payload and the flames licked out at the Urgon. Grisheimer was yelling, "Shit! Back to the ship!"

I spoke harsh words into the com as I ran, "TK, get Starrunner running!" Grisheimer's man got Urgon airborne, even as metal was flying by me. I caught a glimpse of Dolgra scrambling for the silver Sphinx, dodging bullets all the way. Some of his men caught lead and fell like flies.

TK already had the hatch open as Wren and I zigzagged along, dodging shells and firing back over our shoulders.

One of the Gedra air guard flew over us, raining bullets and spraying death. I hunched, crouching behind a dune, my AK trained on some movement to my right. Wren and Raez fell in behind, sucking in labored breaths. The leather on my right arm was torn and blood flowed. Raez had an ugly slash across his left cheek from shrapnel that had grazed him. Good. All of us were soot-covered from the blast.

"You idiot, sabotaging our venture?" I wheezed at the acrid stench. "Whose side are you on?"

"None, from where I'm looking," Wren spat, blood curling from her lip.

Raez spat. "I at least, had the guts to do what neither of you chickenshits did—blast those bitches away."

I lifted a fist. "I could have smoothed it out, fed them a line and given those messenger boys some baksheesh and it would have ended smoothly."

"You think? I highly doubt that given the size of the load they'd—"

"Quit bitching and let's get to the ship," Wren cried.

An opening presented itself. The crouching Gedra were concentrating on the Urgon, raking it with fire.

I grinned. "Lick your wounds later, Raez. Let's shake a leg, get back to the ship, if you want to live."

"I don't take orders from you." Raez lifted his barrel, my eyes darting to a furtive movement several paces away. An enemy creeping up behind my back. For a second there, I thought Raez was going to cap me. Instead he blew the stalker's eyes out.

The Gedra desert men stepped out from behind the sand dunes, spraying fire. That rat-a-tat of enemy fire was a hollow echo of nightmare to me. I knew one day one of those slugs would catch me in the wrong place and it would be all over. Would it be today?

I shook off the pending image. The second enemy ship was in the air, taking sporadic shots at our freighter which nicked the underbelly's cowling. I cringed, my heart lurching. If that ship went down…but obviously they just wanted to paralyze Urgon and spare the expensive cargo. Metal plates fell off her stern.

We came staggering up Starrunner's ramp, as I smashed the hatch button closed. TK got us airborne. How that rat-bastard Raez, huffing at our heels, had managed to survive the shells and bullets and flames mystified me. He'd done some kind of crouching dance, half snaking his way through fire flares and managed to avoid the onslaught. I raced to the bridge, took the controls, and swept TK out of the way. Raez came stumbling in, trailing blood, gaping at the viewport like some dumb animal.

As soon as I had wrested the controls from TK, I veered us about in a desperate hairpin. Wren stayed at the weapons console, sighted on the closest Gedra ship and blasted it to pieces.

Dolgra's T-Arathron Sphinx came looping after us, a silver, glittering T-bone shape with modern engines, souped up forward thrusters, like the old rad-rockets of the first generation. We still hadn't paid the chief Dolgra, so I guessed he'd be pissed. Going to be a shitload of angry parties before this was all over.

Wren aimed her Uzi at Raez. "You stupid ass, you have some gall. What were you trying to pull down there?"

"Things got a little out hand, bitch, no big deal. Mind your manners. Nothing that can't be fixed."

"Fixed? What shit are you pulling? The devil's got new horns, with you wasting Gedra, now the deal's shot to hell."

"No it isn't. We can salvage it," I said. "No thanks to Raez here."

Raez bowed, flashed a cheeky grin. "Cap'n, I am duly sorry and hope you'll accept my humblest apologies."

My fists turned white. "That smug shit isn't going to work here, Raez. It comes out of your share—or Pazarol's."

Raez shrugged. "Kind of like the minnow telling the shark to go bring him some fresh mackerel." He spat a wad on the metal tiles. "Big P ain't going to like that."

"Tough titty on big P," Wren roared.

CHRIS TURNER

CHAPTER 14

We escaped Besi 6's gravity and the freighter limped along, its starboard flank smoking. Dogra's lightweight Ultra dogged us, weaving in and out, weapons spraying fire.

"Rusco," Dolgra's voice screamed over the com. "I want my yols."

"You'll get it," I grumbled. "You expected me to waltz over there and hand it to you in the middle of a firefight?"

"If this is a doublecross—"

"Relax. Let's plan on a rendezvous somewhere near once we clear Gizren's gravity. Say Mora-Vaille, on the way to the dropoff point. You wanted to play escort, so this'll work out for you."

"One condition—" Dolgra's wheezing voice played over the com. "Two of my men go aboard Urgon to ensure safe passage and fair play."

"Fine by me."

"Like hell it's fine!" Raez shook his greasy head as he came crowding behind me, breathing down my neck. "That wasn't the deal."

"It is now," I barked at him. "Get back and let me handle this."

"Gris will never allow it." The man glared about like a wolf, shafting me a venomous look. His gaze shifted to TK, clacking away at the keys. "What're you looking at, old codger?"

TK turned, brows raised.

"Yeah, you—the one who looks like head librarian around here."

TK's lips pressed in a firm line. "Quaint, very quaint."

"Cap'n Jet put you up as a charity case?" He laughed at his own quip. No laughter came back. "Oi..! Are you guys just a bunch of stiffs?"

"No, we just have a higher bar for humor," said Wren.

I wondered if I should be worried about Raez walking around freely with that piece at his hip. I moved over to him. "Hand over your weapon."

"Say what?"

"You heard me. No loaded firearms on my ship."

He scowled down at my R4. "What about your piece then, and hers?"

"I'm the captain and she's the first mate."

Wren covered him while I held out my hand. With reluctance he unstrapped it and tossed it over.

I locked the guns from the weapons rack in the forward bulkhead with Raez's and motioned him back. "I'll show you to your quarters." And here my mouth slackened in a smirk. There being no spare private cabins, I took Raez to the most grimy, cluttered space by the hold with a rat-chewed mattress and rusty pipes rattling on the wall. I threw a couple of old dusty shipping blankets at him. It'd have to do, and I owed this miserable troublemaker nothing. "Head's in the fore, not pretty in there, but I'm sure you'll manage." I left him seething and grumbling in the dimness, then I made my way back to the bridge.

While Starrunner and Urgon had made some distance from Besi 6, we set out for the outer planets with four-fifths of our shipment. I looked over at Wren while the darkening feeling churned in the pit of my stomach. The old maxim of what doesn't feel right, ain't right thundered like a storm. Of course, Gris had refused to let Dolgra's men board Urgon so I ended up parking at the space station orbiting Mora to give Dolgra his yols while Urgon sped ahead at subwarp.

As I charted our course to catch up, while checking and rechecking our rendezvous with Jasmel, something gnawed at me. I knew we'd never make that destination. Why? Call it the voice of intuition that speaks in the dead of night when one wakes in a lucid moment. Everything was in order, and yet that disturbing hunch beamed like a hooker's red light. Things had been barely smoothed over with Pazarol an hour ago! Raez had done his best to highlight how botched our job had been under my direction and we possessed only a portion of our cargo. I explained to Pazarol how it was impossible to go back to Gizren and get the rest of our freight without incurring casualties and risking the rest of the shipment. The Gedra would cap our asses and we'd have nothing to show for it, without less than an army to cut through that rat swarm.

Long story short, the deal would proceed as planned, but with a third less payout. Okay, I could run with that, as this was our highest paying gig thus far, even split three ways, and I didn't want to jeopardize it. Raez didn't seem to care much at the lesser payout; he seemed to be in it for the kicks. A strange sentiment—but a hell of a lot more interesting than hobgoblining around that gloomy warehouse on Tarsus.

I stayed on the bridge. The others had gone off to their quarters, and my tired eyes were seeing fuzzy shapes while the ship stayed steady on Molly's autopilot.

As I was making for my cabin while we kept up with Urgon, I heard voices down the corridor. Wren's husky voice was raised, an audible murmur.

I crept down the passage, paused before the next corridor, my jaw set.

"How about it, Fox?" came a familiar weasely voice. "What's say you and me slip between the sheets, keep each other warm? I know you and the cap may have something going, but no worries. He isn't about to hear it from me and I won't ruin your gig."

I caught the pregnant pause, then guessed Wren, for a second, had considered the sleazy offer and had almost given in.

Then I heard her stony hiss. "Buzz, off, creep. I don't like your smell or your oily smile."

I smiled at that. Raez put up a fuss and spewed a bunch of spuriously offensive words, like 'sloe-eyed bitch', and 'pissy dike', so I stepped in, putting on a look of innocent concern.

"Everything all right here? Wren, you okay?"

Raez's face lit up in a mocking grin. "No worries, cappie. Me and the bosomy lady were just getting to know each other better, weren't we, Wren? I like to get under the skin of the people I'm working with." The man's patronizing, piss-licking grin made me want to plow him.

Raez was one of those ungracious, low-class weasels who hung out at the casinos looking for easy lays—not that there was anything wrong with that—I'd done a few myself. Those feel-good-about-yourself screws, but there was a way to do it, with a certain modicum of class. Everything in this schmuck's aura spoke of loutishness. A regular wise guy with some black and white around the edges. Irritant Raez, egging for a rude awakening. This little soap opera reminded me of some cornball vid back in that ancient earth collection I used to watch when having nothing better to do.

Raez put up a bit of a fuss, me muscling into his game, but it wasn't anything I couldn't handle. He stomped off with a bruised cheek and some ruffled pride to his hidey hole.

I followed Wren back to her cabin, keeping an eye on the lady. "Anything you'd like to tell me?"

"No."

In the end we had a little nightcap, featuring some gin she'd snuck from the hamper. "Didn't think you'd mind, Ruskie, one bottle missing."

I shrugged. "What do you think of our unwanted guest, Mr. Raez?"

"A bottom feeder." She grimaced. "I've known sleaze bags like him before. Think he's trouble."

"Agreed. He almost got us killed."

She snuffled out a noncommittal sound.

"So you think we should—"

"Forget that rat, let's think about us." She crept closer and undid her tight leather then my shirt, her lashes fluttering, full lips parted in a breathless purr.

"Good plan," I murmured.

Wren's tomboyish energy was more feral feline tonight and I had trouble keeping up with her. After a rousing interlude, I stumbled back to my cabin, a bit bowlegged. On contact with the hard foam, I sighed and went to sleep.

I awoke in the middle of the night, victim of a bad dream. Aliens, or some sort of freaks—those shoulder-high walking mantises that TK had described so eloquently—walked unseen. Mixed with that terrifying glimpse I'd seen out on the journey to nowhere with the phaso, it was a lethal combination. I shivered and shook off the memory, sitting up on my bed, wiping my dry eyes. A cold sweat had broken out around my neck. That bad feeling resurfaced, that larger-than-life feeling that something vastly unpleasant was brewing. It seemed contagious. I reached for my bottle of redneck Black Bull gin stashed under the bed and chug-a-lugged. Made my gut sour. Winced. Took another swig. That didn't go down well either. My gut was burning.

I donned my brown captain's leathers and did my patrol rounds, making for the bridge. The console lights burned brightly and I caught the old man hunched over one of the command tables, deep in concentration. Billy was at his side, making little grunting sounds like a curious chimp.

TK jerked up and gave me a guilty look. "Hey, Jet. How's the night watch?"

"What the hell are you doing?" I cried.

"Relax. Just checking out the inscriptions on this device."

My jaw dropped when I saw what he was working on and the iridescent flash of a familiar disc. "You sneaking bastard. I told you to leave that thing alone—"

"Couldn't. Managed to trace some info on the central free store, Mentera lore, and figured I could backtrace some of the coordinates and test it out some."

"Are you fucking insane? That thing's deadly."

"No worries, I've got it all under control."

"You think? I don't give a piss in the wind what you're thinking. Put it back."

"Just another few minutes, Jet. I've almost got a handle on it—"

I pulled my sleeve over my hand and swept the shimmering disc off the table, away from his grasping hand before he could tweezer it with those rods he held.

All the time Billy's watching and getting more agitated, blinking with his googly eyes, moving from side to side like an adder, wringing his wrists and making funny little sounds in the back of his throat.

The kid reached over and grabbed at that spinning top as if it were some toy. The old man cried out. TK lunged to stop him, but it was too late. Some combination of buttons and coordinates the boy touched and he was gone in a crackling haze of dusty color. The disc rolled, spun to a stop, glaring up at us like an evil eye.

The old man's mouth worked in a rictus but no sound came out.

I swore. "I'm locking this destructo up."

"Look at what you've done!" He clutched at his hair.

"You're the bright one brought it out," I stormed. "I told you the thing was dangerous."

He looked at me with shock then began rooting through the bulkheads, rummaging through hatches, searching for Billy like a madman before he dropped to his knees. "No! He's got to be here somewhere!" The halfwit's disappearance was tearing him apart.

I rounded up the strongbox underneath the sensor panel and used my sleeve to put the phaso in there. I locked the lid.

"We've got to get him back!" TK's pathetic wail raised my hackles.

"Fat chance," I gusted. "Move away. Nothing you can do." I knew I should have hid that strongbox better, remembering the eager glint in TK's eye when I locked up that nasty little device, but it had slipped my mind.

I heard bootfall behind me. I whirled to behold *Raez*. Great timing to stroll in. How long had the slug been there eavesdropping?

He gave a low whistle. "A little love squabble? Where's the kid?"

"What do you care?" I growled.

Raez stared at TK hard, hand pressed to his mouth. "Granddad, you gone and done something to him? You dirty old man."

"Shut the fuck up," TK snarled.

I didn't know how much Raez knew or didn't know, but I could only guess it would do us no good. More than ever I wanted to knock that bastard the hell off my ship.

"Where's Billy?" cried Wren, crowding in behind Raez. *Where'd she come from? Was this party night on the Starrunner?*

"Dead," I growled.

"A joke, right? What do you mean 'dead'?" she croaked.

"What part of 'dead' don't you get?"

She looked around in disbelief.

"I told the old man not to mess with the phaso, but what does he do— he goes and starts fucking with it."

"That's not possible—" she frowned, a choked gurgle in her throat.

She saw TK's red eyes, tear-stained face and knew the truth. Unfortunate that Raez had heard all of this. In my anger I couldn't stop the flood of heated words. But he didn't seem to know what we were talking about.

"Some kind of explosives we talking here?" he asked.

"None of your business. It's over and done."

I locked the controls on the bridge and left the others staring there as I took the silver box to my cabin. I was afraid to keep the phaso on my person in case I inadvertently triggered it as Billy had.

What to do with the cursed thing? Part of me wanted to chuck it out in space, forget it ever existed. But it could be money, lots of it. The thing needed a new hiding spot, and my cabin was not the place—it was the first place anybody'd look to steal it.

* * *

No mention of the phase-distorter-shifter or Billy's sad, mysterious disappearance the next morning. No sign of Baer and his ugly goats zooming in on us at our sub-warp vector. The phaso was a sinister episode better left forgotten.

TK took me aside later in the corridor leading to the cabins and spoke in a distraught voice, "I'm still concerned about Billy. Dammit, Rusco, I think he may be still alive. How be I take a quick peek at the phaso and—"

"N-O." I grunted. "A few moments out there, and the kid's toast, let alone a few hours. Believe me, I saw the place."

"You don't know that, Rusco. We've no idea where Billy ended up. Maybe he ended up on some deserted island or in some abandoned city, calling for help."

"Maybe, but I doubt it. Unless the phaso coordinates were reset. Without a manual, we'll never know how the thing works, and without having it on him, he can never leave."

"But I can go there."

I stared at the man with awe, seeing the genuine expression of a fatherly love for a long lost son presumed dead. "Forget it, TK. The thing's jinxed. Anyone who touches it, dies." And I could see the glowering resentment in his eyes, those gray eyes that looked at me with fathomless despair and loathing and under the influence of the instruments working in his sawmill of a mind—and I didn't like what I saw.

CHAPTER 15

It was going to be a long trip to Jasmel. The whole mishap with Billy had me rattled. Maybe I should have tried right then to go in after the kid, or some such insane scheme, but the moment had passed. Water under the bridge. You're a real hero, Rusco. Proud of yourself? Saving an old man from sacrificing himself. What was going to go down next? Three edgy crew members, and Dolgra champing at the bit with Gris incommunicative, whom I didn't trust farther than I could spit.

As I was doing my hall rounds, I went to check on the phaso, something bugging me again. I reached the panel bulkhead where I'd hidden it in the small hallway leading to the utility room, then opened the strongbox. All seemed in order. I shook my head. Paranoia. It played tricks on the brain. I packed up the kit, made doubly sure the box was locked with a combo only I knew and walked away with a weary yawn to my cabin. Wren was watching the bridge; I could count on her. It was time to turn in, get some shut-eye.

I paused. Raez was staring at me, his ugly face catching the dim light from down the hall.

"What do you want?" I growled.

He lifted his hand in greeting. "Out for a little stroll, Rusco. I get insomnia on small space craft. Suffer from it all the time."

"Get back to your cabin. We're keeping strict curfew here. Besides, this area is off limits to all but personnel."

"Oh, and spank my wee bottom, Cap'n. Gonna tuck me into bed too for a good night's sleep?"

"Don't get cute with me, Raez. My ship, I make the rules." I lifted my blaster, trusting the scoundrel less than ever.

He held up his hands. "Okay, Cap'n, I'm hurrying. Don't shoot me. I'm allergic to gunfire."

I saw him skip back to his grungy little cubbyhole and returned to my own digs, doing badly at falling asleep, wondering if I should call on Wren to help me relax. A bit of night play could do wonders for the soul.

But not tonight. That disturbing feeling kept nagging me, even with all my precautions. I rustled on some clothes and staggered down the hall into the bath of dim blue light.

I opened the strongbox. The phaso was missing. *That fucker. Raez, you're a dead man.*

I stalked to the hold looking for him.

He stood by the emergency escape vehicle, fiddling with the hatch as if he meant to take it somewhere. Like over to Urgon. We were nearing Jasmel at the cusp of the asteroid belt and it would be an easy jaunt for a thief on impulse power to get there or over to Urgon.

He was speaking in a low monotone to someone in his ear communicator. Must have hid that device on him.

When he caught sight of me, he cut the connection as if in apology, while reaching for his left hip for a small concealed weapon. I put a bullet through his brain. He dropped like a stone, eyes staring up like glassy pearls. I kicked the body over, turned him about. Discovered the phaso in his black waist belt. Rotten bastard. I had to smile at the irony. The thief calling the beggar a thief. My smile didn't last long.

I ripped off Raez's ear communicator, figured it would be useful down the road. Raez was about to jump ship and take the emergency vessel when we were close to a drop point. How he planned to accomplish this without getting his head blown off, or blasted by Starrunner's fareon beams was beyond me. It kind of insulted my intelligence. But then, Raez was not the brightest bulb in the box. Yet this was the same guy who had stolen the phaso right out from under my eyes and was minutes away from his getaway. I needed a new hiding spot for the damn thing. I began bagging Raez's corpse to jettison it out in the garbage hatch, all the while formulating a story to feed Wren and TK. He was stealing our share? *No, what share?* We got in a fight. He turned into a wise guy, and pulled a gun on me? *Better. Yeah, closer to the truth, maybe I'll stick with that.*

I got the body in the garbage compactor and released the load out to space. Relief. No evidence. Bye bye, Raez.

I'd make some enemies with Pazarol when he got wind. The fat fuck deserved it though. Had he put Raez up to it? The schemer'd be cut out of his share. I'd steal his shipment and double bag the profits, provided his goons didn't hunt me down and pepper us full of holes. There was still the problem of Gris out there in the freighter. A tricky business getting rid of him. The longer we stayed in this system, the more likelihood Pazarol'd catch up and deal with us, for double-timing him and murdering his man. Rusco, you're making enemies like flies. *Can't help it, captain, just who I am.*

I snapped out my reverie. Okay, stop daydreaming and start thinking. Wake up the others and tell them what happened.

We assembled at the bridge, TK groggy and Wren wiping her eyes. "You what?"

"You heard me, Raez caught a bullet, on account of he kind of pulled a weapon on me and was taking Messenger for a ride."

TK groaned, his face in his palms. "Now what? We're dead when Pazarol finds out."

"Not necessarily. Let me think—A longshot, but are you up for a blastfest?"

Wren shrugged. "When haven't I been?"

"If I can figure out how to spin this…" I rubbed my chin, mumbling, letting the ideas run through my crooked mind. "Okay, how's this?" I turned to TK. "Pull up as much data as you can on Urgon, the floor layouts, the sentry posts, weapons deployment, everything you got." What I had in mind, was risky. I didn't like keeping TK back on Starrunner, especially after the disappearance of Billy, but I had no choice. The few I could trust were getting fewer.

Wren caught wind of what I was planning and glowed with enthusiasm. "Take Dolgra along for the ride. We'll need backup."

"Good idea."

I contacted the Tanza crew. "Is this a secure line?"

"I've flipped it to encrypt secure," said Dolgra. "What is it?"

"Raez's meat. Fucker tried to kill me. Trying to make off with the escape pod, so I had to smoke him."

A wheezing groan came over the com. "Why would he do something stupid like that?"

"Who knows what that devious fuckwad was up to? I suggest if we want to save our hides, we either scram, or take over Urgon. Personally I like the second option, as it gives us the flexibility of selling the cargo on our own terms."

There was a long pause. "What do you need from me?"

"Get over here so you can help us take down Gris. We take the shuttle over, fake them out, and kill the crew."

"What, are you berserkers?" Dolgra barked.

"Any other ideas?"

"How do I know you won't scuttle me and take me out like you did Raez?"

"You don't. But who do you trust—me or Pazarol?"

"No contest. Okay, how many men do we need?"

"Wren, me and two of your guys."

"That's all?" He spat out a harsh croak. "Rusco, you're a bold bastard. Well, you only live once."

I cut the channel and called up Urgon on Raez's ear com.

"Gris, it's Raez here." I disguised my voice.

Silence, then a hard-edged mutter. "You got the piece? Did Rusco cause any trouble?"

"I'm heading over in the pod now. Rusco went out like a lamb. He doesn't know a thing. I've some interesting merchandise—think you and Paz might like it. Turn off the video and cut this channel when we're done, in case our boy is on the wire."

"10-4."

I grinned my sour grin. "Let's have ourselves a little rendezvous, Wren. Give a little surprise to our 'partners-in-crime'."

I paused. *Raez...* I tried to understand the man's game. The fuck could pretend he got tired staking out Starrunner and that the old man could be pinned with the theft of the phaso if anything were found out. He'd lie low on Urgon, use it as a shielded fortress to protect his ass and sit tight, keep both prizes, the fareon tech and the phaso. Not a bad plan, but desperate, and flawed. Leaving me a live unknown was as stupid a mistake as he could ever make. Glad I confiscated his R4. Should've checked him more carefully for that concealed pistol. He must have cached it in his boot. No wonder he so easily relinquished his weapon earlier.

I glanced at the clock. 04:07. We had time. Raez wouldn't be checking with anyone on Tarsus anytime soon. I faked a call to summon Dolgra over and piggy-back for refueling, keeping the communication on open channel. This way Gris could overhear.

When Dolgra's ship did dock on ours, Dolgra and two of his men came aboard, armed to the hilts.

We entered the Messenger and reviewed our plans. "Four men we're going to have to take down quickly," I whispered in a raspy voice. We all stared grimly at each other like wolves before the hunt. "Pazarol's going to get wise pretty soon, but if we can take over the freighter quickly, we can be off before Paz can do anything about it."

Dolgra peeled back his black mask. His nose twitched in a grimace. "It's risky, Rusco. About even odds man-for-man in a blast-out, but we have the bonus of surprise."

I remembered Raez and the murderous look on his face which reflected the murderous schemes in his twisted mind. "This big crime business is ugly, Dolgra—risky and ugly."

The Urgon transport carrier grew large as we approached. It dwarfed our vessel like a grey toad floating in space. The monster's hatch opened, mouthing an unpleasant grin. I guided Messenger in with technical ease. "On my signal."

The hatch closed, a dull clink reverberating through layers of steel. I deliberately kept the landing dock lights in our area dim. I hoped to hell this hare-brained scheme worked. The point of return had passed. Four sets of eyes looked on as the cold metal grates of Urgon's docking platform materialized and the landing chamber re-pressurized from vacuum. We crouched, weapons gripped. Only a pool of pale light shone through the port windows from Urgon's teal dockyard. I could see the whites of Wren's and Dolgra's men's eyes gleaming in the half murk.

The hatch peeled back and we hugged the walls of our own vessel, keeping back in the shadows. Gris's first man strode in, the proverbial unsuspecting lamb. "Raez, about time you showed—What the fuck—?"

The man exploded in a fountain of blood as Dolgra's men lay bullets into him, head and chest peppered with R4 fire. He flopped like a puppet to the metal grates. Wren and I burst through, kicking the mangled body aside while I crashed a shoulder into his henchman only a few feet away. But the man's Uzi came up and got off a blast, triggering the ship's alarm.

Shit. I twisted and kicked the weapon aside while Wren stomped on the man's larynx.

Two down. How many more to go?

They'd be watching, closed-circuit video. I aimed my barrel and knocked out the sensor light poised high on the far wall. There could be more. Better to assume Gris had eyes on us; he was the most dangerous of the lot. I could tell by that efficient wastage of Gedra flesh down on Gizren.

Soon blasts raged from around the hallway. Two more came in ducking around the corners, well-trained and fast. How many more of the ferrets manned this freighter? I cursed myself for not querying Paz more about the infrastructure of his ship and its manpower. A mistake that could cost us our lives.

While Gris's men bore down on us, Dolgra ducked around the side of the pod, motioning his men to sneak out and cover him.

Blasts raked the hallway, blue and green beams, pinning us down in the docking area. *Not good.*

"Wren, you fake them out, and I'll try to blow Gris's boys to kingdom come," I whispered. She nodded. I looked to Dolgra. "Now!" I lobbed a hunk of broken pipe fallen from the ceiling at the closest of the men down the hall.

Blue fire came spitting to blast the metal to a pulp. Wren pushed off in a crouching run. She rolled for cover behind a white-paneled wall, aiming a stream of fire at the wall for added subterfuge. *Good girl.* I chose to pepper the place where the other man lurked, my gunfire eating away at the wall. Showers of sparks and metallic rubble covered the wretch. He cried out in pain, a shot catching him high up on the shoulder. The smoke and dust masked my rush for an instant, so I ran through, bold as brass. Dolgra, swift as an ocelot, ran close on my heels. It was now or never. I caught a glimpse of a dark form lurking in the smoke and sprayed it with fire, hoping I could snag even the slightest of body hits. Return fire spat back at me, but I rolled on my belly, moving like a fish out of water. I heard a painful cry and hiss of anger as my assailant fell over. My lips curled in a triumphant grin.

I caught a glimpse of Gris. No mistaking that salt and pepper grey, the ends of the hair trailing at the back. It was a fine mullet for a man of his age, but he had on a gas mask and that alerted me.

The man was good, a cold-blooded killer. Deadly. I saw Dolgra's man, Yeir, lying face down in a smoking heap, blood pooling around his inert form.

A clink of metal sounded in front of me. My head shot around, eyes blinking as a silver cylinder, six inches in length rolled a few feet away. Smoking gray coils rose from its core. My eyes started to burn.

"Tear gas. Get back!" My throat contracted in a wheezing rasp. This was something I hadn't expected.

Dolgra, Wren and I staggered back into the pod. A rain of blue fire came ripping into the shuttle, decimating our only defenses.

Lolling on the rubble-strewn floor, I clawed for the utility panel in the forward bulkhead. Through the clouds of dust, I motioned Wren to grab the masks inside. I sprayed the entrance with fire so that some bright light didn't march in and waste us right there. She and I snatched masks from the bulkhead. Wren tossed extras to Dolgra and others. I lay low, urging Dolgra's two henchmen to curb their wretched, muffled yells.

I knew they'd be advancing through dusty clouds in the murk, protected by masks and breathing tubes. They'd keep low, their weapons aimed to kill anything that moved. Gris, the crafty bastard, knew his assault techniques. Perhaps I'd underestimated his cunning.

More was yet to play out. Gris was about to move in and waste us, but I held Dolgra back, made a small hand signal indicating I would draw them out and he would storm in and kill them. He gave a grim nod and patted me on the shoulder, wishing me luck.

I grabbed a piece of ruined pipe at my feet, knowing I had perhaps seconds to live. The blood pounded in my ears. In a rolling twist, I tossed it out as I frog-hopped along the edge of the shuttle's wall, blasting the grey cloud before me. I heard a cry of anguish, the pad of desperate feet behind me. Dolgra and Wren scrambled forward, taking advantage of the confusion.

My last barrage of blasts must have charred Gris's right side and he stumbled out, like some wounded animal, cursing in the open air, dropping to his knees.

I seized the man's shoulders and jerked him around, gun trained.

Gris croaked, "You fucking popsicle-brain, Rusco. When Paz hears—he'll kill—"

Dolgra jumped in and peppered the man full of holes. "That's for Yeir." The man's last act of contempt. Grisheimer sank in a heap of charred, limp bones.

Silence. Even the alarm had blown itself out.

The ship was ours.

We stripped the bodies of their communicators and weapons. I helped Dolgra drag Gris and the others to the jettison hatch, disposing of the bodies in a brief whoosh of vacuum. Though I had no personal quarrel with any of these thugs, I felt no remorse in seeing any of them go. Too many lowlifes in this universe. The rational part of my brain said it was a cleansing.

Dolgra suffered a broken finger, Wren a scraped elbow, me, my usual battery of cuts and bruises while rolling and shielding my head from falling debris. All in all we were lucky to have survived, but not so lucky, Yeir and Dolgra's other man, Benzit.

Wren looked around with contempt. "Raez or Gris's going dark will signify something went wrong and one or both of them are dead. We're screwed."

I made a low sound. "If we can hide the ship or TK can reprogram the tracking beams, we can be in the clear."

"Where'll we do that?"

"We backtrack, hide the load on Phoros, that large asteroid on the fringe of the belt. No one will look for it there. Once the dust settles, we'll take Urgon elsewhere to sell the product, maybe one of the outer planets. Shouldn't be hard, if this stuff is hot."

"It'll take weeks to get there."

"So? At least we get paid and blow Pazarol off."

Dolgra shrugged. "We ensure that our payload is intact first."

"Agreed." We marched down the companionway to the lower levels, Wren tagging my heels. It was a goldmine of goods: five heaping lodecarts full of crystal and a thousand cylindrical rods, fareon beam enhancers, stacked in upright racks a few inches apart. Even if we didn't fence those tons of Beryllium crystal, the fareon beams were worth millions, and I'd be a fool if I was going to pawn it off on Paz's warlord on Jasmel—

"I'm staying to guard our investment," Dolgra grunted. "I'll radio my ship to have them drop me off a couple of men. Send along this TK fellow of yours to do the tracking alterations."

"Stand by."

I flew Wren back on the Messenger to fetch TK so he could pilot Urgon to Phoros and work his magic on reprogramming the flight plan and the tracking chips.

The Urgon was one of those old freighters that needed to refuel so we charted out Elphi Alpha II, the next planet away. I worked with TK all day to get the Urgon's flight path reprogrammed and disable the home beacons. Then TK and I flew back on Messenger to Starrunner, with a promise to rendezvous with Dolgra and his men on Phoros within a week. I'd quietly informed Dolgra not to get too adventurous, that I'd taken precautions against doublecrossing, and he could expect a big kaboom if he failed to show for the next meet with Urgon. I was a paranoid man. As with Raez who had ill-timed his getaway, he had not counted on my extreme paranoia. It had spelled his doom...

CHAPTER 16

We landed on the outskirts of the capital city Desia on Elphi Alpha II. I needed to get away from my crew. The twists and turns had rattled my nerves, not to mention the bloodshed. TK was gloomy as death with the absence of Billy, absorbed in his own private melancholy. Wren had gotten weird, distant, sullen, but mostly whiny as if pleased with nothing and becoming something of a live-in wife with her high demands between the sheets, cramping my bachelor's style as if we were in some committed relationship after only a few screws. Which kind of astounded me, considering we were hardly soul mates, just a couple of waifs trucking along the harsh road of life, blasting people to death and stealing. My old adage rebounded back on me: Don't mix coital experiences with the hired help.

So, I cooked up some lie to run to port on Desia to get supplies for our next heist. I'd lay over for a day or so, with some cock-and-bull story about needing to scout out the terrain, research what other side scams we could rustle up while on layover. Which wasn't far from the truth.

"I want to tag along too," insisted Wren. "Like you, I need to get off this crate."

"Not today. Find your own entertainment, Wren. Remember we leave at oh-twelve hundred tomorrow."

"Fine, sure." She packed up some gear and left, taking the local air tube into town. TK opted to stay behind. Predictable. *Good luck finding that phaso, pops.*

I disabled the main drive by pulling out a special circuit, the orbigon, or something like that, something even TK couldn't easily figure out. I didn't trust the old man who'd been giving me evil looks ever since Billy had vanished. Either way, I didn't have time to ponder his next move.

There were things to do. Water tanks, new purifier, frozen meal packs: microwaveable, several yummy flavors, including synthetic chicken, fish, stripped steak, liver, no salt. Loaded with nutrients, also synthetic. Of course, scurvy was a bit of a concern out in deep space. Like the old mariners of the ancient Earth, back when humans had first explored the new worlds and faced down the formidable sea beasts, they had suffered. Loved those old classics yarns, *Moby Dick* and *Gulliver's Travels.*

We spiked our drinks with Vit C liquid drops and threw in supplements whenever we could get them: kiwi fruit, apples, genetically engineered and modified. I kind of wondered at the long term effects. Humans hadn't died off as of yet, it seemed. Other things to worry about. Like when the next blood-toothed warlord was going to plug a bomb on our ass.

Ok, Rusco, off topic.

Lack of sunlight was a problem too. To solve that, I had a lamp room installed early on in Starrunner to sunbathe in and soak up rays. Throw on the oil, lay back with the old eye patch, the dark glasses. Hence, my bronzed look. A worthwhile investment. Also a hot tub installed, but rarely used, water being a scarce resource on such a small starship as Starrunner. If I really wanted to impress though, the tub came in handy…

I treated myself to an evening at the hotel Medusa in downtown Desia. Looking forward to something other than protein powder and microwaved patty dinners with TK and Wren's doom and gloom scenarios about the state of the galaxy and their communal trials on Talyon, that garbage pit of a world they'd holed up on for so long. Looking forward to bright lights and space to move around in. Some upbeat human contact.

In the glass lounge I kicked back at the bar and sipped my dry gin. Quite a selection of highbrows here, some fine fillies too. In laced tops and tight skirts, black and white, modular hair styles. The men wore executive type suits. Clean cut, ran the syndicates, the food production and transpo systems of the new age—at least before the gangsters got to them, bombarded them with naphtha. Then there was the run of regular shysters and crime jojos, but fancy ones with classy, gold cufflinks and tailor-made suits. It was a high end place with multiple security webs and high-voltage fencing staked about, electro-grids and a hundred yols cover entrance. We'd made some dough on our prior cons, so I could afford it. The latest in techno music played, live bands with tables and dance. I set my creaking back down in a soft sofa and loosed a whistling breath, trying to release the cobwebs from my head and ease my joints.

But still the old brain buzzed. Many cons and scams worked their course. Outside of the fat wallets to pickpocket, not a lot to move on. I could scavenge the games table in the next room, but there were limits to what I could do solo. My hound ears picked up snatches of conversation, of this merger and that merger, the need for under-the-table investment— gangster money. Wouldn't be too hard to work up some con here, build some contacts with thin bread down the line. Make some friends, rub shoulders with the moneyed players and leverage them with a kick in the ass later.

Give it a rest, Rusco. Is this your day off or what? I grabbed another drink, a tall tuber at the bar.

I chatted up the young brunette sitting two stools down, who intrigued me—Raquel—with long legs and enigmatic smile that was a compelling lure, classic lines to the face, even though the face was a little too lean for my tastes. Seems she was game, while being coy at the same time. They were always like that. I gave the hint of money, dropped some yols on a fancy dinner and some local champagne, which springboarded the rental of the cheapest room in the hotel. Sir, what is your budget? 100 yols? Hmnn, our feature suites are 500 yol rooms, but that's clearly unaffordable. But we have them as cheap as 80. I blinked. The 80 yol room, please, for a night. Another 80 yols. Yeah, it was adding up, but I was worth it.

She moved to the rhythm and thrusts of the moment that had a way of turning me on in a unique way. I roused her higher by not giving into her climax. Was the sex good? Better than average, I'd say. I had a lighter spring to my step, a bit of kick in my bones, a spice in my blood, eyes a little dreamier by the end of it, and my voice a little lower. Our slow gallop to the finish line had moved in synch with the sounds of the alley below from the open window, and the sleazier hotels that ranged appallingly close: a blend of low level techno pop, the sound of breaking glass, wide gas holo screens playing loud movies, a woman's scream, followed by a man's laughter.

My brain spun. Spent and lathered, I lay back in the damp blankets, blinking, contemplating life at this moment. For all its glamor, it was one of those low moments, Raquel's sighing breath, the warm air playing across my bare chest, her slender white fingers on my scarred arm, knowing she would soon age and be forgotten, my own sad ass chased across the galaxy by crime scum, whipped at the heels by fatal impulse, still hoping to be some hero at the end of the day. What a pathetic dream. At least I'd rid the universe of one Raez, and if I had my choice, I'd include Pazarol, Baer and Mong on that list. My implausible excuses for rationalizing my own criminality was like an overused mantra. When I was young, I wanted to be a rocket engineer, build ships, the best that could fly. Then came the gangs and the beat downs and the drugs and rock and roll, and my parents wiped out in a single strike by a warlord's cannon in our humble neighborhood on Jaunus 8. Me scavenging the streets with no family, no friends, driven like all the other poor refugees to some tarped-up camp, starving, hollow-eyed, wondering where to go from here. What a pipe dream. Where did the dream of young Jet Rusco go? The dream about his little rocket engines and do-gooding. Blown away in some ugly tale where the ogre swallows all and stamps out all thoughts of philanthropy.

I dreamed somebody was rapping at the door.

Figuring it was some room service personnel, I staggered half nude to the door. I opened the door, my jaw dropping. Wren? She caught a glimpse of a tangle of naked arms and legs in the white, disheveled sheets, and slapped my face. Cursed like there was no tomorrow.

I awoke to damp sheets.

Just a guilt-ridden dream. I was gone and back on Starrunner before dawn's light with my packs full of supplies on a world with less daylight than what I was used to. Raquel, I'd left a note for and was managing to forget her, as she, no doubt, me.

Wren was all coos and giggles on the bridge, digging through the yummies I'd brought: the protein packs, the flavored meats. Granted, I would too, living off lizards and grasshoppers for so many years.

I watched the mainscreen holo-vid. This maniac Mong again, conducting a cult ceremony. Seems he was all the rage with his planetary takeovers and promises of liberation. He had a murderous dark hero look, emancipating worlds of their oppressive gang control and abject slummery. Some ambitious journalist had done a human interest story on him. Was this mongrel everywhere at once? Gave me the creeps. A big hulking ape of a man with a fatherly face. A flat-topped, amber hat padded his oversized crown. The brute had some power, sure, to have all those people under his thumb. Look at them—tragic sheep, chanting his name, bowing and praising the works of Mong. He stood tall before the colonnaded temple giving a lecture to thousands, maybe tens of thousands, surrounded by a ring of devotees dressed in blue and gold robes with half shaved heads but for a crop of chicken hair sticking up on top. With a slew of thousands more out in the field, holding their hands up in mindless abandon and chanting some Ciros thing—*long live Ciros, long live Ciros, the fortress of Mong! Fortress of Mong!*

TK snapped me out of my reverie. "Ciros is the name of the temple," he explained.

"How would you know?"

"Because they just said."

"Thanks." I turned the set off and told them we had work to do. Starting with an idea I had for our next heist.

"TK, scour the free data store for buyers of cutting edge, high end arms. First we need to unload our cargo. Outfits, organizations, anyone who'll pay premium for Class A hardware. Go as high as you can and dark as you dare, on the Free Store. There're enough low-ballers out there as it is. Don't make contact with anybody," I warned him, "just compile a list. Anywhere but Jasmel. I'll go through your list later and pick the ones I think are good matches."

"Sure enough, sounds easy."

I turned to Wren. "I scoped out some impound shops down Elphi Alpha. A goldmine of hardware there for the picking: ships, shuttles, probes, drones, the works. All arriving illegally, carrying contraband, gangsters caught by local police, mercs, shakedowns, that kind of thing. One branch is city-owned, just a regional office, so it's light on security."

"What's your angle?" she asked.

"We go in, collecting a worthwhile hulk for transfer to a chop shop, bag the ship for our own and sell it cheap for quick yols."

"Sounds promising." Although her voice was doubtful. "What's the risk?"

"Minimal, if we play it right. Good news is, I'll be doing the initial scout, the run ahead and the main con. You help with the packaging and back me up if necessary."

"Whatever you say, Cap'n."

"Atta girl." That's what I liked about Wren, no fuss, no trouble during business. If only all women could be so cooperative.

We'd go in with papers, pretending to be all official and scam us some hefty hardware for half-decent resale. Outfits like city impound send the ships there anyway, at least the seized vessels the bosses didn't commandeer for their own uses. Better we get the money than some other shyster.

The con operated on the loophole that these shops all kept paper copies of their records. Known fact: Breaking into a secure digital system would be much harder and not worth the risk.

The next day I staked out the joint, The RAI: Regional Airspace Impound. I was at the office depot a few days before the heist. Low security there, easy to slip past the sensors. I'd worked on these types of shops before.

I made sure my face was covered by a mask and disabled any cameras in ready sight I could find. Rifled the office while the staff was off duty, photographed the hundreds of letterheads of certain important acquisition forms, serial numbers of impounded crafts and particulars, studied both the names of the impound officers, owners, managers of the local office and those of the local businesses to whom they supplied parts. I hid out in the file room, eavesdropping on the clerks when they arrived in the morning the following day, heard a few names dropped, then listened keenly for more names when transcalls came through: Benzie Krai, Kata Layne, jotted a few down, recorded the rest on my little black recorder. Found out who presided over whom and whose authority made the difference. Tedious work, but necessary. It was enough to bluff my way through two days later, when I came in, all important and business-like, deliberately arriving early in the morning, plopping my forged papers on the wicket counter and dropping the right combination of names I'd memorized the night before.

"Who are you again?" the attendant asked, all squinty-eyed.

"Juss Rambo. Over at Militia Distributing. Seems here that Mr. Kata Layne authorized this requisition. I'll be taking the J-Zen cruiser to Meik's strip yard, parts and wholesale."

"This is irregular, sir. I should get Mr. Layne personally on the line to confirm."

"You can do that," I said with a frown, "but Layne might get upset— no, pissed if you bother him at this hour. The other day he sent me over here to get this job done quickly. Seems as if something slipped through the main branch's wire and now Mr. Layne's weighing on us. There's his signature at the bottom."

"Yes, sir, I see it is. One moment please." The clerk frowned, scrutinized the papers, the seals, signatures and serial number, and scratched his initials on several pages, then fiddled with some files in the back cabinet. Finally he ripped off some yellow pieces of paper and passed me two with a pink slip. "Go ahead, Mr. Rambo. The impound yard is down the way to your left."

"I know, been here before."

The attendant gave a curt nod.

And that was that. A brief moment of nailbiting on the odd chance that sleepy pencil neck decided to call my bluff and summon the big boss Layne. Secret here is to look important and gruff and as confident as possible. Any bit of doubt or hesitation on the con's part and the deal floats south. But I'd planned for that, recalling the hardware under my brown leathers, fingering my blaster and the grenade tucked in my waist pouch. Although that route could get ugly very quickly.

Couldn't work the same scam twice at the same place. No, no. Once they found out they'd been conned, they'd be up to their armpits in security. Somebody's neck would be on the line. I pitied the poor soul to work a scam similar to mine.

I radioed Starrunner in over the impound yard and, while TK hovered overhead, Wren jumped down. After a few moments with a yardman and a flash of pink papers, we attached the four towlines to the vehicle in question and boarded Starrunner, hauling the hulk away. It was a lighter job than her load limit, within her horsepower capabilities. Her impulse engines whirred in a high scream and we carried the J-Zen off across the smoggy skyline and on to the next city, dropped her at Regzie's WR, one of the black market warehouses on the east end of town. 5G cash yols, no question asked. A quick job. We took off into the wild blue yonder, with the blackness of space curling around Starrunner as Elphi Alpha faded behind us like a dwindling star.

CHAPTER 17

TK came through with the compiled list. After a quick review I whittled it down to four possibles. The third was promising, a certain Vee Hars. Said he'd pay cash for everything, especially the manufactured, enhanced weapons. The crystal he'd take as a favor. "Meet us in three days in the capital of Myx on the nearby world of Trellian. Volgrim Enterprises, north end of the city."

Time to rendezvous with Dolgra on Urgon. I varwoled into orbit around Phoros, radioed Dolgra, told him we'd be there in minutes. Dolgra confirmed. I took TK over in the shuttle, where he set up the flight path and we shuttled back.

Next stop Trellian.

A day to arrive at Myx City and some more time to find the drop point. That's a long time on a starship. A man's mind can wander into stray territory. As mine did. Something about the whole affair with Pazarol still rankled. I'd had to kill Raez; Gris was casualty damage, scumbags without question, that was not a problem. But another loose end, some stone left unturned, I couldn't figure it out. The puzzle left me staring up at the plated ceiling, lying in my hard bunk that night in wordless dismay, wondering what wolf was waiting around the next corner. Not even the lusty affections of Wren could assuage that.

I jolted up, knowing there was going to be trouble with that phaso. I whipped on my clothes and staggered down to the hold. There in my workshop, near Raez's former cubby hole, I set about making a clever imitation of it with the materials I had aboard and my budding artistic talent. To foil any eager searchers, I used extra varnish and colored lead tinsel to give it that shiny, iridescent look. I felt better when it was done. I inserted the fake in the strongbox and put it back in the forward bulkhead where it had been and hid the real phaso in a place no one would find it—in the conduit leading to the engine core, the Barenium chambers, taped to the inner wall. Maybe not the safest place for it, but at least out of TK's reach, or anyone else who might be searching. I could trust nobody.

Trellian came up on our sights and we bore down on the single, prominent continent. Starrunner flew over rich woodland—gigantic, three hundred-foot trees with plumed tops like ostrich tails. Beyond the outriders of Myx's towers we coasted where a long patch of industrial lots stretched within the forest confines.

We landed in Volgrim's yard, Urgon first and Starrunner after, spraying up dust and specks of dirt from the grainy tarmac. The sky was overcast and the air slightly muggy. Even these outer worlds seemed to have been terraformed long ago with thick atmospheres to make them habitable. Their air generators had been running for decades to keep the planet warm, in addition to thousands of geothermal stations set up around the globe to pipe heat from the planet's crust into the air. Major acreage of forests had been planted to supply ready oxygen.

Two battered, rusty buildings stood in the foreground, with flat, rectangular roofs. A gravel pit loomed in the back, with several large freighters and smaller range vehicles huddled in the landing yard out front. It looked dead as a graveyard, could as easily have been a gravel yard, or some construction depot. Dolgra's men stayed back to watchdog the shipment while Wren, Dolgra and I debarked to meet Vee Hars and his associates and consummate the transaction. I relished closure on this deal. I packed extra weapons—R4, R3, some explosives—while ensuring Wren and I were carrying trackers that TK could monitor steadily from Starrunner. I wasn't taking any chances. That bad feeling had not abated, even after hiding the phaso in a safe place, so I started to wonder if it was something else that had my imagination piqued.

I motioned to Dolgra. "There, at two o'clock." The equipment yard was bare but for oil drums, fork lifts and some metal skids piled with crates. Four figures came out of the first set of ugly, rust-coated double-doors on the warehouse.

Hars was a medium-boned man of no great stature. A woman kept his stride, wearing a hardhat and two other men in coveralls trailed behind. I sized them up in a second—a set of trade business professionals, black market operators, possibly, but clean. So, why the worry?

"Rusco? Hars, here," the man said, husky of chest, short of leg, and held out a pink hand. "These are my colleagues: Deen, Faber and Lozane." I gave them a salute and they all nodded.

"Pleasure, Hars. My crew, Dolgra and Wren."

Hars tipped his head. "You have my merchandise?"

"In the Urgon over there." I pointed. "Ready for transport."

"Good, let's move it out then. I've got a busy day and there are lots more things to do. There's a spot set out in the warehouse."

"Not so fast," I called. "Where's our yols?"

"Relax, you'll get them, Rusco." He frowned, fingering his jaw at the delay. "All two million of it. Fresh credits."

"Then let's go get them, shall we?"

He shook his head. "Let me take a look first at the merchandise."

"Fair enough. Follow me." I set out at a brisk pace, Wren behind me, Dolgra to my side, forcing Hars and his gang to keep up to my impatient stride. Normally this all this would have been formal, a simultaneous transfer at a more leisure location. But these guys seemed a bit overcautious, even amateur—

My thoughts came to a grinding halt at a deep rumbling sound from the sky. My hand went to my weapons belt. I looked up. Three ships streaked out of the clouds like dive bombers. An XT-5 warship, then a white-gray service freighter, and then one of those grey Markests I'd seen on Talyon, looking suspiciously like one of Baer's.

I swore. Guns from the XT-5 trained on us, reminiscent of the ships I'd seen in raids on civilian territories.

Hars's eyes darted up in sudden terror. "What the hell?—Rusco are you playing us?"

"They're aiming at me as much as you, Hars! Get down!"

He ducked, but too late. Fareon blasts set fire to the oil drums nearby and hot gases licked out at us like chemical bombs. Flames lit the tarmac and sent us flying. I pulled Wren to my side to shield her.

Two bullets slammed between Hars' eyes and he sagged like a rag doll. One of his henchmen went to his knees, blood spraying from his chest. The other, I gather, the woman, was running, but she didn't get far.

A vulpine howl rattled in Wren's throat. Dolgra had a slug in his leg. All this happened so fast, my reflexes could hardly keep up with the unreality of it all.

Starrunner and Urgon were rising in the air. Pulse blasts slammed from the Warhawk, then flashed down to disable our ships' electrical circuits for brief instants. The two ships clunked down on the tarmac like dead weights.

I saw the Warkhawk blast the rear thrusters and struts off Urgon. Armed men stormed out of the Warkhawk and blew the hatch and boarded Urgon. I don't know whether they killed Dolgra's men that instant or took them prisoners. Warhawk crew members were moving crystal out of the freighter on a big load lifter to their freighter. They weren't taking any chances of their cash cow flying away.

Wren was firing rounds into the cloud of smoke, but not getting much action. I was reaching for my grenade pin.

The Warhawk wasn't even on the ground when a dozen men in khaki fatigues jumped out of the hatch, spraying us with fire. We crawled on our bellies like worms, Dolgra moaning in pain. A paralyzer-slug zapped my shoulder. I convulsed, cursing. I looked up to see five grim faces peering down at me with weapons trained on us all. Boots flicked out and kicked the weapons out of our hands. Rough hands seized us and dragged us into the warehouse.

I felt my shell-shocked grip on reality fading. More figures disembarked from the Markest and in my horror, I thought to see big P leisurely making his way down the tarmac with three of his ape-armed escorts.

One of our captors threw a bag over my head while others dragged Wren and Dolgra down the dim-lit hall. I couldn't figure it out. I easily expected we'd all be taken aboard P's bandit cruiser and that would be the end of us. Truncheons slapped down on my neck; my shoulder spasmed and I groaned in pain. Thuds, blows, curses. Wren's wild cries, Dolgra's murmurs of agony—all came in a wild orgy—the opening and slamming of doors, heated arguing of voices, muttered yells, pitched insults. More blunt objects wracked against my body, and I was forced onto a cold, cement floor. Hands seized me by the hair and arms and thrust me into a hard-backed chair. They bound my forearms with twine to the armrests, roped my calves to the leg-rests. The whimpers of my team faded to a primal keening. Only the harsh mutters of violent men accompanied the scuff of booted feet.

The bag was removed from my head, and I gulped in lungfuls of air.

The paralyzer was fading and I reeled to the throes of a splitting headache, my face all puffy and my arms throbbing something awful. I struggled in vain to free myself from that chair in that bare storeroom with no windows.

I recognized the hairy face that leered over me, but it was not who I expected it to be.

"Déjà vu, eh, Rusco?" came Baer's gruff voice. "Wipe that purple grin off your face. Hope your trip wasn't too painful?"

The shadowy figure donned a pair of heavy work gloves, blue-grey industrial grade with raspy edges and steel knit weave, and patted my cheek with a rough caress as if those mitts were made for handling asbestos. His arm seemed to be repaired, assuming he had either some wicked miracle glue or hardcore flesh regen. How about a mechno-arm?

He nodded to the three of his goons with AKs at their belt. "I paid Pazarol to pass you off to us. Or we wouldn't be having this conversation. He wanted to kill you outright. But that would have been a waste of time and useless for our purposes. We still have unfinished business, Rusco, don't you remember?"

"What do you want?"

His bushy brows shot up in inquiry. "I assumed that'd be obvious. We got the phaso, thank you very much. But where's my amalgo? Seems as if Lugi couldn't find it on your ship."

I wondered how long it would take them to figure out I didn't have the amalgo and the phaso was a dud. Wren sprawled on the floor, a sorry sight, coming to with a groggy shake of her head. She was stripped near naked. Dolgra was at her side, splayed in shameless abandon, out cold. I took one look at the two of them and I knew that the jig was up. We were dead regardless of what we did or said.

That sneaky bastard Raez must have bugged the Starrunner before he'd died. How else could that maggot-spawn Paz, in cahoots with Baer, have known so much about our movements? I cursed myself for my carelessness, neglecting to sweep for bugs after I wasted that slime ball.

My mind worked at any desperate plan at all. Needed to figure a way out of this, otherwise we were dead.

Struggle was useless. They'd strapped me in tight. I hated my impotence, but gave my hosts my most defiant look.

Baer grunted in disgust. "What about you, black beauty?" He turned and back-ended Wren with the heel of his boot. "Know anything about a shiny disc, glittering all colors, size of your hand that can take you to faraway places? What about my big horseshoe gadget, like a wonder magnet, something you may have seen in a haute moderne living room?"

She looked away, shook her purpled face, looking as if she was going to vomit.

"Thought so."

Had they gotten to TK? Maybe he was sprawled in another room, getting his face plastered all over the wall.

With cat-like strength, Dolgra shot up and clawed at the nearest thug, bringing him down in a crashing heap. Thumbs caught in his eye. He cried out in pain as fingers worked and he kicked Dolgra off him. The other two pinned Dolgra's arms and began clubbing him.

The one rubbing at his face swore. "That miserable catclawer. Fucked up my eye."

"Whine somewhere else," cried Baer. "Get that trash out of here. I need to have a one-on-one with Rusco."

He peered with critical appraisal at Wren. "And this bitch is a bit mannish for my tastes, so remove her too." He motioned to one of his henchmen who gave an anticipatory growl.

"A woman's a woman, boss." The bald-headed thug grabbed Wren by the ears and hauled her up and dragged her out by what had grown of her hair. Wren kicked and screamed all the way.

Baer shrugged. "Nasty piece of work, Rusco. Such company you keep. Now, I might just let you live, albeit it painfully, if you'll tell me where the amalgo is?"

"What amalgo?"

He gave a weary sigh. "We have to do this the hard way?" He nodded to his other man; they cut my right arm bonds and forced open my palm flat. I struggled but Baer shoved a coin-sized object in it, while the other thug closed and tied my fingers around it.

I protested in horror when I saw what that silver thing was and what they planned to do. On a nod, all three left the room and whispered in anticipation amongst themselves.

"I always repay any favors done to me." Baer gave a last look. He closed the door while I counted the seconds.

Kaboom.

The blast came from far away in my mind as my ears adjusted to the shock, and my fingers were gone in a second and the hand with it. Blood and flesh kicked up in my face. Then the agony came in mountainous waves.

Red hot gallons of it. A minute, two days, a year? How much time passed? I don't know.

I remember a figure larger than life lumbering into that room. Could have been an avatar, a dark angel, some figment of my distorted imagination. He was big, his shoulders so wide, hawk eyes so dark and bright at the same time. The man wore a long, wine-colored trenchcoat, with white stripes down the middle and golden eagles off to the side. His hair was thick and black as buffalo fur and trailed past the middle of his back. The eyes, sightless as a blind crow's eyes, penetrated into my soul, windows into new universes. But the presence of the man was what awed and stunned me most, despite my pain. He made Baer look like a mangy rat. Those ageless eyes scrutinized me as a raptor might bore into a helpless rabbit, but then his eyes went soft and gentle, as if he were trying to coax the truth out of an errant child.

"You've wandered far from the truth, haven't you, child? Empty your soul, become one with the universe."

I must be in heaven, dreaming a benevolent dream. My hand had ceased to throb, just a warm jelly feeling there.

"Yes, the pain is not that crippling, is it?" he asked. "Doesn't last, like all things in this transient world."

His voice changed as he muttered something to Baer who had clumped in, "So this is your darkhorse, the one who's been causing me so much trouble and giving you merry chase?"

With my eyes adjusting to the pink mist of pain, I recognized that face!—*Mong*. The holo screen…I croaked a hang-man's curse.

"Yes, you know me, don't you?" the warlord jeered with a grotesque grin. "You have something of mine. A very important item. Tell us about it, and I'll make sure the pain goes away. Forever."

I shook my blood-stained head, coming in and out of delirium.

He exhaled a sad laugh. "That phaso's nothing but a cheap imitation. You expecting to pawn it off on somebody in a quick sale?" He gave a spitting growl. "Good luck." In impatient, cruel pantomime, he reached in his trenchcoat and pulled out a green vial, which he opened and flicked the caustic liquid on my stump of a wrist. The fires of agony bit into my flesh.

The severed nerves reanimated. A good reminder of the pain to come.

Yet Mong's promise of pain meant the end of me, a bullet to the brain or worse. I'd hold out and die. They'd never get the amalgo, those fucking scavengers.

As if reading my mind, Mong grinned and pulled a pick-hook out of his grab-bag of tricks and approached me from behind. He jabbed it into my stub of a wrist bone and proceeded to carve out the marrow.

I howled in misery, croaking out a rasp as a lunatic might make, hoping for the oblivion of unconsciousness. The warlord paused, his eyes blinking in expectation, his presence a still of death. As he leaned forward, I could not help but cringe—the man was built like a tank, an iron killing machine, a mountain of muscle.

Baer muttered, "The girl might give us a location, Mong. Hold up. Right now Branx and Madler are working her over for the truth, loosening her up, if you know what I mean."

"Fool! I don't care what your slackwit goons are doing to the bitch. I want my merchandise."

"Alright, hold your horses." Baer held up his hand. "I'm working on her. If you hadn't been so impulsive and brought the Megalians to their knees so early, I'd have caught up with this Rusco scum long ago on Skeller's Reach—"

Mong's patience wore thin and his hand flicked out. I blinked as the air went cold and dark. An invisible force seemed to lift Baer up by the throat and slam him against the wall. The thug gurgled, coughed, snorted, his eyes bulging like a frog's. His hairy face went beet red. Mong thundered out a curse. "You stupid bungler! You were the shipping agent. Your job was to secure those Mentera techs back in Hoath. You didn't. The amalgamators were highest priority. It's been weeks since you promised them."

"I—know, M-Mong. S-sure," Baer croaked, his voice a high-pitched twang. His feet dangled inches from the bare floor. "Just a minor detail. Rusco'll be squawking like a hen before long."

"I don't see him squawking like a hen." Mong released the thug with whatever voodoo powers he had, and the hate-mongering Baer fell to his knees, clawing at his throat, like a drowning man.

A prolonged howl came from the adjoining room, a thin wail of helplessness like the cry of a tortured animal. It could have easily been Wren's or Dolgra's, and I shuddered. A lament that might come from my own throat soon enough. Mong seemed to pay no heed.

"I came here on a call that I would get results and my tech in my hand. My devotees are waiting for me on Z-Mezarath—you know that, to rally them to the true path." He thrust a finger high. "One day my religion will spread throughout the galaxy, as popular as the Christ savior of old." His voice had risen to a self-righteous pitch.

"Sure, Mong, sure. You know I'm your staunchest supporter."

"Shut up. That's enough of your fatuous words for one day."

A beeper rang on the warlord's communicator. He snatched at it. "What?" he growled. His face darkened.

"Unacceptable, Ry-yin! Fix it." He cut the connection. "Is there no end to incompetence?" He exhaled a dark breath. "The war on Questra is going badly, Baer. I must go. See that this worm talks or you'll be the next in that chair."

The star lord's contemptuous glance brushed me a warlock's hex as he made for the exit. "A mere flesh baby," he chided in contempt, shaking his head. "A few bruises, a missing hand, and some bodily discomfort and the weakling mewls like a newborn child."

I wanted to fling out an insult but my tongue could form no words, only gurgles.

"If you experienced the primal initiations on my home planet, Rusco, you'd be laughing right now—a man of iron, daring me to bring on more." He gave a final shake of his leonine head and flung open the door. "You are not worthy of my teachings."

He strode out and Baer flinched, his burning bearish eyes raking me with sinister fervor. He reached out with his prosthetic hand to squeeze my stump of a wrist, the exposed bone and purple flesh. The dirty, rough glove reached high, maybe to pour gasoline on the raw wound, I couldn't tell. My eyes circled up in agony, even as blackness overcame me.

CHAPTER 18

I drifted in and out of consciousness, stirred by some distant blast, a thunder clap, or it could have been a faraway mountain exploding. It was all the same.

Wren was beside me, slapping my cheeks, yelling in my ear.

She unstrapped my arms and legs. *No, Wren was dead.* Her scratched, bloodied face gleamed with sweat and blackened soot and grime. Her leathers were torn, but a wild look blazed in her eye, the other swollen nearly shut, as if she'd been to hell and back. Good old Wren! She had come back.

"TK came through, Rusco. If you want to live, let's hurry."

I struggled, hobbling like an eighty year old. Gunfire and blasts echoed down the hall. I was limping with Wren's supporting arm around my waist down the rubble-strewn corridors, the rat-darkened places, doubled over in pain. More booms resounded from the cracked concrete above and the crumpled steel.

It seemed a million miles we staggered, half dragging ourselves along, my head snapping sideways, peering in horror into one of the nearby storerooms. The door was half ajar. I caught a quick glimpse of Dolgra sprawled there, head pulled back, eyes glazed up in terror. The muscular olive skin body lay half stripped, half naked, the small, petal shaped breasts exposed high on the sun-browned chest. I knew that, despite the denial of my instincts on first meeting, she had been a woman, dressed up in costume and posing as a man, jousting, fighting in a world ruled by males, trying to survive and rise up the ranks in a world ruled by iron fists. Metal picks stuck up her arms and pincushioned her ribs like a sewing-box voodoo doll. I couldn't look away, let alone imagine the last minutes of her agony. I grimaced and forced my feet on, vowing that I would avenge that brave woman's sacrifice, if I ever got out of this misery alive. Which didn't look very likely with half an arm, and the ceiling crumbling over our heads. Bomb fire threatened to kill us all.

Even in my daze, I couldn't help but realize that Dolgra's defiance to the end had saved both Wren and me, or at least delayed having our throats cut in ruthless spite.

Wren kicked open the steel door at the end of the hall. We stumbled into the harsh light on the tarmac, my eyes adjusting to the white sunlight as it shafted through a rent in the clouds. I heard the blast of pulse fire, then the roar of engines. Fareon beams sighted on the warehouse roof. Another licked out at the diving Markest and the ship buckled in flames. Its grey bulk crashed into the warehouse. Right on target, TK! Starrunner burst through a cloud of fire and landed beside us, smoking. I looked up to see two of Mong's auxiliary warships screaming in, which he'd left to safeguard the cargo. We were screwed. Wren pushed me through the open hatch, yelling commands. TK lifted off at full impulse, miraculously dodging the sprays of fire left by fareons, even as Wren got the hatch closing. Our reserve shields took major hits. I could hear Molly's voice caterwauling: *"Danger! Warning. Shields at 4%. Structural overload. Expected hull implosion in T minus 30 seconds."*

I shook my head in despair, staggering to the bridge, the ship rocking to TK's clever maneuvering.

The sensors were off the charts. Starrunner was toast. I looked over at Wren, my eyes vacant.

Wren seized the controls and spat fareon fury at the Warkhawk in pursuit. The vessel lit up in red but did not explode.

She gave a wild start. "Aw, fuck it!"

Her hand reached for the Varwol initiate. "No!" TK jerked forward to stop her, but too late. Starrunner's warp engaged. We tumbled end over end in a funland of blinding multicolored light. Mong's ships in immediate pursuit stretched out like pancakes, then flared.

I heard banging like unholy drums, the deafening peals of hell ogres, as if the gongs of oblivion were out there to reduce us to atoms.

Inconceivable forces arced from Varwol to Trellian gravity. Conflicting time and gravitational forces wreaked havoc on the continuum. Our bones were slowly popping from our joints, stretching to infinity. Wren, moving in slow-motion, released the Varwol, her face a rictus of agony. The ship dropped back to impulse, slewing sideways like some rogue comet caught in a collision of 3D and 4D realities. We floated in another realm, one with a black sky drawn like a curtain with pale stars, an eerie globe with craters below us. The ship idled; we blinked as raw agony throbbed all over but we were alive, as the sensors went quiet.

Were we in the same system? In a different time? No. My right hand was still gone. The agony was still there, of course, if not worse.

TK leaned over and vomited. He lifted himself up, pale as a ghost. He flicked some dials, pulled up a 3D visual. "We're orbiting Feldris," he coughed, a trickle of blood seeping at the corner of his mouth. My slow brain made sense of the name. We'd made Trellian's moon in the few light seconds we'd been in marred, warped-up no man's land.

In other circumstances we would have been stretched to nothingness, at the mercy of infathomable physics.

None of Mong's ships showed on our sensors. I hoped they'd all been blown to space dust, entered the horizon of oblivion, but somehow I doubted that. How long would it take our pursuers, if any there were, to pinpoint our coordinates?

I slumped back in the co-pilot's chair, holding my mangled stump under an armpit. The cloth Wren had wrapped around it staunched the blood. I motioned to her to bring the Myscol from the cabinet and every damn painkiller there. She brought down a dozen glass pill bottles. I downed them at once like a starving man. I chased them down with what was left of the whiskey. Wren gobbled a few herself while TK felt too sick to eat anything.

"Get us out of here," I growled at Wren.

"We've got to get you to a surgeon."

"I don't know where the nearest black market op shop is," I croaked hoarsely, "certainly not on that crater below us." My voice, reedy and faraway, sounded alien to my ear.

"Molly," I coughed. "Op shop's nearest to, to—where the hell are we?"

"Feldris."

"Feldris!" I gasped.

"Affirmative. Delta sector. Malron, Malron City on Gainor."

"How long?" I cried.

"Four hours, three minutes, on impulse."

"On Varwol, you silly girl."

"Varwol at 1% light speed capability makes it two hours."

"Set the course."

TK set the coordinates and engaged the drive, what was left of it, and we were in the unreality of sub warp. I looked up through bleary eyes, my arm quivering, my legs spasming, and waves of nausea assaulting my shattered nerves.

Wren looked at me from a bruised face and through a blackened, swollen eye, but with a vindictive gleam and blood on the bowie knife belted at her side.

I could tell the way TK was shivering, it was the bravest thing he ever did, coming back with Starrunner and blasting our enemies.

He saw my incredulous look and gestured. "I hid in the hold, under the mattress and moldy blankets you gave Raez. They searched the ship, eight of them, looking for crew. Didn't find any."

"The phaso?"

"I'm afraid they got it. If it was in that strongbox you hid, it's gone." He bit his bloody lip. "Wren's locator was dead. I knew you were in trouble. But yours was still active."

So, the fact that they had not damaged my locator had saved our hides. It was still plastered to my blood-sprayed jacket, weaved into the fabric to look like a button. I flashed Wren what might have been a grateful, questioning stare.

She grinned. "You saved me from that sorry planet of Talyon, so the least I could do is save your hide."

"You did well. I don't know how you did it, but you pulled it off."

Her shoulders twitched in a shrug. "Those cretins underestimated me, as does every lout, and they all died. I must thank you, TK. Those fareons you showered made them think twice and I grabbed the first scum's knife and cut off his balls. Then I got his gun. Small payback for the pains those lowlifes've caused us."

I flinched and got Wren to bring the metal tin labeled 'regen' from the overhead bulkhead. I got her to smear a generous dose on my throbbing stump. I cried out in agony as the thick orange paste made contact with the exposed bone and the nerve ends. But the glopping goo did its work. A stinging pain, like pepper spray applied to an open wound, then a sizzling of flesh, as it cauterized the flesh and bone. Then came a flood of warm, tingling sensations, as small bits of tissue rebuilt themselves, and I was in heaven—momentarily.

The flesh-regen was good for rebuilding small tissues like a missing ear, damaged tongue or even major skin damage, but not, I knew, for regenerating bones. Ligaments or complex nerve tissue would need a level of regen I did not have. But the orange paste would keep the tissue primed if there was any hope for a new hand—which I seriously doubted at this point.

I began to drift away, my eyes dilating, swinging back in my skull like a church bell, with the loss of blood and Wren slapping my face. She began mouthing words, anything that would keep me from fading into non-existence. I remember a garbled story, out of sync with the words coming from her lips. She was probably trying to keep me from succumbing to shock and bleeding out, despite the regen.

"Stay with us, Rusco, you stupid sod." *Slap, slap.* I blinked. "Think of my daughter before you think of dying. I lost Kela and I was a broken, empty doll. No purpose or direction. The manner of her death messed me up most, Rusco, brought me nightmares every sleepless night. I tucked myself into some safe harbor, away from them, away from harm, knowing that those scumlord sadists were out there hiding in the shadows with their machetes and ships and guns, waiting to rape and torture and wring every bit of goodness out of me and everybody else—my kin and friends. So, I hid like a feral animal, just like what we're doing now, and went back into a deep, dark place, like the sand dervishes, hiding under rock, dunghill, every piece of broken metal, a dirty, scavenging castaway killing anything that threatened us with my sawed-off rod. Once when the thing refused to fire, I used it to beat off two grimy, hooded lowlifes with lust and murder on their minds. Another time four had tried to gang rape me, pulled off all my clothes, bloodied me up, broke my fingers. This one never healed right—" She held up her left hand and in my delirium, I saw how the index finger had been twisted and crooked. But I knew that already, didn't I?

"They failed, Rusco. Not too far off from what the scum tried to do to me today in that storeroom, but they got a surprise."

Her voice faded in and out, as we neared Gainor and she took our earnings from the stash box where I kept the phaso and I mouthed the combination in her ears, not TK's, as I didn't trust the man despite his recent heroics...

I sat there, my mind hallucinating as if I were on psychedelics with the regen and the Myscol.

The next series of events passed in a dream, with a strange bliss punctuated by snippets of conversations and figures I knew must be medics. Concerned faces peered at me. Men and women dressed in white coats, objects of whimsy and perplexity. Echoes of endless speculation and questions arrowed at me. I blinked like a dumb mule, opened my mouth, unable to fire up my vocal chords.

When I came out of the anesthetic, I realized Wren had taken me to some black market shop. A raw ache trickled down my right side. Fingertips alienated from fingers, fingers alienated from hand, hand alienated from wrist, alternating from a dull numbness to rabid agony.

I grunted, rolled over with a curse.

"Careful, sir," the female attendant said. "The circuits will need time to adjust to the nerve signals. I know it is disorienting." I looked down at my duck hand and flexed the mechanical fingers. Pain, lots of it; the effort to get them to flutter, even the minutest, was staggering.

"Therapy will be in-depth and intense," she said. "Two weeks you should have most of your motor control back, but not strength. We installed a Trinbal T4 circuit limber in your wrist. It was within your budget." The orderly's remark seemed to be almost an afterthought.

I flashed Wren a sallow grin. Step right up, kids—JR, mechno man coming through!

I got back to the Starrunner, and we made for the nearby world. I didn't know which one nor did I care. So began the first day of a long series on a road to depression. The worst had finally caught up to me. Maimed for life.

But now was not the time for self pity. I gathered TK and we scoured the bridge. At last we found that tracking bug hidden under the console. Like a tiny black parasite. Raez'd taken a panel off. It was a clever plant; TK's previous searches for the phaso had not found the tracker. I motioned the old man's hand away when he reached to pull it off and destroy it. "No!" A part of me was still Jet Rusco, the cunning fox that never gave up. I knew that miserable device would come in handy one day. "Can you disable it?"

"Probably."

"Do it then."

TK complied without a grumble. An hour later it was done and I took the bug and locked it away in my cabin.

Looking down at my mechno hand, I admired the fake covering of human skin, a hue slightly lighter than my own, the fingers stronger than my fleshy ones, but not my own. Feeling something of dead and wooden weight there.

And with it came the raging urge to strip off my old identity, become the fierce torrent, the unstoppable rush of what I was to become. The old Jet Rusco was gone, kaput. A vengeful one birthed—an avenger to destroy every scumbag crime lord I could get my hands on, starting with Pazarol, Baer and that mad fuck, Mong, who had caused so many senseless miseries and the deaths of so many people. I didn't care who died, who lived, or who got mangled up, or if I got robot parts to replace my whole body. Those fuckers were going down.

We'd lost our payout and our cargo, and our shields were whittled to about zero—as our Varwol.

These details I noted and considered, as we limped along to the next planet, though I was barely there in essence, going through the motions like some sock puppet powered by a clown master. I felt half a man, as if my manhood had been shunted. Biomech Rusco, suffering from implant stress disorder. Mech organ rejection.

Whatever the fuck.

I didn't care and I had to snap out of this downward spiral.

CHAPTER 19

After repairing the Varwol on Gainor, I pushed TK away from the controls and set the course for Merius, the asteroid belt. To a place on the fringe where I remembered Deros the dwarf planet shone with its greenish tinge around its edges.

"Rusco? Are you out of your mind?" TK gasped.

"They fucked with the wrong asshole."

"What're you scheming?"

"Lure those scumbags into a trap they'll wish they'd never sprung."

"How?" TK's mouth twitched. "I don't like that murderous look in your eyes, Rusco. I've seen it in you before and I don't want anything to do with it."

"Tough shit. Get used to it, TK. There's a reckoning to be had."

"With big bad Baer?" he guffawed. "What have you got to bargain with? The phaso's gone. Remember, they got it?"

"Yeah, too bad about that."

He flashed me a perplexed look. "You don't sound too broken up about it." His eyes widened. "Wait, you still got it?"

"Whatever gave you that idea?"

"You're a tricky bastard, Rusco." He slapped me on the back, his lips working in a grin. I pulled away, not liking his overly familiar back slaps.

It was a full scale war I waged now on Baer and Pazarol. Unfair of me to ensnare TK and Wren in it, but I was committed and I knew I'd need their help. Bounty hunters had no doubt been alerted, with a larger price on my head and all our miserable hides. Our ship, bugged, a magnet for slaughter and yet I planned to push the red card a little further.

Time to install the tracker back in the ship. As I tinkered under the console with wires I'd ripped out two weeks ago, TK's jaw went slack.

"What in hell are you doing?"

"Installing the bug back in the transcom, what's it look like?"

"Are you crazy?" He reached down to pull the device out.

I slapped his hand away and told him to back off. "It stays on." I flashed him a dangerous look.

"What do you mean, it stays on?"

"Listen, can you jumpstart this thing, TK, so we can monitor it, where it transmits?"

He blinked, gave me a dazed inspection. "I can, sure. But why? There's a risk you'll tip them off by sending static down the line."

"Just want to know the message is getting through and it's received. A lot depends on this working, like our lives."

He gave me a lip-chewing appraisal when I told him more of my plan. "I can do that."

"I'm banking that they won't kill us, without getting their precious phaso back."

Misinformation. Misdirection. We'll lead the flies to the spider's web. A ghoulish smirk played across my lips. I looked down and flexed my robot hand. Pulling myself to my feet, I recalled all the forsaken derelicts of this solar system floating out in space and an old memory stirred: Belisar One, Primary Ore Station near Deros, the largest of the dwarf planets in the asteroid belt. I tapped some keypads and it came up in the holo field. "There!" I zoomed in and we studied the floor plans. "It's still intact. We can probably rig the place without suits, if the air generators are still operational."

TK muttered under his breath.

I summoned Wren to the bridge and told her the basics of my plan. "The phaso and amalgo are the imaginary bait we use to seed the dropoff point. Some fictional buyer while our gangster friends are listening on the wire. They come running to seize the cargo, but a little surprise awaits them. Simple."

"Sounds doable." She grinned.

"And dangerous," TK snarled. "I don't think it's survivable, Rusco, given the firepower they had on Trellian."

"I wasn't asking you. Now can you study the upper floor plan and map out entrances and exits? It's vast. We need a confined area to work from."

The Varwol kicked out and got us to Deros, a misshapen would-be planet, looming brown and grey under distant Jesra's weak light. On the near side hung Belisar station, an old derelict fish-spine station with multiple bays and landing docks stemming from the main vertebrae—one of those giant outposts left over from yesteryear—a monster of the past no longer operational. Had the works: artificial gravity, ore processing equipment, massive storage, redistribution.

The station grew closer as Starrunner's impulse engines guided us in to its central core, a desolate hulk, which had survived massive wars, now dark and dead. Life support systems? Unlikely. Air, heat, emergency lights, I hoped, if we could activate them.

We approached the top, diamond-shaped crown and landed in a still-open port—Bay D-2. I tried various radio signals hoping to trigger the hatch behind. One of the common bands worked. The hatch closed behind us and sealed the depressurization chamber, letting the air flood back up. A green light showed on the inner wall. So…some of the systems were still online after all these years—incredible. A power source was still connected, solar, I deduced from the array of panels deployed on the station's superstructure.

I got out with Wren, wearing a light mask and suit. At the back of the landing pad, double doors led to a command bay that had been looted over the years. Many ore bins and sorting stations that it overlooked on a lower level caught my attention. A perfect ambush zone. We could stage an explosive web of horrors for our guests. Blow those bastards out of the sky.

Wren and I worked for hours installing explosive packs and trip wires that I'd picked up on Gainor, booby trapping the place nicely. The artificial grav docks were still functional, a definite plus, otherwise we'd be floating off our feet. Heating and air systems had automatically kicked in with our presence. When it was done, we had two sets of fireworks installed in the command bay, fore and aft. All exits were wired to the touch of a button. Both Wren and I would carry remote detonators.

I'd even rigged Starrunner to explode should the worse-case scenario occur, we got boarded, then we'd all go up in a cloud of smoke. Let's hope it didn't come to that. TK's bulging eyes blinked when he saw what we were doing and what I was planning.

"Why don't we just zoom off to a faraway star system? Do we have to be so dramatic?" His voice was a low plaintive mutter.

I snorted. "And have the next ice man waiting around to jab us with a pick? Gotta nip these moguls in the bud, TK, buddy. Do you want to live running in fear for the rest of your days?"

"No, but you're not considering all the risks."

"Trust me. This is the minimum risk. Once we get rid of our bugbears, we're free to roam the galaxy, working our scams."

Wren mumbled her agreement. "I'm fed up with being shadowed by murderous scum."

TK sighed and threw his hands up in the air. The man looked gray and worn around the edges. Arolin, a martial arts expert, once told me the color of a man reflects his aura when his number is up. I think TK was feeling a bit of that. That slight quivering in the left wrist, the nervous tic of eye, the quick labored breathing and grey pallor of face. Perhaps the scrape back on Trellian had been too much, or maybe Billy's death had got to him, or my hand being shot off. Whatever, he looked as gray as a ghost, and I guessed he was on his way to cracking.

I set Starrunner on a course for Elphi Alpha's airspace to stage the call, far away from Deros. I made sure that we were out of warp and the tracker was active and we were speaking within range of its pickup. I had my friend Loue on Elphi Alpha play an imaginary script, rehearsed in advance on an encrypted line. I didn't want to give Baer and his mongrel brood a lot of time to plan an attack on us, so I only gave them two hours lead time.

"Loue? Meet us at the upper dock D-2 on Belisar…yeah, that's the one, the abandoned ore hub orbiting Deros…Yes, that's two hours on the nose, not a minute later or sooner. Don't worry, I'll have both phaso and amalgo ready and waiting for you….Price, an even 40. Any fuckups, or no shows, and the price goes up 50%... Believe me, I've had enough hassles with these pieces of shit and I'll be glad to get rid of them…that cockroach Baer's almost cooked me twice. After this deal I'm going on a long ride to Pegasus or Ramses or whatever…Yeah, bittersweet memories." I cut the line and saw the activating circuit light in yellow and knew the message had gotten through, to whoever, wherever. The signal piggybacked off our own transcom and would be sent through encrypted and unencrypted channels.

"It's done," I said and moved away from the pickup range.

Wren remarked, "Let's just hope they don't seize the opportunity to blast us out of the sky."

"Don't worry, Wren. We'll get our payback."

A particularly dark legend surrounded Belisar station, one of alien origin lost in time. Strange and inexplicable artifacts found down there on the dwarf planet: a squid-like intelligent warlord race, Zakro or Zipri or something, extinct now, whose only legacy was scattered bones with fanned, herring-bone spines turning up on the odd world or two. Made me shiver. All the mine charters came through Belisar at one time, the mining deeds for every jackleg asteroid, no matter how small. But some unknown scourge had infected the dwarf planet, an epidemic or parasite of some sort, made its way into the mined ore and the station had been closed.

"You should be more worried about Mong than Baer," said TK, interrupting my reverie, "at least from what you describe of the man while you were strapped in that chair. If it were me, I'd turn tail and never look back."

"That's you, not me. As I said, TK, there's no bucking necessity." Still I recalled that frightful face of the star lord and his hulking presence and shivered. Mong was a red herring who was impossible to read.

TK's bright bird-like voice chirped. "Mong's lust for the alien tech exceeds what you'd expect from a power monger of his sort. He could have empires, planets, wealth and power beyond measure! Yet he's chasing us all over the galaxy for a tiny piece of hardware. Ever think of that? Something to consider before you leap into the lion's jaws."

I shrugged and focused on the last minute details of the operation. Yet TK's voice had infected me with a bug that had my brain spinning. I pored over all the words I had ever heard from Mong and the news reports on him. So what drove the megalomaniac? Galactic dominion, yes. But why was the amalgo so important to him? Some men, or quasi-humans, desired power over all other beings. Mong was different. He wanted respect also— to be perceived as the next messiah. Go a peg deeper, Rusco. Was the man really that deluded into thinking that he was actually helping the human race by taking over their planets? A poignant snippet came to mind, *They do not know what they want. A unified community and existence, free of warring bandits, free from slums. I will give it to them, Baer. Through hell or high water, I will give it to them.* Vivid was the crusader's manifesto I'd overheard back in that torture room on Trellian…

It seemed that Baer was no crueler or kinder than this master. But Baer was only a peon, a simple minion in the larger scheme of a grander visionary; Mong could have modelled himself on the warlord Genghis Khan, throwing in a twist of the cultist. No matter. The beast was after me, to the death. As was Baer. I'd robbed him of his limb, true, as he had mine. Now we were even, and one of us had to die…

I reviewed my strategies and could find no flaw. Starrunner's shields were low, so I'd spared no expense in replenishing my ship's defenses with a heavy duty Rexar 3 magno-electrovolt mesh, knowing one day the device might save my hide—like the present. Wren was grinning like a cat; TK was shitting bricks. As I punched the hyperdrive to get to Belisar, I wondered what ball I'd started rolling by the simple act of turning on that tracker.

The red lights glowed on the overhead panel, signaling our arrival at Deros as the Varwol cut out.

Asteroid belt, Merius, spread behind us and Deros station loomed below, a half billion miles from Jesra.

From what I had gathered of its operation, all ore and crystals, including Barenium, amassed from the nearby moons, asteroids and space rock, had been collected here for transshipment to neighboring worlds.

If this plan worked, the reapers would come knocking soon.

The camouflaged suit hung still there on the peg by the weapons rack, along with the poison-tipped boots Pazarol had given me. I looked at the garb and cast them a sour grin: Pazarol's gift might come in handy.

I murmured to Wren, "They'll probably try to ambush us when we get settled into the drop point. Let's be ready." I adjusted the straps on the AK custom blaster slung over my shoulder, and the pouch containing the grenades.

"You don't know that," hissed TK, his face grim.

"Your point?"

Wren interceded. "I'm surprised they haven't tried to blow us up already."

"Until Mong and his monkeys get their alien tech, they'll keep us alive. That's what I've been banking on this whole time."

As we came within docking distance of the station, I made out more details: immeasurably long superstructure, shaped like a fish vertebrae with scores of side wings extending ninety degrees outward. The upper tiers of the main hub spread out like a honeycomb: rows for small craft like ours to dock in. Below that, larger octagonal ports spread, gray and sealed now, as they had been for centuries, since the large freighters had come to dock and transfer their payloads. An impressive piece of architecture all said and done. Belisar sprawled like a fantastic ark, the single portal open to the landing bay, just as we had left it. Already our scanners had picked up one bogey on our tail, too far away to do any damage, but proof that the bait had been nibbled. We'd hole up in the mining station before long, ready our explosives and wait for armageddon.

No sooner had we reached docking distance with upper deck loading bay D-2 than a sudden blue blip flashed across the starboard viewport. A black ship vaulted out of nowhere. Wtf? A stealth ship? Drone? It was shaped like a manta ray and had that sleek, streamlined look of new tech and black death, some harbinger of doom. Either way, it had slipped under our radar. A blue beam of destruction came flaring out of its fuselage, one of those long-range fareon rays. With horror, I realized my well-oiled plans were becoming unglued from the onset. Our enemies had timed their strike with just enough force to incapacitate us, rather than destroy us.

Our shields buckled; the ship rocked, sending us in a tailspin as we slewed into the landing port. I jammed the forward thrusters to compensate and save us from colliding with the side of the docking bay. Starrunner ran high up into the open landing bay.

Starrunner spun down on her side, trailing sparks from her underbelly, smoking from her midsection. *What can go wrong, will go wrong*, the universal law of consequences. Molly's voice crackled through the gloom. *"Critical meltdown of engine core. Ship's Barenium unstable."*

At the edge of my vision, the viewscreen showed impending disaster. Baer's ship and her companion vessel, a stealth V-Ray, glided in through the hatch before we could manually trigger the portal closed. *Shit.*

I snapped out of my daze. We were sitting ducks in this smoking coffin. "Out! Now!"

Wren and TK scrambled through the smoke, grabbing R4s and masks and coughing, staggered to the port hatch. The sealed landing dock re-pressurized automatically and I cranked the hatch wheel upon seeing the green lamp blink on the far wall. But it would only turn half way, and I had to kick it several times before it would loosen. We were in a bad place, trapped between the ship's stern and our protective enclave while enemies roved about. The booby-trapped command area with all my careful snares was the only safe area for us at the moment. My synthetic fingers clenched the detonators with tingling desperation.

I did not set any off.

We forced our way through the cold but warming air, toward the double revolving safety doors of the command area. I ran up to the exit, my steel-tipped boots clanking on the grates.

Wren and I dove for the command room, TK lagging behind, puffing for air, his breath coming out in steamy gasps. I got off a few shots, but I wasn't going to trade ammo with the vague figures emerging from both ships and become instant space fodder.

"Into the command bay! Quickly," I hissed. "Let them fall prey to our traps."

"If we don't have a ship," cried TK, "what good will it do?"

I waved a hand. "Messenger shuttle may still by salvageable." *Better to give them hope than futility.*

"We don't have time—"

"Shut up and move!" I cried.

Wren herded the old man on, grumbling for him to tough it up. "We go to plan, TK. Think 'plan'."

I could see the terror writ in the old man's eyes. Under that dim swath of emergency lights, his broken, defeated look mirrored the inevitable, the shadow of looming death.

"Use minimum fire," I barked. "Draw them out with the explosives. Don't give away our positions."

I looked back and Baer and two dozen of his men were pouring out of the first vessel with laser-guided AKs—remodeled blasters with stun capability. Swift, capable men, garbed in loose black fatigues, like modern ninjas, dark skull caps tucked over their ears. I knew in an instant those killers meant to capture us and torture us for the information leading to the amalgo. I was under no illusion that this round of torture would make the last look like a kindergarten picnic. Under no circumstance must any of us get captured.

A group of five of them branched off to search Starrunner. *Good, keep them busy.* The rest moved in after us.

CHAPTER 20

My eyes dilated, adjusting to the murk. The command area of Belisar One was a rubble-strewn sprawl just as we'd left it. A pool of blue-black shadows with lots of places to hide showed itself, rigged with enough booby traps to kill an elephant and several lions thrown in. The place had been looted by bandits over the decades, as evidenced by the hodgepodge of overturned consoles, smashed component boxes, spilled circuits with wires showing. The pillars that supported the honeycombed ceiling had whole sections eaten out of them. By machine gun fire. Wedges were cut out as if drunken bandits had aimed a thousand shots and chewed holes into the walls. At least the idiots had left the port door alone.

The light was so dim as to make it difficult to see. Only a faint ambient bluish glow spilled from the windows overlooking the interior of the station.

I motioned to TK and Wren, urging them to the side wall to duck behind the random wastage while I staggered in a bent-kneed crouch over to the opposite wall to lure the others out and activate the explosives. Good thing the heating and air systems had powered on during our last mission, eliminating the need for suits. I made quick time to the back corner where the paneled glass looked into the interior: a place of silence, brooding and mystery. Below, the lower level showed massive ore bins, sorting stations and holding pods. A vast tangle of machinery, piping, docking stations, catwalks and inky depressions lurked in those confines. The emergency lights dimmed, then cut out. The unearthly blue glow flickered back on again, so recently activated by human presence after many decades.

Despite what I'd told TK about Starrunner, I felt sick at the loss of her.

In her state she was of little use. We were marooned here—like castaways, stuck out in nowhere with no hope of rescue or little chance of making repairs. I thrust that anxiety out of my mind.

A dozen and a half enemy, lean and silent as weasels, came slinking in low on a wide sweep of the area. Their laser sights gave away their position while ours remained dark. We had an advantage, but they had the superior numbers.

I signaled Wren with my silent communicator: lie low. The plan was for me to draw them out, pick off stragglers with explosives, and rely on the camo qualities of my guerrilla suit to keep them at bay.

I chucked a piece of broken circuitry toward the first plant of explosives by the lower level ore carts. Several green laser sights lanced to the spot and eager figures split up to investigate.

My sweat-beaded face curled in a cold grin. I saw a line of them moving toward the sound. *Fools.* My body tingled with expectation. Imminent slaughter was moments away.

Just as the pack was within blasting distance of the far wall, I pinched my thumb on the detonator. Flesh and sinew erupted in a crimson mash. The force took out six of them, shredding them like ripe carrots in a blender. Bloody shreds of arms, legs and torsos sprayed in the immediate vicinity.

Baer's voice rumbled over the flames. "Fan out, you stupid fools! That fuck Rusco's got the place rigged! He wasn't so dumb after all. Flush him out. Quickly. Now!"

"But boss—"

"Shut the fuck up! What am I paying you for, blockhead? Move!" He thrust the man forward. "Don't cluster in too tight and let him take you down."

I pressed the left detonator. *Kabam.* Another bright blast took out four more of the black-masked bastards, leaving a gaping hole in the ore bins and tangle of machinery below. Bright fire licked out at me as I sprang from one hiding place to another behind an overturned console. *Keep them moving.* Make them think there was a rat's nest of snipers and ambushers around them.

I winced. Shit, they were rounding on Wren. Someone must have sighted a flicker of movement. That idiot TK panicked, for he began shooting a spray into the fray. I told the fuck not to fire! Except in an emergency as it gave away location.

A howling cry rose above the mayhem. Another black enemy fell on a knee, shin shattered by the shells.

Wren joined in the firefight. Two more gunmen groaned in anguish and fell face down in the rubble.

We were down to four plus change.

But three of them started firing, and like a death squad, rained a fury of inescapable green at Wren and TK. They were smart, those stalkers; they took out the pillar where Wren and TK had dug in and the ceiling collapsed on them. A ton of metal came crashing down and I heard Wren's sharp cry echo in peaked anguish. The girders folded like a tent around them, offering them some small cocoon—I hoped. All I could see was a dull gleam of metal where she was. I swore silently and acted without hesitation. The explosion had left her pinned behind a mangled ceiling panel.

TK must have managed to wiggle free for I could hear his hoarse grunts and curses. I could vaguely make out a dark outline moving along the shadowy backdrop of the side wall. His or an enemy's?

I scooted closer. Like a thief in the dark, I kept low. My itchy fingers hovered over the last of the detonators. But the enemy was nowhere in my sights, nowhere near my kill zone.

I think the last four heard Wren. I set off the last explosive, only serving as a costly diversion, and while they staggered back, wondering what next booby trap they'd step into, I raced forward, struggling to cover the area to their left side. She was gasping and cursing and banging on the metal that covered her.

I rapped hard, hissing at her to quiet down. I grabbed an old machine tool, a hammer or something, caked with eons of dust and launched it somewhere behind them. One of the stalkers whirled around at the clatter of metal and loosed a shot. I launched out like a cat to a new defensive position, but was forced to dodge around and confuse them before I could come back to her.

"Sh," I hissed at her, trying to imagine the terror she felt trapped under that mangled mess. "Stay silent, you hurt?"

"Pinned, can't get out," her muffled voice came back. "Left arm is throbbing."

I whispered, "Wren, listen to me. Stay put, no noise. Don't try to move. I'll get you out—but not now." I couldn't peel the metal back around her without alerting those fucks to my position.

They were returning. Shit! This was not going well. I backed off, my head in a quandary, a high buzzing in my ear.

"The old subterfuge trick," Baer called out in the murk. "Nice job, Rusco. I expected more from you. Disappointing that you let your arm get blown up like mine. We're two peas in a pod, you and me, two fools in a stew pot."

That's it, you dumb fuck. Keep talking. Draw yourself out like a fat fool and use up your energy.

An assassin had positioned himself between Baer and the tangle of metal. Now he was moving closer. Before long he'd clue in to where Wren was, trapped and helpless.

I slunk away, hoping to draw him away. No luck. The bugger kept sidling closer, weapon trained at the fallen mass of metal. Where the hell was TK? Why wasn't the twit helping?

I sidewinded back and snuck up behind him while the gunman was focused on the debris, weapon aimed at the fallen ceiling. I hoped to neutralize him while he was preparing to take out the two of us whom he thought cowered behind that mound.

I dove at this hulking figure, meaning to kick him in the groin with my poison-tipped boot to avoid firing and giving away my position. But the stalker heard the crunch of glass under my boot and pivoted. I ducked, missing by a hair his stun beam, wrapped my arms about his waist and brought him crashing to the ground. I knocked his weapon away. The man was exceedingly strong and he bent me backward to the point I could feel my spine creaking under the pressure. I pummeled him with my fists and in a mad tangle of arms and legs, we grappled and hooked, grunted and cursed. My hard right lashed out and I caught him with my elbow in his teeth. He loosed a garbled cry. I scrambled to my feet, kicked out a foot while rising, and grazed him high on the thigh. He went down with a howl, shivering for an instant and was dead within seconds. An impressive fast-acting poison. I staggered over the body, panting as I saw his glassy eyes stare up. No time to get Wren. I stumbled away from the booted feet coming closer to my position as they set scarlet sights upon me—scarlet meant moderate to lethal.

Peeow. Peeow. Bright laser fire licked past my ribs, shredding consoles and metal.

I couldn't find my weapon in the dim light. Fuck it. I'd lost it.

I saw the dead man's firearm, a long fat rod of dark length in the shadows. I dove for it, snatching up his modified AK, then rolled flat to fire on the last moving shapes in the dark. But the damn thing jammed. I threw it away in disgust. Laser lines were sighting on me. With a hissing curse, I scrambled crab-wise for cover. *Rat-a-tat-tat.* A death rattle for heart-pumping Rusco. Terror raged at my heels, shredding everything around me. Those were no stun rays. They were real shelled bullets.

"Rusco, give it up," shouted Baer. "You're a dead man. You've no ship and your explosives can't last forever." His panting voice rose above the shell chatter. "Tell you what—give me the phaso, and I'll call it even—"

"Phaso? Why didn't you say so?" I called.

Restless rumblings came from the huddle, like a nest of rats from where I counted three, with weapons cocked, laser sights trained in my direction. I ducked, held my breath behind a mound of shredded tin. Wished I was the invisible man right now.

Baer held up a hand to the others to hold their fire. He advanced like a hairy beast.

"Tell me where it is, Rusco."

"If you really want it, Baer, it's in the conduit leading to the Barenium cylinders in my ship. I hid it there, taped it to the silver metal siding for safe-keeping. Go ahead and check—it's out of harm's reach, and the hands of even my own crew."

"More like a trap," he jeered.

"Believe what you want. Send one of your crew members to check." I ducked down, inching away from there to another overturned console a few yards away.

I hoped they'd fall for the lure as I'd bomb-rigged that conduit. It would mean one or two less thugs for me to kill.

How everything was going to shit right now. It would kill Starrunner's Barenium drive for good but better that than dying here at the hands of these cutthroats. A gamble. I hadn't counted on both TK and Wren being neutralized so soon.

One of them left on quiet feet; I could feel a lightening of presence. It was about the same time I noticed some other dark figure trail after him with a hobbling gait. TK? Where was that sneaky fuck going? Maybe he was going to take down the errand boy. I hoped so.

My explosives were done. I'd been reaching for a fallen hunk of metal a yard away from my defensive position. It lay in open sight, but I was afraid that if they saw the small movement, they'd blow my hand off. And I wasn't about to let that happen again.

I tried to keep Baer talking. Fortunately Wren had made herself quieter than a church mouse. *Make the Baer blunder.* The man had a gun, I didn't. A distinct disadvantage in this miserable situation so any winning trick was a good one. I'd grab onto it like a drowning man grasped for straws.

"I'm not sweet on the phaso, truth be told, Rusco," said Baer. "Just tell us where the amalgo is, and we'll be out of your hair."

Just like that, you slimebitch, as if we were old pals? I grinned. "The amalgo's a little trickier, Baer. Truth be told, it isn't here, hate to tell you. I put it somewhere safe. Thought you'd like that."

He chuckled. "I do, and that's good to hear. For a second, I thought you might have gone and done something stupid like destroy it to spite me. After that unfortunate incident back on Trellian."

"No, nothing like that, Baer. I got better things to do with my time than play the spiteful bitch."

"Haw haw. You'll have to tell me where it is sometime. I got a short temper with this one at the moment."

To my right came a shuffle of feet. I could hear two of them. Flanking me like foxes at the henhouse, moving inch by inch, expecting that I had another detonator to trigger, but I'd drawn my last card.

"Tell your gophers to stay back," I croaked. "Otherwise I'll blow them up like the rest of your tainted meat."

Baer nodded, signaled the two to stop. "So, what do we do now?" he said. "Seems as if we're at a stalemate."

I let the seconds pass. I was running out of options. Just when I was about to do something desperate, I detected a hint of motion back near the landing dock entrance.

TK, the mysterious sod, was slinking by the side wall. The crystal ring clutched in his trembling hand; it radiated that queer iridescent glow that had always mesmerized me. What was the fool up to? Maybe he thought to use the phaso as a bargaining chip? To save his own hide? Why had he left Wren, though? Seemed cowardly in my opinion. I couldn't quite figure it.

The dark animal shape of Baer lunged out of the shadows and intercepted him, speaking low in his ear. "The phase-shifter or I blow your cock off, asshole."

TK whirled, looking as surprised as I'd been. "Stay back or I nuke it," he rasped, twisting on his hips. He jammed his weapon down at the phaso.

"Go ahead, blast it, you muttonhead, you die next."

TK's eyes flicked away, a trickle of anxiety running down his hollow cheeks.

"Don't be stupid, TK," I warned him. "Give him the phaso. Or we all die."

"Shut up, Rusco. We're all dead anyway!" He turned, scowling at me like a fishwife. "You let Billy die. I owe you nothing. You left him out there, you bastard."

"Think again. Billy's dead and you can't save him."

"We might have saved him," he whimpered. The old man was all choked up. "He might have gotten away." He lifted his gun hand to wipe at his running nose.

A moment of distraction that allowed Baer to put a ruby ray between his eyes. TK dropped like a strawman, the phaso rolling out of his hand like a pinwheel. One of Baer's goons reached to snatch it up then disappeared in a haze of multicolored light. The idiot hadn't grabbed it properly, so he winked out of existence much as had Billy and Mitch, unaware of the alien device's potential.

Baer swore as I jumped up and hurled the bar in my hand like a boomerang. Didn't care who I hit. Just that it hit. I clocked the first thug in the neck. He fell choking in his own blood with a crushed windpipe. At the same time, I scuttled out like a crab, grabbed the phaso with my sleeve, and was up and running to the next place of protection. I dove behind a component box just before Baer's fire could eat away at me.

He cursed and I heard muffled cries coming from Wren, still trapped underneath that wretched panel, maybe injured or maybe not. She kicked and cursed, lashed out at the metal. *Shut up, you stupid woman.* Christ, she had a foul tongue.

"Nice move, Rusco. I'm guessing you're right out of explosives by now by the look of that little missile you cast. Makes my job a lot easier."

The bear-man moved forward, emptying fire into the scraps of metal that shielded me and I cried out in pain as a hot flare grazed my side, singeing leather and drawing blood.

"Feel like talking now?" he grunted. "I know you're still there. I can smell your dirty hide. Once I get you, I'm going to cut off your head, then take your squealing bitch back for a ride she'll never forget."

I crouched, my heart beating, counting the moments. *Come on, Rusco, think.*

"Just you and me," laughed Baer. "Your geriatric mechanic is down, but I guess you saw that, didn't you? Sure you did. The girl? Well, she ain't sounding as if she's too available right now." He laughed, an acidy hyena chuckle. "Why don't you just come out like a good boy, and we can settle this like men, instead of rustling around in the dark, shitting in the corners like mice?"

'That's a nice idea for someone with a gun."

"It is what it is, Rusco. Not leaving here until I have your head on a platter. Part of the deal I made with Mong. Either your head or mine. Mong gave me the choice, a month to track your miserable hide down and deliver the phaso. Said he'd make a captain of me in his army, with all the material perks of war."

"That's a nice deal, Baer. Congratulations." *Three down, only one black bear to go.*

My prosthetic hand twitched. A bad time for it to act up. Control it, Rusco. It reached out and clutched the smooth, cool surface of the phaso, my last card.

"You've been duped by a charlatan with psi power, Baer. Parlor tricks that a well-timed hit from a blaster can end in a second."

"You're wrong there," Baer grunted, loosing another spray of fire as he moved closer. "I've seen Mong employ telekinetic powers that you wouldn't believe. Got 'em through his meditation on dark gods, that black religion or whatever he dabbles in. You don't know the power of the man."

"I could give a shit about his powers, if he sucked Adam's dick. Give me a gun and I'll put a bullet in the lizard's brain."

"Tsk, tsk. Now that's no way to badmouth somebody who isn't here to defend himself. Didn't your mother teach you manners? Think Mong would have something to say about that fly-away tongue of yours. Shame on you, Rusco. Plan on getting me back that little phaso. If I don't, the star lord's death warrant awaits."

"You've already mentioned that, Baer. Going Alzheimer on me?"

Hearing my labored breathing, he strode in with a leisurely gait. "Mong told me all about that phaso. The Mentera were stupid enough in how they employed the technology. They could have ruled the universe, and almost did, but lost it at the end. Now they're only passing memories. Mong and I'll not make the same mistake."

Famous last words, reptile brain. All the while I'd been edging around his left side, inching on my stomach like an eel, leaving a small trail of blood and slime behind me. Wren chose that instant to whimper and as Baer turned his ugly head and muttered, "That's right, bitch, you'd better—" I lurched up.

"Peekaboo." I lobbed the phaso at him and he swatted out a hairy hand to block it, or grab it? It amounted to the same. As I dove sideways in a desperate roll, he blinked out of existence, flicked out to nowhere land like his buddy and Mitch and Billy before him. I shuttled forward, snatched up the dead gunman's AK and did a wide sweep, expecting a host of criminals to come at me all at once. They didn't. I loosed a spray of fire and a wolfish howl all around me in a half moon. Heart beating, I stumbled to the place where the phaso was and where Baer had last blinked out, as warily as a wolf who approaches a steel-ringed trap.

I stooped to pick up the glimmering disc with my sleeve and pocketed it. I grinned from ear to ear, familiar Rusco now, raw, crinkly grin. "Okay, good, everything's good," I assured myself. I staggered over to the tented hump of metal where Wren lay trapped and began pulling the sheets back. I had to use the full force of my dwindling strength, legs braced, while the aches crawled up my arms. Wren's obvious distress gave me added haste.

"Okay, kiddo, we're clear." Grunting, with anguished efforts and the augmented strength of my mechano-hand, I pried back the last of the metal and dragged her to her feet. She was a dusty mess, all stooped and haggard, limping and bedraggled, but her dark eyes burned with a fierce light. A dark crust of blood caked her left forearm. She shook her slim body out, blinking. Her right hand massaged the small of her back where I'd guessed she'd lain for too long on her bulky R4.

"Took you long enough," she groused. She looked around, scooping up her weapon from the cramped cubbyhole. "They all dead?"

"Dead."

"Baer?"

"Dead."

"Good." She snuffled out a grunt of satisfaction. "All's fair in love and war. So we've won?"

"I'd say so, outside of having no Starrunner."

Wren swore. "Let's go take a look. TK might be able to work some magic on it. Where is the old complainer?"

"I regret to say TK's no longer with us."

She gave her head a sad, wistful shake. "The man had a death wish right from the start. I almost felt he'd expected to join Billy one way or the other today."

"Those were my very same feelings."

She scowled. "Let's get to the ship then."

She held me tight, and I winced at the pressure of her trembling body, warm and a relief. "Thank you, Jet. You protected me when I thought I was done. You're a good man."

I grunted, not versed in any displays of emotion.

"Rusco, you're quivering and all shot up." She wiped away the blood smear off her hand.

"What about you? That nasty cut on your arm isn't looking too good. Mine could have been worse."

She lifted up my leathers, ignoring her own gash, and tore a strip off her own jacket and wrapped it around my ribs. "We need to get that wound cleaned up. You're going to have a nasty scar there."

"Nothing new." I shrugged, taking only shallow breaths. "Looks as if we both need some patching up."

We limped back to the landing dock.

Starrunner still smoked and crackled as we drew near. Molly's voice, a low garbled robo staccato, rang out from the interior: *"Warning, warning… Barenium irrecoverable leak…"*

"Yeah, I know, Molly."

The computer voice trailed out and died.

I blinked. Starrunner looked crippled beyond repair. I kicked my boot at her hull in despair. I winced at my futile action. "Sorry, Molly. Wherever you are." I ran a caressing finger across the smooth smoking curve of her right wing. Maybe it was time to retire her. The old Rusco too—the one before the mechno hand, and let a new Rusco surface.

"Weeping for your old girlfriend?" she muttered.

"Sort of."

"Sorry to hear, Rusco. She was a good ship to you, I know. She took you places. She brought you to me, and TK and Billy."

"You don't seem too broken up by her demise, considering she's our ride out of here." I clutched my side where the brown leather and makeshift tourniquet bulged and grimaced.

She looked at me with puzzlement. Her gaze shifted to the stealth ship. "What about that one there?"

"Worth a try."

We advanced with caution. The ship was a black sleek killing machine, that manta-ray stealth V. I kept low, weapon ready, in case there were others aboard.

There weren't. No movement, no life. I forced my way through the hatch. Kindly, the crew had left it open. None of the thugs had expected to lose this fight and resort to defending their ship.

We made our way to the bridge. Immaculate. The stealth V was a beauty with state-of-the-art weaponry, compact design, chrome, posh leather seats. Mong must have lent it to the dead Baer, rest his black soul. It would have trackers aboard, and that was a problem. We no longer had TK's expertise to help us out with that. We'd have to make our getaway quickly then ditch the vessel first chance we got.

One more loose end to attend to. I jumped out and dragged two hulks of the shrapneled bodies over to Starrunner and lay them beside her open, smoking hatch. I was worried the Barenium might blow, given Molly's last shrill warning, but risk was risk. I clambered in through the companionways, grabbing some personal effects, regen and the last bottle of whiskey from my smoked-out cabin. I coughed, edged back out in a hurry and dropped my gold watch on one of the charred remains. I aimed my blaster and blackened the remains some more, disfiguring the watch just enough so it could still be recognized. I grabbed Wren's hand and tore off the ring that she still wore on her index finger. She protested, uttering no small number of profane words, but I ignored them. I put the ring on one of the corpse's finger, nearly gagging from the state of the body. I made sure this one was messier than the last, and not easily recognizable as a male versus a female body. TK was next, dragged his sorry hide out, and placed it by the others, face down, what was left of it anyways. Dragged some more pieces of human torsos over to make it look more grisly and authentic. A thrum of voices ran through my head: Where's Baer and the rest of the bodies? Who knows? Where's the stealth ship? Oh, Baer and one or more of his thugs must have gone rogue and stolen it, took the phaso. Rusco and crew? Ha. You're looking at them.

It was a sorrowful business, but anything that'd keep that killer Mong off my tail and make him believe we were dead, was worth the effort.

A sour taste flooded my mouth, surfacing from throat to palate, that bad bit of bile that comes from deep down as I mulled over the sordid events of the day. Up till the end it would remain a mystery to me what exactly TK's motives were. I could only guess that he had some crazy scheme up his sleeve to try to rescue Billy or something. I was sorry he had to die, that the old man had to go and get himself killed, but he did it all under his own free will. For now, I'd give him the benefit of the doubt that he'd come back to help us.

We climbed aboard the stealth V and I slathered the last of the regen on Wren's long gash, wiping the excess on my own ribs. I familiarized myself with the bridge controls while I invited her to take over the weapons console. I never looked back, doubted I'd ever seen Starrunner again.

CHAPTER 21

Maybe not whole, but I was alive and had one last piece of unfinished business to carry out. The prosthetic started to feel like a part of me, more natural. Maybe I was just getting used to the lack of sensations in my right fingers? I had this mechanized hand on the end of my wrist, something that used to be flesh and bone.

The ship crossed the gulfs back to Elphi Alpha. Returning in good time, our first priority was to ditch this stealth craft. We traded our state-of-the-art vehicle for *Bantam*, an Alpha-Omega Beamer similar to my own Explorer. Regzie's WR, whom we'd done business with during the impound scam, was happy to oblige. He and his associates gave us an extra bonus in change—15k yols, citing our current track record of good business relations. I convinced them to throw in a bunch of tools and ship accessories on the side.

"A mighty fine piece of hardware you have there, Mr. Rambo. Any more trades you'd like to propose, bring 'em our way."

"Sure, I'll do that."

It was time to give Jesra and her brood of planets a rest and let Baer and his men's ghosts lie. I took the Beamer on a direct course toward the inner planets, Tarsus.

"Where now?" Wren asked from across the bridge's conference table. A pang of worry flicked across those dark-shadowed eyes.

When I didn't reply, she grew more restless. "Rusco, don't do anything stupid. That fucker Mong will break your legs and pluck out your eyebrows."

"Don't worry, Wren, nothing so dramatic. If I want dear old Mong dead, I'll leave the heavy lifting to Batman and the Boy Wonder."

"Very funny, but seriously, why not let sleeping dogs—"

"Relax." I outlined my plan to her. The fact that Pazarol was still alive was a loose end that couldn't be tolerated. "Dollars to donuts, Mong'll contract Pazarol to be my next executioner." I grimaced, recalling Pazzy's last promise of playing bounty hunter.

Wren shook her head in dim frustration. "Does it ever end?" She rubbed her eyes, heaving a sigh.

We came in smooth and low over the north end of the shell-shocked industrial zone that marked Belgen's business section. Buzzing the haggard clumps of trees, we left Bantam just under a half mile away in an abandoned yard, not far from Pazzy's crib. Close enough to make a mad dash if we needed to, far enough away that our landing would draw no undue attention. I cut the engines, grabbed my gear, the arsenal of weaponry and snips to cut the wire fence guarding the lot, then we'd have an exit hole readily accessible when the time came to hoof it out of there. It'd be nip and tuck. I had a remote control for the ship. I could run and operate Bantam in limited scope in case we needed the fury of her guns if the situation got desperate. I hoped to hell not.

I drew in a deep breath, inhaling the pungent odor of ozone, tar and something else—a far-off reek of petrochemicals lacing the air from some tall, grimed smokestacks farther down the way. A smoky glow lit up the early evening haze.

I convinced myself the main goal of our expedition was a rescue mission, of the workers whom I'd seen so bruised and mistreated. If Pazarol was there and just happened to get in the way, well, too bad. Right, Rusco, who are you kidding?

I slowed up, my determined stride coming to a halt at the sight of the crumbling line of the brick warehouse. Wren paused at my side, limber and relaxed, as if we were just staking out a kid's birthday party. She had recovered nicely from her scrape at Belisar, given the regen and the efficient muscle machine she was. Those years on Talyon had sure toughened her up, surviving those scuttling dervishes and creepo mad boys. They'd blooded her like a SEAL, ironically made her ideal for the purposes I had in mind. Her loyalty was without question. We were like two peas in a pod. I grinned. Bonnie and Clyde, victims of violent disaster, lost family and trauma at an early age.

We moved with low-crouching strides, noiseless, straight toward the warehouse, through the tall, dry prickle-weeds and past the broken crates and skids, the old disused machinery.

The front and side exits we needed to secure. The guards were all inside. The cameras would pose a problem.

There'd be no grand entrance, no bombs or glitter. Just a stealth op, my specialty—the lives in there needed protection and a more delicate touch than the hack and slash fireflares I was used to. Dressed in my ragged camo suit and Wren in her black Kevlar gear, we slunk in like cats, our Uzis and R4s slung on our shoulders, the backup weaponry snug at our belts. I hunched just out of the view of the first overhead camera and aimed my disrupter at it, a thin black rod, bulbed at the end to shoot out a black net of spidery film. The sticky gel covered the lens and would dissolve in three minutes, giving us time to plant our explosives and move on. The lens would revert back to its original state. Enabling the cameras again was a key component in our undetected break-in. *Just a brief outage, Ned. Must have been a technical glitch.*

Wren did the same to the side cam. All this in prep for our exit, if exit there'd be. The tricky part would be getting the workers out, the young women and boys I remembered vividly with their bruised cheeks and blackened, despairing eyes. There was an ample margin of knuckle-gnawing in this excursion. A hair's separation from death. Many things could go wrong.

We crouched before the last side entrance, wasting no time. A part of me knew this venture was insane, but I couldn't back out now. Not if I wanted to sleep easy at night. It was one follow-up promise I'd made to myself. Might even take down Paz in the doing.

The high rusty door was an emergency exit and looked to have been little used. I applied some putty to the cracks around the edges and alongside the metal ring and wired the pulse cylinder. I hoped the door wasn't under alarm. We turned and the silent blast jerked the door ajar.

It wasn't wired. Good thing, otherwise Plan B would have come into effect, and that was a hell of lot messier.

Pazarol's men were nowhere in sight. They were confident, these thugs, as evidenced by their cocksure posturing and loose-limbed gunwielding. Nobody would try to burgle the very place they called home.

Such conceit was a fortunate occurrence. I knew the workers lived there and it was off shift for the guards, having scoped out their movements in advance. Many of them had left, so only a skeleton detail remained.

We crouched, breathless, in a cramped foyer stacked with row upon row of shelves of old junk and open boxes of dusty uniforms and boots—rejects.

The sewing machines had mostly settled down for the day and I set out for the back of the warehouse, motioning Wren to get to the workers' stations fast and move the women and boys back toward the side exit we'd breached. Hers was the harder job, I knew, convincing the laborers not to panic, bolt or raise an alarm. Her presence as a woman would command more trust and compliance. I hoped. If not, Plan C.

Keeping low and out of sight, I threaded my way through the many aisles of random equipment where the victims' daily chores were ever the same: hunched on benches before long tables, cutting, dyeing, sewing the electronic components into fabric, pressing, working the tall, upright mantis-like machines to pump out Paz's guerrilla wear. I dodged the sound of a guard's coarse laugh and the murmur of nearby voices, finally to crouch before the fat, double heating pipes running length-wise three feet above the ground at the back of the sweatshop. I'd seen them in the floor layout and memorized the specs back when TK and I'd scoped the joint. Typical rectangular warehouse, complete with storage areas at the sides. I set my canister of gas down underneath them and armed it for thirty seconds. I pressed the mask over my face. The hiss grew as I beetled away, for soon it'd blow and the funland of hell would begin. We'd have seven minutes before the toxic gas spread throughout the compound and rendered the air unbreathable.

When I heard a distinct pop behind me as the canister released, I knew the die was cast. I scrambled back the way I'd come.

Gray clouds of hot steam hissed from the piping area, simulating a burst pipe, obscuring the view. This mix had tear gas in it for added effect. We'd have to get the workers out with speed, otherwise they'd choke to death.

I heard shouts to my right and the thuds of booted feet of big Paz's guards, converging from their diverse locations. They'd be wondering what was up: a main pipe rupture or thinking the worst, some spontaneous fire. I snuck off in the opposite direction, keeping low between the lanes of dyeing equipment and the presses, blending in with the shadows. Confuse and misdirect; that was the name of the game, for as long as possible while Wren and I got the workers out.

I ran nose to nose with Pazarol and a few of his boys before long in the cleaning area on the way back to join up with Wren: a blur of dark suits, mustachios, Uzi blasters, foul tempers and tongues. I pegged off the first of his entourage, a bewildered bodyguard, his mouth wide and gaping, before answering fire sent me spinning under a worktable.

Shots ricocheted off the shiny metal. I found myself pinned down before the dye vats. One beam nearly clipped me and I jerked away from a whoosh of green fire that nearly grazed my Adam's apple. Both far too perilously close. Feet scrabbled around me. I shouldered in behind a large vat of toxic green dye, the chemical reek making my eyes water and my throat seize up. My mask had jiggled loose. I fumbled to secure it and shook out the chemical sting from my eyes. The gunmen weren't equipped with masks, so I sent green dye pouring their way by blasting out the bottom far side of the vat. Soon they were reeling on the ground as the fumes from the dye stung their noses and throats while the more toxic billows of steam crept up on them like snakes through the aisles.

So began a shooting spree in a wild free-for-all that the gambler in me knew was bad odds at five to one. Yet gradually big Paz's gunmen started to cough and reel back, snarling and cursing.

I slipped out of my hiding spot, my mask snug on my nose now. I picked them off one by one so there'd be no blasting us in the back while we were making our escape.

Pazarol, the fat fuck, lolled in the curling swirls of mist, wiping his eyes, drooling and spitting curses all the way. So, he was here. Bonus. Someone had thrown him a mask, the strap still dangling in his pudgy hands. I kicked the weapon out of his grip and beat him down to the ground with the end of my blaster. I looked down at him with little love.

His priceless expression was one of white-faced surprise. Rusco, a grinning pumpkin man returned from the grave.

"It can't be! You're dead!" he choked and sputtered, as if he'd been struck in the head. Wish I could frame that image and pin it on my cabin wall. "I saw you hauled off by Baer," he croaked. "Then that Mong striding down the hall."

He lunged up at me between phlegmy drools, spitting out blood. "Is that cropped he-bitch woman of yours alive too?" he gasped. "Should've plowed her while I had the chance."

"Would have thought this little exchange had given you more humility."

"Fuck off, dogshit asshole. I hope you and that broad get wasted—"

I finished him off with a single shot. He lay still, with a gaping, smoking hole in his forehead. Good riddance. Couldn't stand the man.

A death was a death, and this was no less gruesome, though more like putting a rabid hound out of its misery. But the cost of taking a life always stirred the hairs on the back of my neck.

I caught up with Wren. She and the others were hustling toward the east wall, the workers frightened out of their wits at the echoes of gunfire blasting away and the hint of white steam floating ever closer toward them. "Out the side door!" I grunted. "This area'll be gassed out in minutes."

A group of fifty of them looked at me with dilated eyes of terror. "Who are you?" they cried.

"Pazarol's nemesis. Get moving! This is your lucky day. I've a ship waiting." Blinking in astonishment, they stumbled on trembling legs and I bunted them toward the side exit. Wren sighed with relief at the sight of me, alive and whole.

Some of them were too frightened to take action and stood immobile. Others gaped like fish, cowering behind the rows of khaki wear they had toiled so hard to produce. I gave a croak of frustration. "Do you want to stay here enslaved, victims of these scumlords?" A lean, hollow-cheeked woman with dark circles under her eyes visibly trembled. She wrapped her bruised arms around her chest, gave a choked sob and a call of action to others. Then took to her heels after Wren. Some I had to leave behind, blinking in the dim emergency light as the alarms rang. So be it. I joined in a mad scramble, prodding the others from behind down the main corridor, blaster in hand. When more rats with foul teeth came out to play, I stayed back as their rounds clipped out toward us, and rolled under equipment tables, using the gathering smoke as a screen through which I shot at will. Tools and instruments skidded off tables; khaki fatigues lined up on hangers shredded around us to the rat-tat-tat of gunfire. Wren was somewhere ahead of us, gesticulating with her R4, herding the mob forward through the double doors, three and four abreast so undernourished they were.

It was a wild rush. Desperate figures burst out into the damp air onto the weed-ridden tarmac, the grey light of dusk hitting us, and the smell of chemicals in our noses. Down the service yard, past rusty forklifts. Again I had to drop back as five others came out of the emergency exit we'd booby-trapped, staggering like strawmen in a gale. I fired shots back at them.

I hit the detonator switch. All disappeared in a cloud of white flames as their charred limbs flew, severed from torsos.

More stumbled out of the side door closer to the back. This time caustic smoke billowed out at their heels like sidewinders' tails. I jammed down the detonator. It didn't fire. "Fucking hell!" The canister was a dud. I threw the useless thing away.

They chased after us. Gunmen rained fire like cannons. Two women fell, shot in the back. I cried out in dismay. A tousle-haired boy tripped and crashed to his knees, sobbing. I winced and hauled the featherweight up on his feet, urging him to run like he'd never before. Like panicked sheep, they all ran after Wren through the weeds and cracked tarmac toward the distant fenced yard. I thought some would expire from sheer exhaustion and terror before they made it to the hold. They kept apace each other, some women gripping boys' hands.

I stayed back, kneeling, pegging off those who came within range. Blaster fire kicked up. One caught me in the left foot and I cursed, felt a zinging burning sensation in my toe. *Shit, this was not progressing well.*

"Move your asses!" Wren cried, swatting at them with the flat of her gun. She crowded them forth, through the fence toward the ship, herding them in the direction of the hold like cattle at a roundup.

When the last worker was in the ship, I came hobbling, sucking in lungfuls of air. I closed the hatch. All were secured and Wren already had Bantam circling in the air. I raced to the bridge, used the remote to fire her front cannons, bright lasers which licked at the snipers retreating in haste back to the compound. I grimaced in triumph as bodies fell.

I scanned the ground. Some survivors piled into the dormant X-R Rover craft sitting out in Pazarol's dilapidated yard. The V-winged tri-fighter whisked up at us, fareon beams pouring out, catching our shields, but Wren was pounding them with our own pulse beams. We were already well ahead, engaged, and I maxed Bantam's impulse out to the twin moons, past the atmosphere and out into space. The go indicator flashed yellow and free of Tarsus's gravity, the Varwol engaged. The universe slipped sideways. Stars, light flashes, multicolored beams sheared on impossible angles that bent in wrong places and made no sense to any waking eye.

We were off to the stars, and I could only breathe a gasp of relief.

* * *

I came down into the hold, limping with Wren at my side. There they all crouched in a miserable huddle, murmuring and sniffling like lost orphans, some in shock. The women held each other like frightened sisters, consoling each other and some of the younger boys. Wish I'd had a rescue like this when the bombs and pulse beams were going off and dropping on us during my teens. I let the memories slide by, shaking loose those frightful, estranged years of a lost youth. I blinked, emotionally spent, such feelings suppressed for decades now.

I'd take these victims to a far off world and let them start fresh, give them a second chance like Wren. They deserved it. The boy I had set right came hesitantly forward, touched my mechno hand. He smiled. I placed my good hand over his with a startled glance.

I felt a stir tingle in my breast. Seeing those grateful, teary-eyed faces affected me. A wave of something memorable and wholesome blossomed in the depraved chaos of this world for a change. It was a spark of some miniscule change. So much different from the killing and the violence, the cons and blowing everything to shit. It had been so long since I had experienced anything comparable.

Wren came beside me and curled an arm about my waist. She flashed me her lopsided grin.

I thought of that tech hid in the warehouse north of Hoath and a derisive rumble caught in my throat. Let Mong search the universe for it. The bastard'd never find it and I'd never go back to retrieve it.

The phaso I'd keep as a souvenir to remind me of what I had lost. But the other half of the amalgamator would sit there and rot in the darkness. No place for that evil caricature of bug-alien engineering in a human world. I thought of Billy's demise and TK's grief-stricken face before he died. It sent chills down my spine. No less that harrowing glimpse I'd caught out in nowhere land when I touched the phaso. All together, it had cost me my hand and taken a year off my life, or more. But it had given me something else—a sense of purpose. A spur that had driven me to liberate these downtrodden people, whom I never would have met or helped otherwise.

Somehow I knew there'd be more victims squirming like worms on the hooks of evil scumbags like Baer, Pazarol and the fanatic Mong.

I gave a gusty sigh and swung back to the bridge with Wren. "Going all maudlin on us, Rusco? Need to step up your game, I think." I croaked out a laugh and drew nearer to my companion-in-arms, a crooked grin pasted on my haggard face and my eyes agleam. "Wren, you ever hear of Xerxes station out in Perseus?"

"No, should I?"

"Well, it's remote, certainly off the radar of the big moguls. Far from Mong, far from terror. Easy pickings. We could work ourselves a master con. Dress you up real pretty. Minimum risk. That boy shows plenty of promise too."

"Leave the boy out of it. But I'm game."

OTHER BOOKS IN THE STARSHIP ROGUE SERIES:

STAR RUNAWAY
STAR WANDERER
STAR REBEL
STAR REAPER
STARVENGER

https://innersky.ca/starship

ABOUT THE AUTHOR

Chris is a prolific author of fantasy, adventure, and science fiction. His writing spans many genres: heroic fantasy, sword and sorcery and speculative fiction.

Browse Chris's books at:

https://innersky.ca/books